JOAN OF ARC - VOLUME 1

Mark Twain

Chapter 1.

When Wolves Ran Free in Paris

I, THE SIEUR LOUIS DE CONTE, was born in Neufchateau, on
the 6th of January, 1410; that is to say, exactly two years before Joan of Arc was born in Domremy. My family had fled to those distant regions from the neighborhood of Paris in the first years of the century. In politics they were Armagnacspatriots; they were for our own French King, crazy and impotent as he was. The Burgundian party, who were for the English, had stripped them, and done it well. They took everything but my father's small nobility, and when he reached Neufchateau he reached it in poverty and with a broken spirit. But the political atmosphere there was the sort he liked, and that was something. He came to a region of comparative quiet; he
left behind him a region peopled with furies, madmen, devils, where slaughter was a daily pastime and no man's life safe for a moment. In Paris, mobs roared through the streets nightly, sacking, burning, killing, unmolested, uninterrupted. The sun rose upon wrecked and smoking buildings, and upon mutilated corpses lying here, there, and yonder about the streets, just as they fell, and stripped naked by thieves, the unholy gleaners after the mob. None had the courage to gather these dead for burial; they were left there to rot and create plagues.

And plagues they did create. Epidemics swept away the people like flies, and the burials were conducted secretly and by night, for public funerals were not allowed, lest the revelation of the magnitude of the plague's work unman the people and plunge them into despair. Then came, finally, the bitterest winter which had visited France in five hundred years. Famine, pestilence, slaughter, ice, snowParis had all these at once. The dead lay in heaps about the streets, and wolves entered the city in daylight and devoured them.

Ah, France had fallen lowso low! For more than three quarters of a century the English fangs had been bedded in her flesh, and so cowed had her armies become by ceaseless rout and defeat that it was said and accepted that the mere sight of an English army was sufficient to put a French one to flight.

When I was five years old the prodigious disaster of Agincourt fell upon France; and although the English King went home to enjoy his glory, he left the country prostrate and a prey to roving bands of Free Companions in the service of the Burgundian party, and one of these bands came raiding through Neufchateau one night, and by the light of our burning roof–thatch I saw all that were dear to me in this
world (save an elder brother, your ancestor, left behind with the court) butchered while they begged for mercy, and heard the butchers laugh at their prayers and mimic their pleadings. I was overlooked, and escaped without hurt. When the savages were gone I crept out and cried the night away watching the burning houses; and I was all alone, except for the company of the dead and the wounded, for the rest had taken flight and hidden themselves.

I was sent to Domremy, to the priest, whose housekeeper became a loving mother to me. The priest, in the course of time, taught me to read and write, and he and I were the only persons in the village who possessed this learning.

At the time that the house of this good priest, Guillaume Fronte, became my home, I was six years old. We lived close by the village church, and the small garden of Joan's parents was behind the church. As to that family there were Jacques d'Arc the father, his wife Isabel Romee; three sonsJacques, ten years old, Pierre, eight, and Jean, seven; Joan, four, and her baby sister Catherine, about a year old. I had these children for playmates from the beginning. I had some other playmates besidesparticularly four boys: Pierre Morel, Etienne Roze, Noel Rainguesson, and Edmond Aubrey,
whose father was maire at that time; also two girls, about Joan's age, who by and by became her favorites; one was named Haumetter, the other was called Little Mengette. These girls were common peasant children, like Joan herself. When they grew up, both married
common laborers. Their estate was lowly enough, you see; yet a time came, many years after, when no passing stranger, howsoever great he might be, failed to go and pay his reverence to those two humble

old women who had been honored in their youth by the friendship of Joan of Arc.

These were all good children, just of the ordinary peasant type; not bright, of course—you would not expect that—but good-hearted and companionable, obedient to their parents and the priest; and as they grew up they became properly stocked with narrowness and prejudices got at second hand from their elders, and adopted without reserve; and without examination also—which goes without saying. Their religion was inherited, their politics the same. John Huss and his sort might find fault with the Church, in Domremy it disturbed nobody's faith; and when the split came, when I was fourteen, and we had three Popes at once, nobody in Domremy was worried about how to choose among them—the Pope of Rome was the right one, a Pope outside of Rome was no Pope at all. Every human creature in the village was an Armagnac—a patriot—and if we children hotly hated nothing else in the world, we did certainly hate the English and Burgundian name and polity in that way.

Chapter 2.

The Fairy Tree of Domremy

OUR DOMREMY was like any other humble little hamlet of that remote time and region. It was a maze of crooked, narrow lanes and alleys shaded and sheltered by the overhanging thatch roofs of the barnlike houses. The houses were dimly lighted by wooden– shuttered windowsthat is, holes in the walls which served for windows. The floors were dirt, and there was very little furniture. Sheep and cattle grazing was the main industry; all the young folks tended flocks.

The situation was beautiful. From one edge of the village a flowery plain extended in a wide sweep to the riverthe Meuse; from the rear edge of the village a grassy slope rose gradually, and at the top was the great oak foresta forest that was deep and gloomy and dense, and full of interest for us children, for many murders had been done in it by outlaws in old times, and in still earlier times prodigious dragons that spouted fire and poisonous vapors from their nostrils had their homes in there. In fact, one was still living in there in our own time. It was as long as a tree, and had a body as big around as a tierce, and scales like overlapping great tiles, and deep ruby eyes as large as a cavalier's hat, and an anchor–fluke on its tail as big as I don't know what, but very big, even unusually so for a dragon, as everybody
said who knew about dragons. It was thought that this dragon was of a brilliant blue color, with gold mottlings, but no one had ever seen it, therefore this was not known to be so, it was only an opinion. It was not my opinion; I think there is no sense in forming an opinion when there is no evidence to form it on. If you build a person
without any bones in him he may look fair enough to the eye, but he will be limber and cannot stand up; and I consider that evidence is the bones of an opinion. But I will take up this matter more at large at another time, and try to make the justness of my position appear.
As to that dragon, I always held the belief that its color was gold and without blue, for that has always been the color of dragons. That this

dragon lay but a little way within the wood at one time is shown by the fact that Pierre Morel was in there one day and smelt it, and recognized it by the smell. It gives one a horrid idea of how near to us the deadliest danger can be and we not suspect it.

In the earliest times a hundred knights from many remote places in the earth would have gone in there one after another, to kill the dragon and get the reward, but in our time that method had gone out, and the priest had become the one that abolished dragons. Pere Guillaume Fronte did it in this case. He had a procession, with candles and incense and banners, and marched around the edge of
the wood and exorcised the dragon, and it was never heard of again, although it was the opinion of many that the smell never wholly passed away. Not that any had ever smelt the smell again, for none had; it was only an opinion, like that otherand lacked bones, you see. I know that the creature was there before the exorcism, but whether
it was there afterward or not is a thing which I cannot be so positive about.

In a noble open space carpeted with grass on the high ground toward Vaucouleurs stood a most majestic beech tree with wide-reaching arms and a grand spread of shade, and by it a limpid spring of cold water; and on summer days the children went thereoh, every summer for more than five hundred yearswent there and sang and danced around the tree for hours together, refreshing themselves at the spring from time to time, and it was most lovely and enjoyable. Also they made wreaths of flowers and hung them upon the tree and about the spring to please the fairies that lived there; for they liked that, being idle innocent little creatures, as all fairies are, and fond of anything delicate and pretty like wild flowers put together in that way. And in return for this attention the fairies did any friendly thing they could for the children, such as keeping the spring always full
and clear and cold, and driving away serpents and insects that sting; and so there was never any unkindness between the fairies and the children during more than five hundred yearstradition said a thousandbut only the warmest affection and the most perfect trust and confidence; and whenever a child died the fairies mourned just as that child's playmates did, and the sign of it was there to see; for before the dawn on the day of the funeral they hung a little

immortelle over the place where that child was used to sit under the tree. I know this to be true by my own eyes; it is not hearsay. And the reason it was known that the fairies did it was this—that it was made all of black flowers of a sort not known in France anywhere.

Now from time immemorial all children reared in Domremy were called the Children of the Tree; and they loved that name, for it carried with it a mystic privilege not granted to any others of the children of this world. Which was this: whenever one of these came to die, then beyond the vague and formless images drifting through his darkening mind rose soft and rich and fair a vision of the Tree—if all was well with his soul. That was what some said. Others said the vision came in two ways: once as a warning, one or two years in advance of death, when the soul was the captive of sin, and then the Tree appeared in its desolate winter aspect—then that soul was smitten with an awful fear. If repentance came, and purity of life, the vision came again, this time summer–clad and beautiful; but if it were otherwise with that soul the vision was withheld, and it passed from life knowing its doom. Still others said that the vision came but
once, and then only to the sinless dying forlorn in distant lands and pitifully longing for some last dear reminder of their home. And what reminder of it could go to their hearts like the picture of the Tree that was the darling of their love and the comrade of their joys and comforter of their small griefs all through the divine days of their vanished youth?

Now the several traditions were as I have said, some believing one and some another. One of them I knew to be the truth, and that was the last one. I do not say anything against the others; I think they were true, but I only know that the last one was; and it is my thought that if one keep to the things he knows, and not trouble about the things which he cannot be sure about, he will have the steadier mind for it—and there is profit in that. I know that when the Children of the Tree die in a far land, then—if they be at peace with God—they turn their longing eyes toward home, and there, far–shining, as through a rift
in a cloud that curtains heaven, they see the soft picture of the Fairy Tree, clothed in a dream of golden light; and they see the bloomy mead sloping away to the river, and to their perishing nostrils is blown faint and sweet the fragrance of the flowers of home. And

then the vision fades and passes—but they know, they know! and by their transfigured faces you know also, you who stand looking on; yes, you know the message that has come, and that it has come from heaven.

Joan and I believed alike about this matter. But Pierre Morel and Jacques d'Arc, and many others believed that the vision appeared twice—to a sinner. In fact, they and many others said they knew it. Probably because their fathers had known it and had told them; for one gets most things at second hand in this world.

Now one thing that does make it quite likely that there were really two apparitions of the Tree is this fact: From the most ancient times if one saw a villager of ours with his face ash–white and rigid with a ghastly fright, it was common for every one to whisper to his neighbor, "Ah, he is in sin, and has got his warning." And the neighbor would shudder at the thought and whisper back, "Yes, poor soul, he has seen the Tree."

Such evidences as these have their weight; they are not to be put aside with a wave of the hand. A thing that is backed by the cumulative evidence of centuries naturally gets nearer and nearer to being proof all the time; and if this continue and continue, it will some day become authority—and authority is a bedded rock, and will abide.

In my long life I have seen several cases where the tree appeared announcing a death which was still far away; but in none of these was the person in a state of sin. No; the apparition was in these cases only a special grace; in place of deferring the tidings of that soul's redemption till the day of death, the apparition brought them long before, and with them peace—peace that might no more be disturbed—the eternal peace of God. I myself, old and broken, wait with serenity; for I have seen the vision of the Tree. I have seen it, and am content.

Always, from the remotest times, when the children joined hands and danced around the Fairy Tree they sang a song which was the Tree's song, the song of L'Arbre fée de Bourlemont. They sang it to a quaint sweet aira solacing sweet air which has gone murmuring through my dreaming spirit all my life when I was weary and troubled, resting me and carrying me through night and distance home again. No stranger can know or feel what that song has been, through the drifting centuries, to exiled Children of the Tree, homeless and heavy of heart in countries foreign to their speech and ways. You will think it a simple thing, that song, and poor, perchance; but if you will remember what it was to us, and what it brought before our eyes when it floated through our memories, then you will respect it. And you will understand how the water wells up in our eyes and makes all things dim, and our voices break and we cannot sing the last lines:

"And when, in Exile wand'ring, we Shall fainting yearn for glimpse of thee, Oh, rise upon our sight!"

And you will remember that Joan of Arc sang this song with us around the Tree when she was a little child, and always loved it. And that hallows it, yes, you will grant that:

L'ARBRE FEE DE BOURLEMONT SONG OF

THE CHILDREN

>Now what has kept your leaves so green, Arbre Fee de Bourlemont?

>The children's tears! They brought each grief, And you did comfort them and cheer
>Their bruised hearts, and steal a tear
>That, healed, rose a leaf.

>And what has built you up so strong, Arbre Fee de Bourlemont?

>The children's love! They've loved you long
>Ten hundred years, in sooth,
>They've nourished you with praise and song, And warmed your heart and kept it young

A thousand years of youth!

Bide always green in our young hearts, Arbre Fee de
Bourlemont!
And we shall always youthful be, Not heeding
Time his flight;
And when, in exile wand'ring, we
Shall fainting yearn for glimpse of thee, Oh, rise upon
our sight!

The fairies were still there when we were children, but we never saw them; because, a hundred years before that, the priest of Domremy had held a religious function under the tree and denounced them as being blood–kin to the Fiend and barred them from redemption; and then he warned them never to show themselves again, nor hang any more immortelles, on pain of perpetual banishment from that parish.

All the children pleaded for the fairies, and said they were their good friends and dear to them and never did them any harm, but the priest would not listen, and said it was sin and shame to have such friends. The children mourned and could not be comforted; and they made an agreement among themselves that they would always continue to hang flower–wreaths on the tree as a perpetual sign to the fairies that they were still loved and remembered, though lost to sight.

But late one night a great misfortune befell. Edmond Aubrey's mother passed by the Tree, and the fairies were stealing a dance, not thinking anybody was by; and they were so busy, and so intoxicated with the wild happiness of it, and with the bumpers of dew sharpened up with honey which they had been drinking, that they noticed nothing; so Dame Aubrey stood there astonished and admiring, and saw the little fantastic atoms holding hands, as many
as three hundred of them, tearing around in a great ring half as big as an ordinary bedroom, and leaning away back and spreading their mouths with laughter and song, which she could hear quite
distinctly, and kicking their legs up as much as three inches from the ground in perfect abandon and hilarityoh, the very maddest and witchingest dance the woman ever saw.

But in about a minute or two minutes the poor little ruined creatures discovered her. They burst out in one heartbreaking squeak of grief and terror and fled every which way, with their wee hazel–nut fists in their eyes and crying; and so disappeared.

The heartless womanno, the foolish woman; she was not heartless, but only thoughtlesswent straight home and told the neighbors all about it, whilst we, the small friends of the fairies, were asleep and not witting the calamity that was come upon us, and all unconscious that we ought to be up and trying to stop these fatal tongues. In the morning everybody knew, and the disaster was complete, for where everybody knows a thing the priest knows it, of course. We all flocked to Pere Fronte, crying and beggingand he had to cry, too, seeing our sorrow, for he had a most kind and gentle nature; and he did not want to banish the fairies, and said so; but said he had no choice, for it had been decreed that if they ever revealed themselves to man again, they must go. This all happened at the worst time possible, for Joan of Arc was ill of a fever and out of her head, and what could we do who had not her gifts of reasoning and persuasion? We flew in a swarm to her bed and cried out, "Joan, wake! Wake, there is no moment to lose! Come and plead for the fairiescome and save them; only you can do it!"

But her mind was wandering, she did not know what we said nor what we meant; so we went away knowing all was lost. Yes, all was lost, forever lost; the faithful friends of the children for five hundred years must go, and never come back any more.

It was a bitter day for us, that day that Pere Fronte held the function under the tree and banished the fairies. We could not wear mourning that any could have noticed, it would not have been allowed; so we had to be content with some poor small rag of black tied upon our garments where it made no show; but in our hearts we wore mourning, big and noble and occupying all the room, for our hearts were ours; they could not get at them to prevent that.

The great treel'Arbre Fee de Bourlemont was its beautiful namewas never afterward quite as much to us as it had been before, but it was always dear; is dear to me yet when I go there now, once a year in my old age, to sit under it and bring back the lost playmates of my youth and group them about me and look upon their faces through my tears and break my heart, oh, my God! No, the place was not quite the same afterward. In one or two ways it could not be; for, the fairies' protection being gone, the spring lost much of its freshness and coldness, and more than two-thirds of its volume, and the banished serpents and stinging insects returned, and multiplied, and became a torment and have remained so to this day.

When that wise little child, Joan, got well, we realized how much her illness had cost us; for we found that we had been right in believing she could save the fairies. She burst into a great storm of anger, for
so little a creature, and went straight to Pere Fronte, and stood up before him where he sat, and made reverence and said:

"The fairies were to go if they showed themselves to people again, is it not so?"

"Yes, that was it, dear."

"If a man comes prying into a person's room at midnight when that person is half-naked, will you be so unjust as to say that that person is showing himself to that man?"

"Well—no." The good priest looked a little troubled and uneasy when he said it.

"Is a sin a sin, anyway, even if one did not intend to commit it?" Pere Fronte

threw up his hands and cried out:

"Oh, my poor little child, I see all my fault," and he drew her to his side and put an arm around her and tried to make his peace with her, but her temper was up so high that she could not get it down right away, but buried her head against his breast and broke out crying
and said:

"Then the fairies committed no sin, for there was no intention to commit one, they not knowing that any one was by; and because
they were little creatures and could not speak for themselves and say

the law was against the intention, not against the innocent act, because they had no friend to think that simple thing for them and say it, they have been sent away from their home forever, and it was wrong, wrong to do it!"

The good father hugged her yet closer to his side and said:

"Oh, out of the mouths of babes and sucklings the heedless and unthinking are condemned; would God I could bring the little creatures back, for your sake. And mine, yes, and mine; for I have been unjust. There, there, don't crynobody could be sorrier than your poor old frienddon't cry, dear."

"But I can't stop right away, I've got to. And it is no little matter, this thing that you have done. Is being sorry penance enough for such an act?"

Pere Fronte turned away his face, for it would have hurt her to see him laugh, and said:

"Oh, thou remorseless but most just accuser, no, it is not. I will put on sackcloth and ashes; thereare you satisfied?"

Joan's sobs began to diminish, and she presently looked up at the old man through her tears, and said, in her simple way:

"Yes, that will doif it will clear you."

Pere Fronte would have been moved to laugh again, perhaps, if he had not remembered in time that he had made a contract, and not a very agreeable one. It must be fulfilled. So he got up and went to the fireplace, Joan watching him with deep interest, and took a shovelful of cold ashes, and was going to empty them on his old gray head when a better idea came to him, and he said:

"Would you mind helping me, dear?" "How,

father?"

He got down on his knees and bent his head low, and said:

"Take the ashes and put them on my head for me."

The matter ended there, of course. The victory was with the priest. One can imagine how the idea of such a profanation would strike Joan or any other child in the village. She ran and dropped upon her knees by his side and said:

"Oh, it is dreadful. I didn't know that that was what one meant by sackcloth and ashes—do please get up, father."

"But I can't until I am forgiven. Do you forgive me?"

"I? Oh, you have done nothing to me, father; it is yourself that must forgive yourself for wronging those poor things. Please get up, father, won't you?"

"But I am worse off now than I was before. I thought I was earning your forgiveness, but if it is my own, I can't be lenient; it would not become me. Now what can I do? Find me some way out of this with your wise little head."

The Pere would not stir, for all Joan's pleadings. She was about to cry again; then she had an idea, and seized the shovel and deluged her own head with the ashes, stammering out through her chokings and suffocations:

"There—now it is done. Oh, please get up, father."

The old man, both touched and amused, gathered her to his breast and said:

"Oh, you incomparable child! It's a humble martyrdom, and not of a sort presentable in a picture, but the right and true spirit is in it; that I testify."

Then he brushed the ashes out of her hair, and helped her scour her face and neck and properly tidy herself up. He was in fine spirits now, and ready for further argument, so he took his seat and drew Joan to his side again, and said:

"Joan, you were used to make wreaths there at the Fairy Tree with the other children; is it not so?"

That was the way he always started out when he was going to corner me up and catch me in something—just that gentle, indifferent way
that fools a person so, and leads him into the trap, he never noticing which way he is traveling until he is in and the door shut on him. He enjoyed that. I knew he was going to drop corn along in front of Joan now. Joan answered:

"Yes, father."

"Did you hang them on the tree?" "No, father."

"Didn't hang them there?" "No."

"Why didn't you?" "I—well, I didn't

wish to." "Didn't wish to?"

"No, father."

"What did you do with them?" "I hung them

in the church."

"Why didn't you want to hang them in the tree?"

"Because it was said that the fairies were of kin to the Fiend, and that it was sinful to show them honor."

"Did you believe it was wrong to honor them so?" "Yes. I

thought it must be wrong."

"Then if it was wrong to honor them in that way, and if they were of kin to the Fiend, they could be dangerous company for you and the other children, couldn't they?"

"I suppose soyes, I think so."

He studied a minute, and I judged he was going to spring his trap, and he did. He said:

"Then the matter stands like this. They were banned creatures, of fearful origin; they could be dangerous company for the children. Now give me a rational reason, dear, if you can think of any, why you call it a wrong to drive them into banishment, and why you would have saved them from it. In a word, what loss have you suffered by it?"

How stupid of him to go and throw his case away like that! I could have boxed his ears for vexation if he had been a boy. He was going along all right until he ruined everything by winding up in that
foolish and fatal way. What had she lost by it! Was he never going to find out what kind of a child Joan of Arc was? Was he never going
to learn that things which merely concerned her own gain or loss she cared nothing about? Could he never get the simple fact into his
head that the sure way and the only way to rouse her up and set her on fire was to show her where some other person was going to suffer wrong or hurt or loss? Why, he had gone and set a trap for himselfthat was all he had accomplished.

The minute those words were out of his mouth her temper was up, the indignant tears rose in her eyes, and she burst out on him with an energy and passion which astonished him, but didn't astonish me, for I knew he had fired a mine when he touched off his ill–chosen climax.

"Oh, father, how can you talk like that? Who owns France?" "God and the

King."

"Not Satan?"

"Satan, my child? This is the footstool of the Most High—Satan owns no handful of its soil."

"Then who gave those poor creatures their home? God. Who protected them in it all those centuries? God. Who allowed them to dance and play there all those centuries and found no fault with it? God. Who disapproved of God's approval and put a threat upon them? A man. Who caught them again in harmless sports that God allowed and a man forbade, and carried out that threat, and drove the poor things away from the home the good God gave them in His mercy and His pity, and sent down His rain and dew and sunshine upon it five hundred years in token of His peace? It was their home—theirs, by the grace of God and His good heart, and no man had a right to rob them of it. And they were the gentlest, truest friends that children ever had, and did them sweet and loving service all these five long centuries, and never any hurt or harm; and the children loved them, and now they mourn for them, and there is no healing for their grief. And what had the children done that they should suffer this cruel stroke? The poor fairies could have been dangerous company for the children? Yes, but never had been; and could is no argument. Kinsmen of the Fiend? What of it? Kinsmen
of the Fiend have rights, and these had; and children have rights, and these had; and if I had been there I would have spoken—I would have begged for the children and the fiends, and stayed your hand and saved them all. But now—oh, now, all is lost; everything is lost, and there is no help more!"

Then she finished with a blast at that idea that fairy kinsmen of the Fiend ought to be shunned and denied human sympathy and friendship because salvation was barred against them. She said that for that very reason people ought to pity them, and do every humane and loving thing they could to make them forget the hard fate that had been put upon them by accident of birth and no fault of their own. "Poor little creatures!" she said. "What can a person's heart be made of that can pity a Christian's child and yet can't pity a devil's child, that a thousand times more needs it!"

She had torn loose from Pere Fronte, and was crying, with her knuckles in her eyes, and stamping her small feet in a fury; and now she burst out of the place and was gone before we could gather our senses together out of this storm of words and this whirlwind of passion.

The Pere had got upon his feet, toward the last, and now he stood there passing his hand back and forth across his forehead like a person who is dazed and troubled; then he turned and wandered toward the door of his little workroom, and as he passed through it I heard him murmur sorrowfully:

"Ah, me, poor children, poor fiends, they have rights, and she said true I never thought of that. God forgive me, I am to blame."

When I heard that, I knew I was right in the thought that he had set a trap for himself. It was so, and he had walked into it, you see. I seemed to feel encouraged, and wondered if mayhap I might get him into one; but upon reflection my heart went down, for this was not my gift.

Chapter 3.

All Aflame With Love of France

SPEAKING of this matter reminds me of many incidents, many things that I could tell, but I think I will not try to do it now. It will be more to my present humor to call back a little glimpse of the simple and colorless good times we used to have in our village homes in those peaceful days—especially in the winter. In the summer we children were out on the breezy uplands with the flocks from dawn till night, and then there was noisy frolicking and all that; but winter was the cozy time, winter was the snug time. Often we gathered in old Jacques d'Arc's big dirt-floored apartment, with a great fire going, and played games, and sang songs, and told fortunes, and listened to the old villagers tell tales and histories and lies and one thing and another till twelve o'clock at night.

One winter's night we were gathered there—it was the winter that for years afterward they called the hard winter—and that particular night was a sharp one. It blew a gale outside, and the screaming of the wind was a stirring sound, and I think I may say it was beautiful, for I think it is great and fine and beautiful to hear the wind rage and storm and blow its clarions like that, when you are inside and comfortable. And we were. We had a roaring fire, and the pleasant spit-spit of the snow and sleet falling in it down the chimney, and the yarning and laughing and singing went on at a noble rate till about ten o'clock, and then we had a supper of hot porridge and beans, and meal cakes with butter, and appetites to match.

Little Joan sat on a box apart, and had her bowl and bread on another one, and her pets around her helping. She had more than was usual
of them or economical, because all the outcast cats came and took up with her, and homeless or unlovable animals of other kinds heard about it and came, and these spread the matter to the other creatures, and they came also; and as the birds and the other timid wild things
of the woods were not afraid of her, but always had an idea she was

a friend when they came across her, and generally struck up an acquaintance with her to get invited to the house, she always had samples of those breeds in stock. She was hospitable to them all, for an animal was an animal to her, and dear by mere reason of being an animal, no matter about its sort or social station; and as she would allow of no cages, no collars, no fetters, but left the creatures free to come and go as they liked, that contented them, and they came; but they didn't go, to any extent, and so they were a marvelous nuisance, and made Jacques d'Arc swear a good deal; but his wife said God gave the child the instinct, and knew what He was doing when He did it, therefore it must have its course; it would be no sound prudence to meddle with His affairs when no invitation had been extended. So the pets were left in peace, and here they were, as I have said, rabbits, birds, squirrels, cats, and other reptiles, all around the child, and full of interest in her supper, and helping what they could. There was a very small squirrel on her shoulder, sitting up, as those creatures do, and turning a rocky fragment of prehistoric chestnut–cake over and over in its knotty hands, and hunting for the less indurated places, and giving its elevated bushy tail a flirt and its pointed ears a toss when it found one significant thankfulness and surprise and then it filed that place off with those two slender front teeth which a squirrel carries for that purpose and not for ornament, for ornamental they never could be, as any will admit that have noticed them.

Everything was going fine and breezy and hilarious, but then there came an interruption, for somebody hammered on the door. It was one of those ragged road–stragglers the eternal wars kept the country full of them. He came in, all over snow, and stamped his feet, and shook, and brushed himself, and shut the door, and took off his limp ruin of a hat, and slapped it once or twice against his leg to knock off its fleece of snow, and then glanced around on the company with a pleased look upon his thin face, and a most yearning and famished one in his eye when it fell upon the victuals, and then he gave us a humble and conciliatory salutation, and said it was a blessed thing to have a fire like that on such a night, and a roof overhead like this,
and that rich food to eat, and loving friends to talk with ah, yes, this was true, and God help the homeless, and such as must trudge the roads in this weather.

Nobody said anything. The embarrassed poor creature stood there and appealed to one face after the other with his eyes, and found no welcome in any, the smile on his own face flickering and fading and perishing, meanwhile; then he dropped his gaze, the muscles of his face began to twitch, and he put up his hand to cover this womanish sign of weakness.

"Sit down!"

This thunder–blast was from old Jacques d'Arc, and Joan was the object of it. The stranger was startled, and took his hand away, and there was Joan standing before him offering him her bowl of porridge. The man said:

"God Almighty bless you, my darling!" and then the tears came, and ran down his cheeks, but he was afraid to take the bowl.

"Do you hear me? Sit down, I say!"

There could not be a child more easy to persuade than Joan, but this was not the way. Her father had not the art; neither could he learn it. Joan said:

"Father, he is hungry; I can see it."

"Let him work for food, then. We are being eaten out of house and home by his like, and I have said I would endure it no more, and will keep my word. He has the face of a rascal anyhow, and a villain. Sit down, I tell you!"

"I know not if he is a rascal or no, but he is hungry, father, and shall have my porridgeI do not need it."

"If you don't obey me I'llRascals are not entitled to help from honest people, and no bite nor sup shall they have in this house. Joan!"

She set her bowl down on the box and came over and stood before her scowling father, and said:

"Father, if you will not let me, then it must be as you say; but I would that you would think—then you would see that it is not right to punish one part of him for what the other part has done; for it is that poor stranger's head that does the evil things, but it is not his head that is hungry, it is his stomach, and it has done no harm to anybody, but is without blame, and innocent, not having any way to do a wrong, even if it was minded to it. Please let"

"What an idea! It is the most idiotic speech I ever heard."

But Aubrey, the maire, broke in, he being fond of an argument, and having a pretty gift in that regard, as all acknowledged. Rising in his place and leaning his knuckles upon the table and looking about him with easy dignity, after the manner of such as be orators, he began, smooth and persuasive:

"I will differ with you there, gossip, and will undertake to show the company"—here he looked around upon us and nodded his head in a confident way—"that there is a grain of sense in what the child has said; for look you, it is of a certainty most true and demonstrable that it is a man's head that is master and supreme ruler over his whole body. Is that granted? Will any deny it?" He glanced around again; everybody indicated assent. "Very well, then; that being the case, no part of the body is responsible for the result when it carries out an order delivered to it by the head; ergo, the head is alone responsible for crimes done by a man's hands or feet or stomach—do you get the idea? am I right thus far?" Everybody said yes, and said it with enthusiasm, and some said, one to another, that the maire was in great form to–night and at his very best—which pleased the maire exceedingly and made his eyes sparkle with pleasure, for he overheard these things; so he went on in the same fertile and brilliant way. "Now, then, we will consider what the term responsibility means, and how it affects the case in point. Responsibility makes a man responsible for only those things for which he is properly responsible"—and he waved his spoon around in a wide sweep to indicate the comprehensive nature of that class of responsibilities which render people responsible, and several exclaimed, admiringly, "He is right!—he has put that whole tangled thing into a nutshell—it is wonderful!" After a little pause to give the interest opportunity to gather and grow, he went on: "Very good. Let us suppose the case of a pair of tongs that falls upon a man's foot, causing a cruel hurt. Will you claim that the tongs are punishable for that? The question is answered; I see by your faces that you would call such a claim absurd. Now, why is it absurd? It is absurd because, there being no reasoning faculty—that is to say, no faculty of personal command—in a pair of tongs, personal responsibility for the acts of the tongs is wholly absent from the tongs; and, therefore, responsibility being absent, punishment cannot ensue. Am I right?" A hearty burst of applause was his answer. "Now, then, we arrive at a man's stomach. Consider how exactly, how marvelously, indeed, its situation corresponds to that of a pair of tongs. Listen—and take careful note, I beg you. Can a man's stomach plan a murder? No. Can it plan a theft? No. Can it plan an incendiary fire? No. Now answer me—can a pair of tongs?" (There were admiring shouts of "No!" and "The cases are just exact!" and "Don't he do it splendid!") "Now, then, friends and neighbors, a stomach which cannot plan a crime cannot be a principal in the commission of it—that is plain, as you see. The matter is narrowed down by that much; we will narrow it further. Can a stomach, of its own motion, assist at a crime? The answer is no, because command is absent, the reasoning faculty is absent, volition is absent—as in the case of the tongs. We perceive now, do we not, that the stomach is totally irresponsible for crimes committed, either in whole or in part, by it?" He got a rousing cheer for response. "Then what do we arrive at as our verdict? Clearly this: that there is no

such thing in this world as a guilty stomach; that in the body of the veriest rascal resides a pure and innocent stomach; that, whatever it's owner may do, it at least should be sacred in our eyes; and that while God gives us minds to think just and charitable and honorable thoughts, it should be, and is, our privilege, as well as our duty, not only to feed the hungry stomach that resides in a rascal, having pity for its sorrow and its need, but to do it gladly, gratefully, in recognition of its sturdy and loyal maintenance of its purity and innocence in the midst of temptation and in company so repugnant to its better feelings. I am done."

Well, you never saw such an effect! They rose—the whole house rose—an clapped, and cheered, and praised him to the skies; and one after another, still clapping and shouting, they crowded forward, some with moisture in their eyes, and wrung his hands, and said such glorious things to him that he was clear overcome with pride and happiness, and couldn't say a word, for his voice would have broken, sure. It was splendid to see; and everybody said he had never come up to that speech in his life before, and never could do it again. Eloquence is a power, there is no question of that. Even old Jacques d'Arc was carried away, for once in his life, and shouted out:

"It's all right, Joangive him the porridge!"

She was embarrassed, and did not seem to know what to say, and so didn't say anything. It was because she had given the man the porridge long ago and he had already eaten it all up. When she was asked why she had not waited until a decision was arrived at, she said the man's stomach was very hungry, and it would not have been wise to wait, since she could not tell what the decision would be. Now that was a good and thoughtful idea for a child.

The man was not a rascal at all. He was a very good fellow, only he was out of luck, and surely that was no crime at that time in France. Now that his stomach was proved to be innocent, it was allowed to make itself at home; and as soon as it was well filled and needed nothing more, the man unwound his tongue and turned it loose, and it was really a noble one to go. He had been in the wars for years, and the things he told and the way he told them fired everybody's patriotism away up high, and set all hearts to thumping and all pulses to leaping; then, before anybody rightly knew how the change was made, he was leading us a sublime march through the ancient glories of France, and in fancy we saw the titanic forms of the twelve paladins rise out of the mists of the past and face their fate; we heard the tread of the innumerable hosts sweeping down to shut them in; we saw this human tide flow and ebb, ebb and flow, and waste away before that little band of heroes; we saw each detail pass before us of that most stupendous, most disastrous, yet most adored and glorious day in French legendary history; here and there and yonder, across that vast field of the dead and dying, we saw this and that and the other paladin dealing his prodigious blows with weary arm and failing strength, and one by one we saw them fall, till only one remainedhe that was without peer, he whose name gives name to the Song of Songs, the song which no Frenchman can hear and keep his feelings down and his pride of country cool; then, grandest and pitifulest scene of all, we saw his own pathetic death; and our stillness, as we sat with parted lips and breathless, hanging upon this man's words, gave us a sense of the awful stillness that reigned in that field of slaughter when that last surviving soul had passed.

And now, in this solemn hush, the stranger gave Joan a pat or two on the head and said:

"Little maid whom God keep! you have brought me from death to life this night; now listen: here is your reward," and at that supreme time for such a heart-melting, soul-rousing surprise, without another word he lifted up the most noble and pathetic voice that was ever heard, and began to pour out the great Song of Roland!

Think of that, with a French audience all stirred up and ready. Oh, where was your spoken eloquence now! what was it to this! How
fine he looked, how stately, how inspired, as he stood there with that mighty chant welling from his lips and his heart, his whole body transfigured, and his rags along with it.

Everybody rose and stood while he sang, and their faces glowed and their eyes burned; and the tears came and flowed down their cheeks and their forms began to sway unconsciously to the swing of the song, and their bosoms to heave and pant; and moanings broke out, and deep ejaculations; and when the last verse was reached, and Roland lay dying, all alone, with his face to the field and to his slain, lying there in heaps and winrows, and took off and held up his gauntlet to God with his failing hand, and breathed his beautiful prayer with his paling pips, all burst out in sobs and wailings. But when the final great note died out and the song was done, they all flung themselves in a body at the singer, stark mad with love of him and love of France and pride in her great deeds and old renown, and smothered him with their embracings; but Joan was there first, hugged close to his breast, and covering his face with idolatrous kisses.

The storm raged on outside, but that was no matter; this was the stranger's home now, for as long as he might please.

Chapter 4.

Joan Tames the Mad Man

ALL CHILDREN have nicknames, and we had ours. We got one apiece early, and they stuck to us; but Joan was richer in this matter, for, as time went on, she earned a second, and then a third, and so
on, and we gave them to her. First and last she had as many as half a dozen. Several of these she never lost. Peasant–girls are bashful naturally; but she surpassed the rule so far, and colored so easily,
and was so easily embarrassed in the presence of strangers, that we nicknamed her the Bashful. We were all patriots, but she was called the Patriot, because our warmest feeling for our country was cold beside hers. Also she was called the Beautiful; and this was not merely because of the extraordinary beauty of her face and form, but because of the loveliness of her character. These names she kept, and one other—the Brave.

We grew along up, in that plodding and peaceful region, and got to be good–sized boys and girls—big enough, in fact, to begin to know as much about the wars raging perpetually to the west and north of us
as our elders, and also to feel as stirred up over the occasional news from these red fields as they did. I remember certain of these days very clearly. One Tuesday a crowd of us were romping and singing around the Fairy Tree, and hanging garlands on it in memory of our lost little fairy friends, when Little Mengette cried out:

"Look! What is that?"

When one exclaims like that in a way that shows astonishment and apprehension, he gets attention. All the panting breasts and flushed faces flocked together, and all the eager eyes were turned in one direction—down the slope, toward the village.

"It's a black flag."

"A black flag! Nois it?"

"You can see for yourself that it is nothing else."

"It is a black flag, sure! Now, has any ever seen the like of that before?"

"What can it mean?"

"Mean? It means something dreadful—what else?"

"That is nothing to the point; anybody knows that without the telling. But what?—that is the question."

"It is a chance that he that bears it can answer as well as any that are here, if you contain yourself till he comes."

"He runs well. Who is it?"

Some named one, some another; but presently all saw that it was Etienne Roze, called the Sunflower, because he had yellow hair and a round pock–marked face. His ancestors had been Germans some centuries ago. He came straining up the slope, now and then projecting his flag–stick aloft and giving his black symbol of woe a wave in the air, whilst all eyes watched him, all tongues discussed him, and every heart beat faster and faster with impatience to know his news. At last he sprang among us, and struck his flag–stick into the ground, saying:

"There! Stand there and represent France while I get my breath. She needs no other flag now."

All the giddy chatter stopped. It was as if one had announced a death. In that chilly hush there was no sound audible but the panting of the breath–blown boy. When he was presently able to speak, he said:

"Black news is come. A treaty has been made at Troyes between France and the English and Burgundians. By it France is betrayed and delivered over, tied hand and foot, to the enemy. It is the work of the Duke of Burgundy and that she–devil, the Queen of France. It marries Henry of England to Catharine of France"

"Is not this a lie? Marries the daughter of France to the Butcher of Agincourt? It is not to be believed. You have not heard aright."

"If you cannot believe that, Jacques d'Arc, then you have a difficult task indeed before you, for worse is to come. Any child that is born of that marriageif even a girlis to inherit the thrones of both England and France, and this double ownership is to remain with its posterity forever!"

"Now that is certainly a lie, for it runs counter to our Salic law, and so is not legal and cannot have effect," said Edmond Aubrey, called the Paladin, because of the armies he was always going to eat up some day. He would have said more, but he was drowned out by the clamors of the others, who all burst into a fury over this feature of the treaty, all talking at once and nobody hearing anybody, until presently Haumette persuaded them to be still, saying:

"It is not fair to break him up so in his tale; pray let him go on. You find fault with his history because it seems to be lies. That were reason for satisfactionthat kind of liesnot discontent. Tell the rest, Etienne."

"There is but this to tell: Our King, Charles VI., is to reign until he dies, then Henry V. of England is to be Regent of France until a child of his shall be old enough to"

"That man is to reign over usthe Butcher? It is lies! all lies!" cried the Paladin. "Besides, look youwhat becomes of our Dauphin? What says the treaty about him?"

"Nothing. It takes away his throne and makes him an outcast."

Then everybody shouted at once and said the news was a lie; and all began to get cheerful again, saying, "Our King would have to sign the treaty to make it good; and that he would not do, seeing how it serves his own son."

But the Sunflower said: "I will ask you this: Would the Queen sign a treaty disinheriting her son?"

"That viper? Certainly. Nobody is talking of her. Nobody expects better of her. There is no villainy she will stick at, if it feed her spite; and she hates her son. Her signing it is of no consequence. The King must sign."

"I will ask you another thing. What is the King's condition? Mad, isn't he?"

"Yes, and his people love him all the more for it. It brings him near to them by his sufferings; and pitying him makes them love him."

"You say right, Jacques d'Arc. Well, what would you of one that is mad? Does he know what he does? No. Does he do what others make him do? Yes. Now, then, I tell you he has signed the treaty."

"Who made him do it?"

"You know, without my telling. The Queen."

Then there was another uproar—everybody talking at once, and all heaping execrations upon the Queen's head. Finally Jacques d'Arc said:

"But many reports come that are not true. Nothing so shameful as this has ever come before, nothing that cuts so deep, nothing that has dragged France so low; therefore there is hope that this tale is but another idle rumor. Where did you get it?"

The color went out of his sister Joan's face. She dreaded the answer; and her instinct was right.

"The cure of Maxey brought it."

There was a general gasp. We knew him, you see, for a trusty man. "Did he believe it?"

The hearts almost stopped beating. Then came the answer: "He did. And that is not all. He said he knew it to be true."

Some of the girls began to sob; the boys were struck silent. The distress in Joan's face was like that which one sees in the face of a dumb animal that has received a mortal hurt. The animal bears it, making no complaint; she bore it also, saying no word. Her brother Jacques put his hand on her head and caressed her hair to indicate his sympathy, and she gathered the hand to her lips and kissed it for thanks, not saying anything. Presently the reaction came, and the boys began to talk. Noel Rainguesson said:

"Oh, are we never going to be men! We do grow along so slowly, and France never needed soldiers as she needs them now, to wipe out this black insult."

"I hate youth!" said Pierre Morel, called the Dragon–fly because his eyes stuck out so. "You've always got to wait, and wait, and wait—and here are the great wars wasting away for a hundred years, and you never get a chance. If I could only be a soldier now!"

"As for me, I'm not going to wait much longer," said the Paladin; "and when I do start you'll hear from me, I promise you that. There are some who, in storming a castle, prefer to be in the rear; but as for me, give me the front or none; I will have none in front of me but the officers."

Even the girls got the war spirit, and Marie Dupont said:

"I would I were a man; I would start this minute!" and looked very proud of herself, and glanced about for applause.

"So would I," said Cecile Letellier, sniffing the air like a war–horse that smells the battle; "I warrant you I would not turn back from the field though all England were in front of me."

"Pooh!" said the Paladin; "girls can brag, but that's all they are good for. Let a thousand of them come face to face with a handful of soldiers once, if you want to see what running is like. Here's little

Joan—next she'll be threatening to go for a soldier!"

The idea was so funny, and got such a good laugh, that the Paladin gave it another trial, and said: "Why you can just see her!—see her plunge into battle like any old veteran. Yes, indeed; and not a poor shabby common soldier like us, but an officer—an officer, mind you, with armor on, and the bars of a steel helmet to blush behind and hide her embarrassment when she finds an army in front of her that she hasn't been introduced to. An officer? Why, she'll be a captain! A captain, I tell you, with a hundred men at her back—or maybe girls. Oh, no common–soldier business for her! And, dear me, when she starts for that other army, you'll think there's a hurricane blowing it away!"

Well, he kept it up like that till he made their sides ache with laughing; which was quite natural, for certainly it was a very funny idea—at that time—I mean, the idea of that gentle little creature, that wouldn't hurt a fly, and couldn't bear the sight of blood, and was so girlish and shrinking in all ways, rushing into battle with a gang of soldiers at her back. Poor thing, she sat there confused and ashamed to be so laughed at; and yet at that very minute there was something about to happen which would change the aspect of things, and make those young people see that when it comes to laughing, the person that laughs last has the best chance. For just then a face which we all knew and all feared projected itself from behind the Fairy Tree, and the thought that shot through us all was, crazy Benoist has gotten loose from his cage, and we are as good as dead! This ragged and hairy and horrible creature glided out from behind the tree, and
raised an ax as he came. We all broke and fled, this way and that, the girls screaming and crying. No, not all; all but Joan. She stood up
and faced the man, and remained so. As we reached the wood that borders the grassy clearing and jumped into its shelter, two or three of us glanced back to see if Benoist was gaining on us, and that is what we saw—Joan standing, and the maniac gliding stealthily toward her with his ax lifted. The sight was sickening. We stood where we were, trembling and not able to move. I did not want to see the murder done, and yet I could not take my eyes away. Now I saw Joan step forward to meet the man, though I believed my eyes must be deceiving me. Then I saw him stop. He threatened her with his

ax, as if to warn her not to come further, but she paid no heed, but went steadily on, until she was right in front of him right under his ax. Then she stopped, and seemed to begin to talk with him. It made me sick, yes, giddy, and everything swam around me, and I could not see anything for a time whether long or brief I do not know.
When this passed and I looked again, Joan was walking by the man's side toward the village, holding him by his hand. The ax was in her other hand.

One by one the boys and girls crept out, and we stood there gazing, open-mouthed, till those two entered the village and were hid from sight. It was then that we named her the Brave.

We left the black flag there to continue its mournful office, for we had other matter to think of now. We started for the village on a run, to give warning, and get Joan out of her peril; though for one, after seeing what I had seen, it seemed to me that while Joan had the ax the man's chance was not the best of the two. When we arrived the danger was past, the madman was in custody. All the people were flocking to the little square in front of the church to talk and exclaim and wonder over the event, and it even made the town forget the black news of the treaty for two or three hours.

All the women kept hugging and kissing Joan, and praising her, and crying, and the men patted her on the head and said they wished she was a man, they would send her to the wars and never doubt but that she would strike some blows that would be heard of. She had to tear herself away and go and hide, this glory was so trying to her diffidence.

Of course the people began to ask us for the particulars. I was so ashamed that I made an excuse to the first comer, and got privately away and went back to the Fairy Tree, to get relief from the embarrassment of those questionings. There I found Joan, but she was there to get relief from the embarrassment of glory. One by one the others shirked the inquirers and joined us in our refuge. Then we gathered around Joan, and asked her how she had dared to do that thing. She was very modest about it, and said:

"You make a great thing of it, but you mistake; it was not a great matter. It was not as if I had been a stranger to the man. I know him, and have known him long; and he knows me, and likes me. I have
fed him through the bars of his cage many times; and last December, when they chopped off two of his fingers to remind him to stop seizing and wounding people passing by, I dressed his hand every day till it was well again."

"That is all well enough," said Little Mengette, "but he is a madman, dear, and so his likings and his gratitude and friendliness go for nothing when his rage is up. You did a perilous thing."

"Of course you did," said the Sunflower. "Didn't he threaten to kill you with the ax?"

"Yes."

"Didn't he threaten you more than once?" "Yes."

"Didn't you feel afraid?"

"No at least not much very little." "Why didn't

you?"

She thought a moment, then said, quite simply: "I don't

know."

It made everybody laugh. Then the Sunflower said it was like a lamb trying to think out how it had come to eat a wolf, but had to give it up.

Cecile Letellier asked, "Why didn't you run when we did?" "Because it was

necessary to get him to his cage; else he would kill
some one. Then he would come to the like harm himself."

It is noticeable that this remark, which implies that Joan was entirely forgetful of herself and her own danger, and had thought and wrought for the preservation of other people alone, was not challenged, or criticized, or commented upon by anybody there, but was taken by all as matter of course and true. It shows how clearly her character was defined, and how well it was known and established.

There was silence for a time, and perhaps we were all thinking of the same thingnamely, what a poor figure we had cut in that adventure as contrasted with Joan's performance. I tried to think up some good way of explaining why I had run away and left a little girl at the mercy of a maniac armed with an ax, but all of the explanations that offered themselves to me seemed so cheap and shabby that I gave the matter up and remained still. But others were less wise. Noel Rainguesson fidgeted awhile, then broke out with a remark which showed what his mind had been running on:

"The fact is, I was taken by surprise. That is the reason. If I had had a moment to think, I would no more have thought of running that I would think of running from a baby. For, after all, what is Theophile Benoist, that I should seem to be afraid of him? Pooh! the idea of being afraid of that poor thing! I only wish he would come along nowI'd show you!"

"So do I!" cried Pierre Morel. "If I wouldn't make him climb this tree quicker thanwell, you'd see what I would do! Taking a person by surprise, that waywhy, I never meant to run; not in earnest, I mean. I never thought of running in earnest; I only wanted to have some fun, and when I saw Joan standing there, and him threatening her, it was all I could do to restrain myself from going there and just tearing the livers and lights out of him. I wanted to do it bad enough, and if it was to do over again, I would! If ever he comes fooling around me again, I'll"

"Oh, hush!" said the Paladin, breaking in with an air of disdain; "the way you people talk, a person would think there's something heroic about standing up and facing down that poor remnant of a man. Why, it's nothing! There's small glory to be got in facing him down, I should say. Why, I wouldn't want any better fun than to face down a hundred like him. If he was to come along here now, I would walk up to him just as I am now—I wouldn't care if he had a thousand axes—and say"

And so he went on and on, telling the brave things he would say and the wonders he would do; and the others put in a word from time to time, describing over again the gory marvels they would do if ever that madman ventured to cross their path again, for next time they would be ready for him, and would soon teach him that if he thought he could surprise them twice because he had surprised them once, he would find himself very seriously mistaken, that's all.

And so, in the end, they all got back their self–respect; yes, and even added somewhat to it; indeed when the sitting broke up they had a finer opinion of themselves than they had ever had before.

Chapter 5.

Domremy Pillaged and Burned

THEY WERE peaceful and pleasant, those young and smoothly flowing days of ours; that is, that was the case as a rule, we being remote from the seat of war; but at intervals roving bands approached near enough for us to see the flush in the sky at night which marked where they were burning some farmstead or village, and we all knew, or at least felt, that some day they would come yet nearer, and we should have our turn. This dull dread lay upon our spirits like a physical weight. It was greatly augmented a couple of years after the Treaty of Troyes.

It was truly a dismal year for France. One day we had been over to have one of our occasional pitched battles with those hated Burgundian boys of the village of Maxey, and had been whipped, and were arriving on our side of the river after dark, bruised and weary, when we heard the bell ringing the tocsin. We ran all the way, and when we got to the square we found it crowded with the excited villagers, and weirdly lighted by smoking and flaring torches.

On the steps of the church stood a stranger, a Burgundian priest, who was telling the people news which made them weep, and rave, and rage, and curse, by turns. He said our old mad King was dead, and that now we and France and the crown were the property of an English baby lying in his cradle in London. And he urged us to give that child our allegiance, and be its faithful servants and well- wishers; and said we should now have a strong and stable
government at last, and that in a little time the English armies would start on their last march, and it would be a brief one, for all that it would need to do would be to conquer what odds and ends of our country yet remained under that rare and almost forgotten rag, the banner of France.

The people stormed and raged at him, and you could see dozens of them stretch their fists above the sea of torch–lighted faces and shake them at him; and it was all a wild picture, and stirring to look at; and the priest was a first–rate part of it, too, for he stood there in the strong glare and looked down on those angry people in the blandest and most indifferent way, so that while you wanted to burn him at the stake, you still admired the aggravating coolness of him. And his winding–up was the coolest thing of all. For he told them how, at the funeral of our old King, the French King–at–Arms had broken his staff of office over the coffin of "Charles VI. and his dynasty," at the same time saying, in a loud voice, "God grant long life to Henry, King of France and England, our sovereign lord!" and then he asked them to join him in a hearty Amen to that! The people were white with wrath, and it tied their tongues for the moment, and they could not speak. But Joan was standing close by, and she looked up in his face, and said in her sober, earnest way:

"I would I might see thy head struck from thy body!"then, after a pause, and crossing herself"if it were the will of God."

This is worth remembering, and I will tell you why: it is the only harsh speech Joan ever uttered in her life. When I shall have revealed to you the storms she went through, and the wrongs and persecutions, then you will see that it was wonderful that she said but one bitter thing while she lived.

From the day that that dreary news came we had one scare after another, the marauders coming almost to our doors every now and then; so that we lived in ever–increasing apprehension, and yet were somehow mercifully spared from actual attack. But at last our turn did really come. This was in the spring of '28. The Burgundians swarmed in with a great noise, in the middle of a dark night, and we had to jump up and fly for our lives. We took the road to Neufchateau, and rushed along in the wildest disorder, everybody
trying to get ahead, and thus the movements of all were impeded; but Joan had a cool headthe only cool head thereand she took command and brought order out of that chaos. She did her work quickly and with decision and despatch, and soon turned the panic flight into a quite steady–going march. You will grant that for so young a person,

and a girl at that, this was a good piece of work.

She was sixteen now, shapely and graceful, and of a beauty so extraordinary that I might allow myself any extravagance of language in describing it and yet have no fear of going beyond the truth. There was in her face a sweetness and serenity and purity that justly reflected her spiritual nature. She was deeply religious, and this is a thing which sometimes gives a melancholy cast to a person's countenance, but it was not so in her case. Her religion made her inwardly content and joyous; and if she was troubled at times, and showed the pain of it in her face and bearing, it came of distress for her country; no part of it was chargeable to her religion.

A considerable part of our village was destroyed, and when it became safe for us to venture back there we realized what other people had been suffering in all the various quarters of France for many yearsyes, decades of years. For the first time we saw wrecked and smoke-blackened homes, and in the lanes and alleys carcasses of dumb creatures that had been slaughtered in pure wantonnessamong them calves and lambs that had been pets of the children; and it was pity to see the children lament over them.

And then, the taxes, the taxes! Everybody thought of that. That burden would fall heavy now in the commune's crippled condition, and all faces grew long with the thought of it. Joan said:

"Paying taxes with naught to pay them with is what the rest of France has been doing these many years, but we never knew the bitterness of that before. We shall know it now."

And so she went on talking about it and growing more and more troubled about it, until one could see that it was filling all her mind.

At last we came upon a dreadful object. It was the madmanhacked and stabbed to death in his iron cage in the corner of the square. It was a bloody and dreadful sight. Hardly any of us young people had ever seen a man before who had lost his life by violence; so this cadaver had an awful fascination for us; we could not take our eyes from it. I mean, it had that sort of fascination for all of us but one. That one was Joan. She turned away in horror, and could not be persuaded to go near it again. Thereit is a striking reminder that we are but creatures of use and custom; yes, and it is a reminder, too, of how harshly and unfairly fate deals with us sometimes. For it was so ordered that the very ones among us who were most fascinated with mutilated and bloody death were to live their lives in peace, while that other, who had a native and deep horror of it, must presently go forth and have it as a familiar spectacle every day on the field of battle.

You may well believe that we had plenty of matter for talk now, since the raiding of our village seemed by long odds the greatest event that had really ever occurred in the world; for although these dull peasants may have thought they recognized the bigness of some of the previous occurrences that had filtered from the world's history dimly into their minds, the truth is that they hadn't. One biting little fact, visible to their eyes of flesh and felt in their own personal
vitals, became at once more prodigious to them than the grandest remote episode in the world's history which they had got at second hand and by hearsay. It amuses me now when I recall how our elders talked then. They fumed and fretted in a fine fashion.

"Ah, yes," said old Jacques d'Arc, "things are come to a pretty pass, indeed! The King must be informed of this. It is time that he cease from idleness and dreaming, and get at his proper business." He meant our young disinherited King, the hunted refugee, Charles VII.

"You say well," said the maire. "He should be informed, and that at once. It is an outrage that such things would be permitted. Why, we are not safe in our beds, and he taking his ease yonder. It shall be made known, indeed it shallall France shall hear of it!"

To hear them talk, one would have imagined that all the previous ten thousand sackings and burnings in France had been but fables, and this one the only fact. It is always the way; words will answer as
long as it is only a person's neighbor who is in trouble, but when that person gets into trouble himself, it is time that the King rise up and do something.

The big event filled us young people with talk, too. We let it flow in a steady stream while we tended the flocks. We were beginning to feel pretty important now, for I was eighteen and the other youths were from one to four years older—young men, in fact. One day the Paladin was arrogantly criticizing the patriot generals of France and said:

"Look at Dunois, Bastard of Orleans—call him a general! Just put me in his place once—never mind what I would do, it is not for me to say, I have no stomach for talk, my way is to act and let others do the talking—but just put me in his place once, that's all! And look at Saintrailles—pooh! and that blustering La Hire, now what a general that is!"

It shocked everybody to hear these great names so flippantly handled, for to us these renowned soldiers were almost gods. In their far-off splendor they rose upon our imaginations dim and huge, shadowy and awful, and it was a fearful thing to hear them spoken of as if they were mere men, and their acts open to comment and criticism. The color rose in Joan's face, and she said:

"I know not how any can be so hardy as to use such words regarding these sublime men, who are the very pillars of the French state, supporting it with their strength and preserving it at daily cost of
their blood. As for me, I could count myself honored past all deserving if I might be allowed but the privilege of looking upon them once—at a distance, I mean, for it would not become one of my degree to approach them too near."

The Paladin was disconcerted for a moment, seeing by the faces around him that Joan had put into words what the others felt, then he pulled his complacency together and fell to fault-finding again. Joan's brother Jean said:

"If you don't like what our generals do, why don't you go to the great wars yourself and better their work? You are always talking about going to the wars, but you don't go."

"Look you," said the Paladin, "it is easy to say that. Now I will tell you why I remain chafing here in a bloodless tranquillity which my reputation teaches you is repulsive to my nature. I do not go because

I am not a gentleman. That is the whole reason. What can one
private soldier do in a contest like this? Nothing. He is not permitted to rise from
the ranks. If I were a gentleman would I remain here? Not one moment. I can save
Franceah, you may laugh, but I know what is in me, I know what is hid under this
peasant cap. I can save France, and I stand ready to do it, but not under these
present conditions. If they want me, let them send for me; otherwise, let them take
the consequences; I shall not budge but as an officer."

"Alas, poor FranceFrance is lost!" said Pierre d'Arc.

"Since you sniff so at others, why don't you go to the wars yourself, Pierre
d'Arc?"

"Oh, I haven't been sent for, either. I am no more a gentleman than you. Yet I will
go; I promise to go. I promise to go as a private under your orderswhen you are
sent for."

They all laughed, and the Dragon–fly said:

"So soon? Then you need to begin to get ready; you might be called for in five
yearswho knows? Yes, in my opinion you'll march for the wars in five years."

"He will go sooner," said Joan. She said it in a low voice and musingly,
but several heard it.

"How do you know that, Joan?" said the Dragon–fly, with a surprised
look. But Jean d'Arc broke in and said:

"I want to go myself, but as I am rather young yet, I also will wait, and march
when the Paladin is sent for."

"No," said Joan, "he will go with Pierre."

She said it as one who talks to himself aloud without knowing it, and none heard it
but me. I glanced at her and saw that her knitting– needles were idle in her hands,
and that her face had a dreamy and absent look in it. There were fleeting
movements of her lips as if she might be occasionally saying parts of sentences to
herself. But there

was no sound, for I was the nearest person to her and I heard nothing. But I set my ears open, for those two speeches had affected me uncannily, I being superstitious and easily troubled by any little thing of a strange and unusual sort.

Noel Rainguesson said:

"There is one way to let France have a chance for her salvation. We've got one gentleman in the commune, at any rate. Why can't the Scholar change name and condition with the Paladin? Then he can
be an officer. France will send for him then, and he will sweep these
English and Burgundian armies into the sea like flies."

I was the Scholar. That was my nickname, because I could read and write. There was a chorus of approval, and the Sunflower said:

"That is the very thing—it settles every difficulty. The Sieur de Conte will easily agree to that. Yes, he will march at the back of Captain Paladin and die early, covered with common–soldier glory."

"He will march with Jean and Pierre, and live till these wars are forgotten," Joan muttered; "and at the eleventh hour Noel and the Paladin will join these, but not of their own desire." The voice was so low that I was not perfectly sure that these were the words, but they seemed to be. It makes one feel creepy to hear such things.

"Come, now," Noel continued, "it's all arranged; there's nothing to do but organize under the Paladin's banner and go forth and rescue France. You'll all join?"

All said yes, except Jacques d'Arc, who said:

"I'll ask you to excuse me. It is pleasant to talk war, and I am with you there, and I've always thought I should go soldiering about this time, but the look of our wrecked village and that carved–up and bloody madman have taught me that I am not made for such work and such sights. I could never be at home in that trade. Face swords and the big guns and death? It isn't in me. No, no; count me out. And besides, I'm the eldest son, and deputy prop and protector of the family. Since you are going to carry Jean and Pierre to the wars, somebody must be left behind to take care of our Joan and her sister. I shall stay at home, and grow old in peace and tranquillity."

"He will stay at home, but not grow old," murmured Joan.

The talk rattled on in the gay and careless fashion privileged to youth, and we got the Paladin to map out his campaigns and fight his battles and win his victories and extinguish the English and put our King upon his throne and set his crown upon his head. Then we asked him what he was going to answer when the King should require him to name his reward. The Paladin had it all arranged in his head, and brought it out promptly:

"He shall give me a dukedom, name me premier peer, and make me Hereditary Lord High Constable of France."

"And marry you to a princess—you're not going to leave that out, are you?"

The Paladin colored a trifle, and said, brusquely:

"He may keep his princesses—I can marry more to my taste." Meaning Joan,

though nobody suspected it at that time. If any had, the Paladin would have been finely ridiculed for his vanity. There was no fit mate in that village for Joan of Arc. Every one would have said that.

In turn, each person present was required to say what reward he would demand of the King if he could change places with the Paladin and do the wonders the Paladin was going to do. The answers were given in fun, and each of us tried to outdo his predecessors in the extravagance of the reward he would claim; but when it came to Joan's turn, and they rallied her out of her dreams and asked her to testify, they had to explain to her what the question was, for her thought had been absent, and she had heard none of this latter part of our talk. She supposed they wanted a serious answer, and she gave it. She sat considering some moments, then she said:

"If the Dauphin, out of his grace and nobleness, should say to me,

'Now that I am rich and am come to my own again, choose and have,' I should kneel and ask him to give command that our village should nevermore be taxed."

It was so simple and out of her heart that it touched us and we did not laugh, but fell to thinking. We did not laugh; but there came a day when we remembered that speech with a mournful pride, and were glad that we had not laughed, perceiving then how honest her words had been, and seeing how faithfully she made them good when the time came, asking just that boon of the King and refusing to take even any least thing for herself.

Chapter 6.

Joan and Archangel Michael

ALL THROUGH her childhood and up to the middle of her fourteenth year, Joan had been the most light–hearted creature and the merriest in the village, with a hop–skip–and–jump gait and a happy and catching laugh; and this disposition, supplemented by her warm and sympathetic nature and frank and winning ways, had
made her everybody's pet. She had been a hot patriot all this time, and sometimes the war news had sobered her spirits and wrung her heart and made her acquainted with tears, but always when these interruptions had run their course her spirits rose and she was her old self again.

But now for a whole year and a half she had been mainly grave; not melancholy, but given to thought, abstraction, dreams. She was carrying France upon her heart, and she found the burden not light. I knew that this was her trouble, but others attributed her abstraction
to religious ecstasy, for she did not share her thinkings with the village at large, yet gave me glimpses of them, and so I knew, better than the rest, what was absorbing her interest. Many a time the idea crossed my mind that she had a secreta secret which she was keeping wholly to herself, as well from me as from the others. This idea had come to me because several times she had cut a sentence in two and changed the subject when apparently she was on the verge of a revelation of some sort. I was to find this secret out, but not just yet.

The day after the conversation which I have been reporting we were together in the pastures and fell to talking about France, as usual. For her sake I had always talked hopefully before, but that was mere lying, for really there was not anything to hang a rag of hope for France upon. Now it was such a pain to lie to her, and cost me such shame to offer this treachery to one so snow–pure from lying and treachery, and even from suspicion of such baseness in others, as she was, that I was resolved to face about now and begin over again, and never insult her more with deception. I started on the new policy by saying—still opening up with a small lie, of course, for habit is habit, and not to be flung out of the window by any man, but coaxed downstairs a step at a time:

"Joan, I have been thinking the thing all over last night, and have concluded that we have been in the wrong all this time; that the case of France is desperate; that it has been desperate ever since Agincourt; and that to-day it is more than desperate, it is hopeless."

I did not look her in the face while I was saying it; it could not be expected of a person. To break her heart, to crush her hope with a so frankly brutal speech as that, without one charitable soft place in it—it seemed a shameful thing, and it was. But when it was out, the weight gone, and my conscience rising to the surface, I glanced at her face
to see the result.

There was none to see. At least none that I was expecting. There was a barely perceptible suggestion of wonder in her serious eyes, but
that was all; and she said, in her simple and placid way:

"The case of France hopeless? Why should you think that? Tell me." It is a most

pleasant thing to find that what you thought would inflict
a hurt upon one whom you honor, has not done it. I was relieved now, and could say all my say without any furtivenesses and without embarrassment. So I began:

"Let us put sentiment and patriotic illusions aside, and look at the facts in the face. What do they say? They speak as plainly as the figures in a merchant's account-book. One has only to add the two columns up to see that the French house is bankrupt, that one-half of its property is already in the English sheriff's hands and the other
half in nobody's—except those of irresponsible raiders and robbers confessing allegiance to nobody. Our King is shut up with his favorites and fools in inglorious idleness and poverty in a narrow little patch of the kingdom—a sort of back lot, as one may say—and has no authority there or anywhere else, hasn't a farthing to his name, nor a regiment of soldiers; he is not fighting, he is not intending to fight, he means to make no further resistance; in truth, there is but

one thing that he is intending to do—give the whole thing up, pitch his crown into the sewer, and run away to Scotland. There are the facts. Are they correct?"

"Yes, they are correct."

"Then it is as I have said: one needs but to add them together in order to realize what they mean."

She asked, in an ordinary, level tone: "What—that the case

of France is hopeless?"

"Necessarily. In face of these facts, doubt of it is impossible." "How can

you say that? How can you feel like that?"

"How can I? How could I think or feel in any other way, in the circumstances? Joan, with these fatal figures before, you, have you really any hope for France—really and actually?"

"Hope—oh, more than that! France will win her freedom and keep it. Do not doubt it."

It seemed to me that her clear intellect must surely be clouded to–day. It must be so, or she would see that those figures could mean only one thing. Perhaps if I marshaled them again she would see. So I said:

"Joan, your heart, which worships France, is beguiling your head. You are not perceiving the importance of these figures. Here—I want
to make a picture of them, here on the ground with a stick. Now, this rough outline is France. Through its middle, east and west, I draw a river."

"Yes, the Loire."

"Now, then, this whole northern half of the country is in the tight grip of the English."

"Yes."

"And this whole southern half is really in nobody's hands at all–as our King confesses by meditating desertion and flight to a foreign land. England has armies here; opposition is dead; she can assume full possession whenever she may choose. In very truth, all France is gone, France is already lost, France has ceased to exist. What was France is now but a British province. Is this true?"

Her voice was low, and just touched with emotion, but distinct: "Yes, it is

true."

"Very well. Now add this clinching fact, and surely the sum is complete: When have French soldiers won a victory? Scotch
soldiers, under the French flag, have won a barren fight or two a few years back, but I am speaking of French ones. Since eight thousand Englishmen nearly annihilated sixty thousand Frenchmen a dozen years ago at Agincourt, French courage has been paralyzed. And so
it is a common saying to–day that if you confront fifty French soldiers with five English ones, the French will run."

"It is a pity, but even these things are true." "Then

certainly the day for hoping is past."

I believed the case would be clear to her now. I thought it could not fail to be clear to her, and that she would say, herself, that there was no longer any ground for hope. But I was mistaken; and disappointed also. She said, without any doubt in her tone:

"France will rise again. You shall see."

"Rise?with this burden of English armies on her back!"

"She will cast it off; she will trample it under foot!" This with spirit. "Without

soldiers to fight with?"

"The drums will summon them. They will answer, and they will march."

"March to the rear, as usual?"

"No; to the front—ever to the front—always to the front! You shall see." "And the pauper King?"

"He will mount his throne—he will wear his crown."

"Well, of a truth this makes one's head dizzy. Why, if I could believe that in thirty years from now the English domination would be broken and the French monarch's head find itself hooped with a real crown of sovereignty"

"Both will have happened before two years are sped." "Indeed? and who is going to perform all these sublime impossibilities?" "God."

It was a reverent low note, but it rang clear.

What could have put those strange ideas in her head? This question kept running in my mind during two or three days. It was inevitable that I should think of madness. What other way was there to account for such things? Grieving and brooding over the woes of France had weakened that strong mind, and filled it with fantastic phantoms—yes, that must be it.

But I watched her, and tested her, and it was not so. Her eye was clear and sane, her ways were natural, her speech direct and to the point. No, there was nothing the matter with her mind; it was still the soundest in the village and the best. She went on thinking for others, planning for others, sacrificing herself for others, just as always before. She went on ministering to her sick and to her poor, and still stood ready to give the wayfarer her bed and content herself with the floor. There was a secret somewhere, but madness was not the key to it. This was plain.

Now the key did presently come into my hands, and the way that it happened was this. You have heard all the world talk of this matter which I am about to speak of, but you have not heard an eyewitness talk of it before.

I was coming from over the ridge, one day—it was the 15th of May, '28—and when I got to the edge of the oak forest and was about to step out of it upon the turfy open space in which the haunted beech tree stood, I happened to cast a glance from cover, first—then I took a step backward, and stood in the shelter and concealment of the foliage. For I had caught sight of Joan, and thought I would devise some sort of playful surprise for her. Think of it—that trivial conceit was neighbor, with but a scarcely measurable interval of time between, to an event destined to endure forever in histories and songs.

The day was overcast, and all that grassy space wherein the Tree stood lay in a soft rich shadow. Joan sat on a natural seat formed by gnarled great roots of the Tree. Her hands lay loosely, one reposing in the other, in her lap. Her head was bent a little toward the ground, and her air was that of one who is lost to thought, steeped in dreams, and not conscious of herself or of the world. And now I saw a most strange thing, for I saw a white shadow come slowly gliding along the grass toward the Tree. It was of grand proportions—a robed form, with wings—and the whiteness of this shadow was not like any other whiteness that we know of, except it be the whiteness of lightnings, but even the lightnings are not so intense as it was, for one can look at them without hurt, whereas this brilliancy was so blinding that it pained my eyes and brought the water into them. I uncovered my head, perceiving that I was in the presence of something not of this world. My breath grew faint and difficult, because of the terror and the awe that possessed me.

Another strange thing. The wood had been silent—smitten with that deep stillness which comes when a storm–cloud darkens a forest,
and the wild creatures lose heart and are afraid; but now all the birds burst forth into song, and the joy, the rapture, the ecstasy of it was beyond belief; and was so eloquent and so moving, withal, that it was plain it was an act of worship. With the first note of those birds Joan cast herself upon her knees, and bent her head low and crossed

her hands upon her breast.

She had not seen the shadow yet. Had the song of the birds told her it was coming? It had that look to me. Then the like of this must have happened before. Yes, there might be no doubt of that.

The shadow approached Joan slowly; the extremity of it reached her, flowed over her, clothed her in its awful splendor. In that immortal light her face, only humanly beautiful before, became divine;
flooded with that transforming glory her mean peasant habit was become like to the raiment of the sun–clothed children of God as we see them thronging the terraces of the Throne in our dreams and imaginings.

Presently she rose and stood, with her head still bowed a little, and with her arms down and the ends of her fingers lightly laced together in front of her; and standing so, all drenched with that wonderful light, and yet apparently not knowing it, she seemed to listenbut I heard nothing. After a little she raised her head, and looked up as
one might look up toward the face of a giant, and then clasped her hands and lifted them high, imploringly, and began to plead. I heard some of the words. I heard her say:

"But I am so young! oh, so young to leave my mother and my home and go out into the strange world to undertake a thing so great! Ah, how can I talk with men, be comrade with men?soldiers! It would give me over to insult, and rude usage, and contempt. How can I go to the great wars, and lead armies?I a girl, and ignorant of such things, knowing nothing of arms, nor how to mount a horse, nor ride it.... Yetif it is commanded"

Her voice sank a little, and was broken by sobs, and I made out no more of her words. Then I came to myself. I reflected that I had been intruding upon a mystery of Godand what might my punishment be? I was afraid, and went deeper into the wood. Then I carved a mark in
the bark of a tree, saying to myself, it may be that I am dreaming and have not seen this vision at all. I will come again, when I know that I am awake and not dreaming, and see if this mark is still here; then I shall know.

Chapter 7.

She Delivers the Divine Command

I HEARD my name called. It was Joan's voice. It startled me, for how could she know I was there? I said to myself, it is part of the dream; it is all dreamvoice, vision and all; the fairies have done this. So I crossed myself and pronounced the name of God, to break the enchantment. I knew I was awake now and free from the spell, for
no spell can withstand this exorcism. Then I heard my name called again, and I stepped at once from under cover, and there indeed was Joan, but not looking as she had looked in the dream. For she was
not crying now, but was looking as she had used to look a year and a half before, when her heart was light and her spirits high. Her old-time energy and fire were back, and a something like exaltation showed itself in her face and bearing. It was almost as if she had
been in a trance all that time and had come awake again. Really, it was just as if she had been away and lost, and was come back to us at last; and I was so glad that I felt like running to call everybody and have them flock around her and give her welcome. I ran to her excited and said:

"Ah, Joan, I've got such a wonderful thing to tell you about! You would never imagine it. I've had a dream, and in the dream I saw you right here where you are standing now, and"

But she put up her hand and said: "It was not a

dream."

It gave me a shock, and I began to feel afraid again.

"Not a dream?" I said, "how can you know about it, Joan?" "Are you

dreaming now?"

"II suppose not. I think I am not."

"Indeed you are not. I know you are not. And yow were not dreaming when you cut the mark in the tree."

I felt myself turning cold with fright, for now I knew of a certainty that I had not been dreaming, but had really been in the presence of a dread something not of this world. Then I remembered that my
sinful feet were upon holy groundthe ground where that celestial shadow had rested. I moved quickly away, smitten to the bones with fear. Joan followed, and said:

"Do not be afraid; indeed there is no need. Come with me. We will sit by the spring and I will tell you all my secret."

When she was ready to begin, I checked her and said:

"First tell me this. You could not see me in the wood; how did you know I cut a mark in the tree?"

"Wait a little; I will soon come to that; then you will see."

"But tell me one thing now; what was that awful shadow that I saw?" "I will tell

you, but do not be disturbed; you are not in danger. It was
the shadow of an archangelMichael, the chief and lord of the armies of heaven."

I could but cross myself and tremble for having polluted that ground with my feet.

"You were not afraid, Joan? Did you see his facedid you see his form?"

"Yes; I was not afraid, because this was not the first time. I was afraid the first time."

"When was that, Joan?"

"It is nearly three years ago now."

"So long? Have you seen him many times?" "Yes, many times."

"It is this, then, that has changed you; it was this that made you thoughtful and not as you were before. I see it now. Why did you not tell us about it?"

"It was not permitted. It is permitted now, and soon I shall tell all. But only you, now. It must remain a secret for a few days still."

"Has none seen that white shadow before but me?"

"No one. It has fallen upon me before when you and others were present, but none could see it. To–day it has been otherwise, and I was told why; but it will not be visible again to any."

"It was a sign to me, then and a sign with a meaning of some kind?" "Yes, but I may not speak of that."

"Strange that that dazzling light could rest upon an object before one's eyes and not be visible."

"With it comes speech, also. Several saints come, attended by myriads of angels, and they speak to me; I hear their voices, but others do not. They are very dear to me my Voices; that is what I call them to myself."

"Joan, what do they tell you?"

"All manner of things about France, I mean." "What things have they been used to tell you?" She sighed, and said:

"Disasters only disasters, and misfortunes, and humiliation. There was naught else to foretell."

"They spoke of them to you beforehand?" "Yes. So that I knew what was going to happen before it happened. It made me grave as you saw. It could not be otherwise. But always there was a word of hope, too. More than that: France was to be rescued, and made great and free again. But how and by whom that was not told. Not until to-day." As she said those last words a sudden deep glow shone in her eyes, which I was to see there many times in after-days when the bugles sounded the charge and learn to call it the battle-light. Her breast heaved, and the color rose in her face. "But to-day I know. God has chosen the meanest of His creatures for this work; and by His command, and in His protection, and by His strength, not mine, I am to lead His armies, and win back France, and set the crown upon the head of His servant that is Dauphin and shall be King."

I was amazed, and said:

"You, Joan? You, a child, lead armies?"

"Yes. For one little moment or two the thought crushed me; for it is as you say I am only a child; a child and ignorant ignorant of everything that pertains to war, and not fitted for the rough life of camps and the companionship of soldiers. But those weak moments passed; they will not come again. I am enlisted, I will not turn back, God helping me, till the English grip is loosed from the throat of France. My Voices have never told me lies, they have not lied to-day. They say I am to go to Robert de Baudricourt, governor of Vaucouleurs, and he will give me men-at-arms for escort and send me to the King. A year from now a blow will be struck which will be the beginning of the end, and the end will follow swiftly."

"Where will it be struck?"

"My Voices have not said; nor what will happen this present year, before it is struck. It is appointed me to strike it, that is all I know; and follow it with others, sharp and swift, undoing in ten weeks England's long years of costly labor, and setting the crown upon the Dauphin's head for such is God's will; my Voices have said it, and shall I doubt it? No; it will be as they have said, for they say only that which is true."

These were tremendous sayings. They were impossibilities to my reason, but to my heart they rang true; and so, while my reason doubted, my heart believedbelieved, and held fast to the belief from that day. Presently I said:

"Joan, I believe the things which you have said, and now I am glad that I am to march with you to the great warsthat is, if it is with you I am to march when I go."

She looked surprised, and said:

"It is true that you will be with me when I go to the wars, but how did you know?"

"I shall march with you, and so also will Jean and Pierre, but not Jacques."

"All trueit is so ordered, as was revealed to me lately, but I did not know until to–day that the marching would be with me, or that I should march at all. How did you know these things?"

I told her when it was that she had said them. But she did not remember about it. So then I knew that she had been asleep, or in a trance or an ecstasy of some kind, at that time. She bade me keep these and the other revelations to myself for the present, and I said I would, and kept the faith I promised.

None who met Joan that day failed to notice the change that had come over her. She moved and spoke with energy and decision; there was a strange new fire in her eye, and also a something wholly new and remarkable in her carriage and in the set of her head. This new light in the eye and this new bearing were born of the authority and leadership which had this day been vested in her by the decree of God, and they asserted that authority as plainly as speech could have done it, yet without ostentation or bravado. This calm consciousness of command, and calm unconscious outward expression of it, remained with her thenceforth until her mission was accomplished.

Like the other villagers, she had always accorded me the deference due my rank; but now, without word said on either side, she and I changed places; she gave orders, not suggestions. I received them with the deference due a superior, and obeyed them without comment. In the evening she said to me:

"I leave before dawn. No one will know it but you. I go to speak with the governor of Vaucouleurs as commanded, who will despise me and treat me rudely, and perhaps refuse my prayer at this time. I go first to Burey, to persuade my uncle Laxart to go with me, it not being meet that I go alone. I may need you in Vaucouleurs; for if the governor will not receive me I will dictate a letter to him, and so must have some one by me who knows the art of how to write and spell the words. You will go from here to–morrow in the afternoon, and remain in Vaucouleurs until I need you."

I said I would obey, and she went her way. You see how clear a head she had, and what a just and level judgment. She did not order me to go with her; no, she would not subject her good name to gossiping remark. She knew that the governor, being a noble, would grant me, another noble, audience; but no, you see, she would not have that, either. A poor peasant–girl presenting a petition through a young noblemanhow would that look? She always protected her modesty from hurt; and so, for reward, she carried her good name unsmirched to the end. I knew what I must do now, if I would have her approval: go to Vaucouleurs, keep out of her sight, and be ready when wanted.

I went the next afternoon, and took an obscure lodging; the next day I called at the castle and paid my respects to the governor, who invited me to dine with him at noon of the following day. He was an ideal soldier of the time; tall, brawny, gray–headed, rough, full of strange oaths acquired here and there and yonder in the wars and treasured as if they were decorations. He had been used to the camp all his life, and to his notion war was God's best gift to man. He had his steel cuirass on, and wore boots that came above his knees, and was equipped with a huge sword; and when I looked at this martial figure, and heard the marvelous oaths, and guessed how little of poetry and sentiment might be looked for in this quarter, I hoped the little peasant–girl would not get the privilege of confronting this battery, but would have to content herself with the dictated letter.

I came again to the castle the next day at noon, and was conducted to the great dining–hall and seated by the side of the governor at a
small table which was raised a couple of steps higher than the general table. At the small table sat several other guests besides myself, and at the general table sat the chief officers of the garrison. At the entrance door stood a guard of halberdiers, in morion and breastplate.

As for talk, there was but one topic, of coursethe desperate situation of France. There was a rumor, some one said, that Salisbury was making preparations to march against Orleans. It raised a turmoil of excited conversation, and opinions fell thick and fast. Some believed he would march at once, others that he could not accomplish the investment before fall, others that the siege would be long, and bravely contested; but upon one thing all voices agreed: that Orleans must eventually fall, and with it France. With that, the prolonged discussion ended, and there was silence. Every man seemed to sink himself in his own thoughts, and to forget where he was. This
sudden and profound stillness, where before had been so much animation, was impressive and solemn. Now came a servant and whispered something to the governor, who said:

"Would talk with me?" "Yes, your

Excellency."

"H'm! A strange idea, certainly. Bring them in."

It was Joan and her uncle Laxart. At the spectacle of the great people the courage oozed out of the poor old peasant and he stopped
midway and would come no further, but remained there with his red nightcap crushed in his hands and bowing humbly here, there, and everywhere, stupefied with embarrassment and fear. But Joan came steadily forward, erect and self–possessed, and stood before the governor. She recognized me, but in no way indicated it. There was
a buzz of admiration, even the governor contributing to it, for I heard him mutter, "By God's grace, it is a beautiful creature!" He inspected her critically a moment or two, then said:

"Well, what is your errand, my child?"

"My message is to you, Robert de Baudricourt, governor of Vaucouleurs, and it is this: that you will send and tell the Dauphin to wait and not give battle to his enemies, for God will presently send him help."

This strange speech amazed the company, and many murmured, "The poor young thing is demented." The governor scowled, and said:

"What nonsense is this? The King—or the Dauphin, as you call him—needs no message of that sort. He will wait, give yourself no uneasiness as to that. What further do you desire to say to me?"

"This. To beg that you will give me an escort of men–at–arms and send me to the Dauphin."

"What for?"

"That he may make me his general, for it is appointed that I shall drive the English out of France, and set the crown upon his head."

"What—you? Why, you are but a child!"

"Yet am I appointed to do it, nevertheless." "Indeed!

And when will all this happen?"

"Next year he will be crowned, and after that will remain master of France."

There was a great and general burst of laughter, and when it had subsided the governor said:

"Who has sent you with these extravagant messages?" "My Lord."

"What Lord?"

"The King of Heaven."

Many murmured, "Ah, poor thing, poor thing!" and others, "Ah, her mind is but a wreck!" The governor hailed Laxart, and said:

"Harkye!take this mad child home and whip her soundly. That is the best cure for her ailment."

As Joan was moving away she turned and said, with simplicity: "You refuse me
the soldiers, I know not why, for it is my Lord that
has commanded you. Yes, it is He that has made the command; therefore I must come again, and yet again; then I shall have the men–at–arms."

There was a great deal of wondering talk, after she was gone; and the guards and servants passed the talk to the town, the town passed
it to the country; Domremy was already buzzing with it when we got back.

Chapter 8.

Why the Scorners Relented

HUMAN NATURE is the same everywhere: it defies success, it has nothing but scorn for defeat. The village considered that Joan had disgraced it with her grotesque performance and its ridiculous failure; so all the tongues were busy with the matter, and as bilious and bitter as they were busy; insomuch that if the tongues had been teeth she would not have survived her persecutions. Those persons who did not scold did what was worse and harder to bear; for they ridiculed her, and mocked at her, and ceased neither day nor night from their witticisms and jeerings and laughter. Haumette and Little Mengette and I stood by her, but the storm was too strong for her other friends, and they avoided her, being ashamed to be seen with her because she was so unpopular, and because of the sting of the
taunts that assailed them on her account. She shed tears in secret, but none in public. In public she carried herself with serenity, and showed no distress, nor any resentmentconduct which should have softened the feeling against her, but it did not. Her father was so incensed that he could not talk in measured terms about her wild project of going to the wars like a man. He had dreamed of her doing such a thing, some time before, and now he remembered that dream with apprehension and anger, and said that rather than see her unsex herself and go away with the armies, he would require her brothers
to drown her; and that if they should refuse, he would do it with his own hands.

But none of these things shook her purpose in the least. Her parents kept a strict watch upon her to keep her from leaving the village, but she said her time was not yet; that when the time to go was come she should know it, and then the keepers would watch in vain.

The summer wasted along; and when it was seen that her purpose continued steadfast, the parents were glad of a chance which finally offered itself for bringing her projects to an end through marriage.

The Paladin had the effrontery to pretend that she had engaged herself to him several years before, and now he claimed a ratification of the engagement.

She said his statement was not true, and refused to marry him. She was cited to appear before the ecclesiastical court at Toul to answer for her perversity; when she declined to have counsel, and elected to conduct her case herself, her parents and all her ill–wishers rejoiced, and looked upon her as already defeated. And that was natural enough; for who would expect that an ignorant peasant–girl of sixteen would be otherwise than frightened and tongue–tied when standing for the first time in presence of the practised doctors of the law, and surrounded by the cold solemnities of a court? Yet all these people were mistaken. They flocked to Toul to see and enjoy this fright and embarrassment and defeat, and they had their trouble for their pains. She was modest, tranquil, and quite at her ease. She called no witnesses, saying she would content herself with
examining the witnesses for the prosecution. When they had testified, she rose and reviewed their testimony in a few words, pronounced it vague, confused, and of no force, then she placed the Paladin again on the stand and began to search him. His previous testimony went rag by rag to ruin under her ingenious hands, until at last he stood bare, so to speak, he that had come so richly clothed in fraud and falsehood. His counsel began an argument, but the court declined to hear it, and threw out the case, adding a few words of grave compliment for Joan, and referring to her as "this marvelous child."

After this victory, with this high praise from so imposing a source added, the fickle village turned again, and gave Joan countenance, compliment, and peace. Her mother took her back to her heart, and even her father relented and said he was proud of her. But the time hung heavy on her hands, nevertheless, for the siege of Orleans was begun, the clouds lowered darker and darker over France, and still her Voices said wait, and gave her no direct commands. The winter set in, and wore tediously along; but at last there was a change.

Book II: In Court and Camp

Chapter 1.

Joan Says Good-by

THE 5th of January, 1429, Joan came to me with her uncle Laxart, and said:

"The time is come. My Voices are not vague now, but clear, and they have told me what to do. In two months I shall be with the Dauphin."

Her spirits were high, and her bearing martial. I caught the infection and felt a great impulse stirring in me that was like what one feels when he hears the roll of the drums and the tramp of marching men.

"I believe it," I said.

"I also believe it," said Laxart. "If she had told me before, that she was commanded of God to rescue France, I should not have believed; I should have let her seek the governor by her own ways and held myself clear of meddling in the matter, not doubting she was mad. But I have seen her stand before those nobles and mighty men unafraid, and say her say; and she had not been able to do that
but by the help of God. That I know. Therefore with all humbleness I am at her command, to do with me as she will."

"My uncle is very good to me," Joan said. "I sent and asked him to come and persuade my mother to let him take me home with him to tend his wife, who is not well. It is arranged, and we go at dawn to- morrow. From his house I shall go soon to Vaucouleurs, and wait and strive until my prayer is granted. Who were the two cavaliers who sat to your left at the governor's table that day?"

"One was the Sieur Jean de Novelonpont de Metz, the other the Sieur Bertrand de Poulengy."

"Good metal—good metal, both. I marked them for men of mine.... What is it I see in your face? Doubt?"

I was teaching myself to speak the truth to her, not trimming it or polishing it; so I said:

"They considered you out of your head, and said so. It is true they pitied you for being in such misfortune, but still they held you to be mad."

This did not seem to trouble her in any way or wound her. She only said:

"The wise change their minds when they perceive that they have been in error. These will. They will march with me. I shall see them presently.. .. You seem to doubt again? Do you doubt?"

"N–no. Not now. I was remembering that it was a year ago, and that they did not belong here, but only chanced to stop a day on their journey."

"They will come again. But as to matters now in hand; I came to leave with you some instructions. You will follow me in a few days. Order your affairs, for you will be absent long."

"Will Jean and Pierre go with me?"

"No; they would refuse now, but presently they will come, and with them they will bring my parents' blessing, and likewise their consent that I take up my mission. I shall be stronger, then—stronger for that; for lack of it I am weak now." She paused a little while, and the tears gathered in her eyes; then she went on: "I would say good–by to Little Mengette. Bring her outside the village at dawn; she must go with me a little of the way"

"And Haumette?"

She broke down and began to cry, saying:

"No, oh, no—she is too dear to me, I could not bear it, knowing I should never look upon her face again."

Next morning I brought Mengette, and we four walked along the road in the cold dawn till the village was far behind; then the two girls said their good–bys, clinging about each other's neck, and pouring out their grief in loving words and tears, a pitiful sight to see. And Joan took one long look back upon the distant village, and the Fairy Tree, and the oak forest, and the flowery plain, and the river, as if she was trying to print these scenes on her memory so that they would abide there always and not fade, for she knew she would not see them any more in this life; then she turned, and went from
us, sobbing bitterly. It was her birthday and mine. She was seventeen years old.

Chapter 2.

The Governor Speeds Joan

After a few days, Laxart took Joan to Vaucouleurs, and found lodging and guardianship for her with Catherine Royer, a wheelwright's wife, an honest and good woman. Joan went to mass regularly, she helped do the housework, earning her keep in that way, and if any wished to talk with her about her mission and many did she talked freely, making no concealments regarding the matter now. I was soon housed near by, and witnessed the effects which
followed. At once the tidings spread that a young girl was come who was appointed of God to save France. The common people flocked
in crowds to look at her and speak with her, and her fair young loveliness won the half of their belief, and her deep earnestness and transparent sincerity won the other half. The well–to–do remained away and scoffed, but that is their way.

Next, a prophecy of Merlin's, more than eight hundred years old,
was called to mind, which said that in a far future time France would be lost by a woman and restored by a woman. France was now, for the first time, lost and by a woman, Isabel of Bavaria, her base
Queen; doubtless this fair and pure young girl was commissioned of
Heaven to complete the prophecy.

This gave the growing interest a new and powerful impulse; the excitement rose higher and higher, and hope and faith along with it; and so from Vaucouleurs wave after wave of this inspiring enthusiasm flowed out over the land, far and wide, invading all the villages and refreshing and revivifying the perishing children of France; and from these villages came people who wanted to see for themselves, hear for themselves; and they did see and hear, and believe. They filled the town; they more than filled it; inns and lodgings were packed, and yet half of the inflow had to go without shelter. And still they came, winter as it was, for when a man's soul is starving, what does he care for meat and roof so he can but get that nobler hunger fed? Day after day, and still day after day the great tide rose. Domremy was dazed, amazed, stupefied, and said to itself, "Was this world-wonder in our familiar midst all these years and we too dull to see it?" Jean and Pierre went out from the village, stared at and envied like the great and fortunate of the earth, and their progress to Vaucouleurs was like a triumph, all the country-side flocking to see and salute the brothers of one with whom angels had spoken face to face, and into whose hands by command of God they had delivered the destinies of France.

The brothers brought the parents' blessing and godspeed to Joan, and their promise to bring it to her in person later; and so, with this culminating happiness in her heart and the high hope it inspired, she went and confronted the governor again. But he was no more tractable than he had been before. He refused to send her to the
King. She was disappointed, but in no degree discouraged. She said:

"I must still come to you until I get the men-at-arms; for so it is commanded, and I may not disobey. I must go to the Dauphin, though I go on my knees."

I and the two brothers were with Joan daily, to see the people that came and hear what they said; and one day, sure enough, the Sieur Jean de Metz came. He talked with her in a petting and playful way, as one talks with children, and said:

"What are you doing here, my little maid? Will they drive the King out of France, and shall we all turn English?"

She answered him in her tranquil, serious way:

"I am come to bid Robert de Baudricourt take or send me to the
King, but he does not heed my words."

"Ah, you have an admirable persistence, truly; a whole year has not turned you from your wish. I saw you when you came before."

Joan said, as tranquilly as before:

"It is not a wish, it is a purpose. He will grant it. I can wait."

"Ah, perhaps it will not be wise to make too sure of that, my child. These governors are stubborn people to deal with. In case he shall not grant your prayer"

"He will grant it. He must. It is not a matter of choice."

The gentleman's playful mood began to disappear—one could see that, by his face. Joan's earnestness was affecting him. It always happened that people who began in jest with her ended by being in earnest. They soon began to perceive depths in her that they had not suspected; and then her manifest sincerity and the rocklike steadfastness of her convictions were forces which cowed levity, and it could not maintain its self–respect in their presence. The Sieur de Metz was thoughtful for a moment or two, then he began, quite soberly:

"Is it necessary that you go to the King soon?that is, I mean" "Before Mid–Lent,

even though I wear away my legs to the knees!" She said it with that sort of

repressed fieriness that means so much
when a person's heart is in a thing. You could see the response in
that nobleman's face; you could see his eye light up; there was sympathy
there. He said, most earnestly:

"God knows I think you should have the men–at–arms, and that somewhat would come of it. What is it that you would do? What is your hope and purpose?"

"To rescue France. And it is appointed that I shall do it. For no one else in the world, neither kings, nor dukes, no any other, can recover the kingdom of France, and there is no help but in me."

The words had a pleading and pathetic sound, and they touched that good nobleman. I saw it plainly. Joan dropped her voice a little, and said: "But indeed I would rather spin with my poor mother, for this is not my calling; but I must go and do it, for it is my Lord's will."

"Who is your Lord?"

"He is God."

Then the Sieur de Metz, following the impressive old feudal fashion, knelt and laid his hands within Joan's in sign of fealty, and made oath that by God's help he himself would take her to the king.

The next day came the Sieur Bertrand de Poulengy, and he also pledged his oath and knightly honor to abide with her and follow her witherosever she might lead.

This day, too, toward evening, a great rumor went flying abroad through the townnamely, that the very governor himself was going to visit the young girl in her humble lodgings. So in the morning the streets and lanes were packed with people waiting to see if this strange thing would indeed happen. And happen it did. The governor rode in state, attended by his guards, and the news of it went everywhere, and made a great sensation, and modified the scoffings of the people of quality and raised Joan's credit higher than ever.

The governor had made up his mind to one thing: Joan was either a witch or a saint, and he meant to find out which it was. So he brought a priest with him to exorcise the devil that was in her in case there was one there. The priest performed his office, but found no devil. He merely hurt Joan's feelings and offended her piety without need, for he had already confessed her before this, and should have known, if he knew anything, that devils cannot abide the confessional, but utter cries of anguish and the most profane and furious cursings whenever they are confronted with that holy office.

The governor went away troubled and full of thought, and not knowing what to do. And while he pondered and studied, several days went by and the 14th of February was come. Then Joan went to the castle and said:

"In God's name, Robert de Baudricourt, you are too slow about sending me, and have caused damage thereby, for this day the Dauphin's cause has lost a battle near Orleans, and will suffer yet greater injury if you do not send me to him soon."

The governor was perplexed by this speech, and said:

"To-day, child, to-day? How can you know what has happened in that region to-day? It would take eight or ten days for the word to come."

"My Voices have brought the word to me, and it is true. A battle was lost to-day, and you are in fault to delay me so."

The governor walked the floor awhile, talking within himself, but letting a great oath fall outside now and then; and finally he said:

"Harkye! go in peace, and wait. If it shall turn out as you say, I will give you the letter and send you to the King, and not otherwise."

Joan said with fervor:

"Now God be thanked, these waiting days are almost done. In nine days you will fetch me the letter."

Already the people of Vaucouleurs had given her a horse and had armed and equipped her as a soldier. She got no chance to try the horse and see if she could ride it, for her great first duty was to abide at her post and lift up the hopes and spirits of all who would come to talk with her, and prepare them to help in the rescue and
regeneration of the kingdom. This occupied every waking moment she had. But it was no matter. There was nothing she could not learnand in the briefest time, too. Her horse would find this out in
the first hour. Meantime the brothers and I took the horse in turn and began to learn to ride. And we had teaching in the use of the sword and other arms also.

On the 20th Joan called her small army togetherthe two knights and her two brothers and mefor a private council of war. No, it was not a council, that is not the right name, for she did not consult with us,
she merely gave us orders. She mapped out the course she would travel toward the King, and did it like a person perfectly versed in geography; and this itinerary of daily marches was so arranged as to avoid here and there peculiarly dangerous regions by flank movementswhich showed that she knew her political geography as intimately as she knew her physical geography; yet she had never had a day's schooling, of course, and was without education. I was

astonished, but thought her Voices must have taught her. But upon reflection I saw that this was not so. By her references to what this and that and the other person had told her, I perceived that she had been diligently questioning those crowds of visiting strangers, and that out of them she had patiently dug all this mass of invaluable knowledge. The two knights were filled with wonder at her good sense and sagacity.

She commanded us to make preparations to travel by night and sleep by day in concealment, as almost the whole of our long journey would be through the enemy's country.

Also, she commanded that we should keep the date of our departure a secret, since she meant to get away unobserved. Otherwise we should be sent off with a grand demonstration which would advertise us to the enemy, and we should be ambushed and captured somewhere. Finally she said:

"Nothing remains, now, but that I confide to you the date of our departure, so that you may make all needful preparation in time, leaving nothing to be done in haste and badly at the last moment. We march the 23d, at eleven of the clock at night."

Then we were dismissed. The two knights were startledyes, and troubled; and the Sieur Bertrand said:

"Even if the governor shall really furnish the letter and the escort, he still may not do it in time to meet the date she has chosen. Then how can she venture to name that date? It is a great riska great risk to select and decide upon the date, in this state of uncertainty."

I said:

"Since she has named the 23d, we may trust her. The Voices have told her, I think. We shall do best to obey."

We did obey. Joan's parents were notified to come before the 23d, but prudence forbade that they be told why this limit was named.

All day, the 23d, she glanced up wistfully whenever new bodies of strangers entered the house, but her parents did not appear. Still she was not discouraged, but hoped on. But when night fell at last, her hopes perished, and the tears came; however, she dashed them away, and said:

"It was to be so, no doubt; no doubt it was so ordered; I must bear it, and will."

De Metz tried to comfort her by saying:

"The governor sends no word; it may be that they will come to–morrow, and"

He got no further, for she interrupted him, saying: "To what

good end? We start at eleven to–night."

And it was so. At ten the governor came, with his guard and arms, with horses and equipment for me and for the brothers, and gave Joan a letter to the King. Then he took off his sword, and belted it about her waist with his own hands, and said:

"You said true, child. The battle was lost, on the day you said. So I have kept my word. Now gocome of it what may." Joan gave

him thanks, and he went his way.

The lost battle was the famous disaster that is called in history the Battle of the Herrings.

All the lights in the house were at once put out, and a little while after, when the streets had become dark and still, we crept stealthily through them and out at the western gate and rode away under whip and spur.

Chapter 3.

The Paladin Groans and Boasts

WE WERE twenty-five strong, and well equipped. We rode in double file, Joan and her brothers in the center of the column, with Jean de Metz at the head of it and the Sieur Bertrand at its extreme rear. In two or three hours we should be in the enemy's country, and then none would venture to desert. By and by we began to hear groans and sobs and execrations from different points along the line, and upon inquiry found that six of our men were peasants who had never ridden a horse before, and were finding it very difficult to stay in their saddles, and moreover were now beginning to suffer considerable bodily torture. They had been seized by the governor at the last moment and pressed into the service to make up the tale, and he had placed a veteran alongside of each with orders to help him stick to the saddle, and kill him if he tried to desert.

These poor devils had kept quiet as long as they could, but their physical miseries were become so sharp by this time that they were obliged to give them vent. But we were within the enemy's country now, so there was no help for them, they must continue the march, though Joan said that if they chose to take the risk they might depart. They preferred to stay with us. We modified our pace now, and moved cautiously, and the new men were warned to keep their sorrows to themselves and not get the command into danger with their curses and lamentations.

Toward dawn we rode deep into a forest, and soon all but the sentries were sound asleep in spite of the cold ground and the frosty air.

I woke at noon out of such a solid and stupefying sleep that at first my wits were all astray, and I did not know where I was nor what had been happening. Then my senses cleared, and I remembered. As I lay there thinking over the strange events of the past month or two the thought came into my mind, greatly surprising me, that one of Joan's prophecies had failed; for where were Noel and the Paladin, who were to join us at the eleventh hour? By this time, you see, I had gotten used to expecting everything Joan said to come true. So,

being disturbed and troubled by these thoughts, I opened my eyes. Well, there stood the Paladin leaning against a tree and looking down on me! How often that happens; you think of a person, or speak of a person, and there he stands before you, and you not dreaming he is near. It looks as if his being near is really the thing that makes you think of him, and not just an accident, as people imagine. Well, be that as it may, there was the Paladin, anyway, looking down in my face and waiting for me to wake. I was ever so glad to see him, and jumped up and shook him by the hand, and led him a little way from the camphe limping like a crippleand told him to sit down, and said:

"Now, where have you dropped down from? And how did you happen to light in this place? And what do the soldier–clothes mean? Tell me all about it."

He answered:

"I marched with you last night."

"No!" (To myself I said, "The prophecy has not all failedhalf of it has come true.") "Yes, I did. I hurried up from Domremy to join, and was within a half a minute of being too late. In fact, I was too late, but I begged so hard that the governor was touched by my brave devotion to my country's causethose are the words he usedand so he yielded, and allowed me to come."

I thought to myself, this is a lie, he is one of those six the governor recruited by force at the last moment; I know it, for Joan's prophecy said he would join at the eleventh hour, but not by his own desire. Then I said aloud:

"I am glad you came; it is a noble cause, and one should not sit at home in times like these."

"Sit at home! I could no more do it than the thunderstone could stay hid in the clouds when the storm calls it." "That is the

right talk. It sounds like you." That pleased him.

"I'm glad you know me. Some don't. But they will, presently. They will know me well enough before I get done with this war."

"That is what I think. I believe that wherever danger confronts you you will make yourself conspicuous."

He was charmed with this speech, and it swelled him up like a bladder. He said:

"If I know myselfand I think I domy performances in this campaign will give you occasion more than once to remember those words."

"I were a fool to doubt it. That I know."

"I shall not be at my best, being but a common soldier; still, the country will hear of me. If I were where I belong; if I were in the place of La Hire, or Saintrailles, or the Bastard of Orleanswell, I say nothing. I am not of the talking kind, like Noel Rainguesson and his sort, I thank God. But it will be something, I take ita novelty in this world, I should sayto raise the fame of a private soldier above theirs, and extinguish the glory of their names with its shadow."

"Why, look here, my friend," I said, "do you know that you have hit out a most remarkable idea there? Do you realize the gigantic proportions of it? For look you; to be a general of vast renown, what is that? Nothinghistory is clogged and confused with them; one cannot keep their names in his memory, there are so many. But a common soldier of supreme renownwhy, he would stand alone! He would the be one moon in a firmament of mustard–seed stars; his name would outlast the human race! My friend, who gave you that idea?"

He was ready to burst with happiness, but he suppressed betrayal of it as well as he could. He simply waved the compliment aside with his hand and said, with complacency:

"It is nothing. I have them often—ideas like that—and even greater ones. I do not consider this one much."

"You astonish me; you do, indeed. So it is really your own?" "Quite. And

there is plenty more where it came from"—tapping his
head with his finger, and taking occasion at the same time to cant his morion over his right ear, which gave him a very self-satisfied air—"I do not need to borrow my ideas, like Noel Rainguesson."

"Speaking of Noel, when did you see him last?"

"Half an hour ago. He is sleeping yonder like a corpse. Rode with us last night."

I felt a great upleap in my heart, and said to myself, now I am at rest and glad; I will never doubt her prophecies again. Then I said aloud:

"It gives me joy. It makes me proud of our village. There is not keeping our lion-hearts at home in these great times, I see that."

"Lion-heart! Who—that baby? Why, he begged like a dog to be let off. Cried, and said he wanted to go to his mother. Him a lion-heart!—that tumble-bug!"

"Dear me, why I supposed he volunteered, of course. Didn't he?" "Oh, yes, he

volunteered the way people do to the headsman. Why,
when he found I was coming up from Domremy to volunteer, he asked me to let him come along in my protection, and see the crowds and the excitement. Well, we arrived and saw the torches filing out
at the Castle, and ran there, and the governor had him seized, along with four more, and he begged to be let off, and I begged for his place, and at last the governor allowed me to join, but wouldn't let Noel off, because he was disgusted with him, he was such a cry- baby. Yes, and much good he'll do the King's service; he'll eat for six and run for sixteen. I hate a pygmy with half a heart and nine stomachs!"

"Why, this is very surprising news to me, and I am sorry and disappointed to hear it. I thought he was a very manly fellow."

The Paladin gave me an outraged look, and said:

"I don't see how you can talk like that, I'm sure I don't. I don't see how you could have got such a notion. I don't dislike him, and I'm not saying these things out of prejudice, for I don't allow myself to have prejudices against people. I like him, and have always comraded with him from the cradle, but he must allow me to speak my mind about his faults, and I am willing he shall speak his about mine, if I have any. And, true enough, maybe I have; but I reckon they'll bear inspectionI have that idea, anyway. A manly fellow! You should have heard him whine and wail and swear, last night, because the saddle hurt him. Why didn't the saddle hurt me? PoohI was as much at home in it as if I had been born there. And yet it was the first time I was ever on a horse. All those old soldiers admired my riding; they said they had never seen anything like it. But himwhy, they had to hold him on, all the time."

An odor as of breakfast came stealing through the wood; the Paladin unconsciously inflated his nostrils in lustful response, and got up and limped painfully away, saying he must go and look to his horse.

At bottom he was all right and a good–hearted giant, without any harm in him, for it is no harm to bark, if one stops there and does not bite, and it is no harm to be an ass, if one is content to bray and not kick. If this vast structure of brawn and muscle and vanity and foolishness seemed to have a libelous tongue, what of it? There was no malice behind it; and besides, the defect was not of his own creation; it was the work of Noel Rainguesson, who had nurtured it, fostered it, built it up and perfected it, for the entertainment he got out of it. His careless light heart had to have somebody to nag and chaff and make fun of, the Paladin had only needed development in order to meet its requirements, consequently the development was taken in hand and diligently attended to and looked after, gnat–and– bull fashion, for years, to the neglect and damage of far more important concerns. The result was an unqualified success. Noel prized the society of the Paladin above everybody else's; the Paladin preferred anybody's to Noel's. The big fellow was often seen with the little fellow, but it was for the same reason that the bull is often seen with the gnat.

With the first opportunity, I had a talk with Noel. I welcomed him to our expedition, and said:

"It was fine and brave of you to volunteer, Noel." His eye

twinkled, and he answered:

"Yes, it was rather fine, I think. Still, the credit doesn't all belong to me; I had help."

"Who helped you?" "The

governor." "How?"

"Well, I'll tell you the whole thing. I came up from Domremy to see the crowds and the general show, for I hadn't ever had any experience of such things, of course, and this was a great opportunity; but I hadn't any mind to volunteer. I overtook the Paladin on the road and let him have my company the rest of the way, although he did not want it and said so; and while we were gawking and blinking in the glare of the governor's torches they seized us and four more and added us to the escort, and that is really how I came to volunteer. But, after all, I wasn't sorry, remembering how dull life would have been in the village without the Paladin."

"How did he feel about it? Was he satisfied?" "I think he

was glad."

"Why?"

"Because he said he wasn't. He was taken by surprise, you see, and it is not likely that he could tell the truth without preparation. Not that he would have prepared, if he had had the chance, for I do not think he would. I am not charging him with that. In the same space of time that he could prepare to speak the truth, he could also prepare to lie; besides, his judgment would be cool then, and would warn him against fooling with new methods in an emergency. No, I am sure he was glad, because he said he wasn't."

"Do you think he was very glad?"

"Yes, I know he was. He begged like a slave, and bawled for his mother. He said his health was delicate, and he didn't know how to ride a horse, and he knew he couldn't outlive the first march. But really he wasn't looking as delicate as he was feeling. There was a cask of wine there, a proper lift for four men. The governor's temper got afire, and he delivered an oath at him that knocked up the dust where it struck the ground, and told him to shoulder that cask or he would carve him to cutlets and send him home in a basket. The Paladin did it, and that secured his promotion to a privacy in the escort without any further debate."

"Yes, you seem to make it quite plain that he was glad to join—that is, if your premises are right that you start from. How did he stand the march last night?"

"About as I did. If he made the more noise, it was the privilege of his bulk. We stayed in our saddles because we had help. We are equally lame to—day, and if he likes to sit down, let him; I prefer to stand."

Chapter 4.

Joan Leads Us Through the Enemy

WE WERE called to quarters and subjected to a searching inspection by Joan. Then she made a short little talk in which she said that even the rude business of war could be conducted better without profanity and other brutalities of speech than with them, and that she should strictly require us to remember and apply this admonition. She ordered half an hour's horsemanship drill for the novices then, and appointed one of the veterans to conduct it. It was a ridiculous exhibition, but we learned something, and Joan was satisfied and complimented us. She did not take any instruction herself or go through the evolutions and manoeuvres, but merely sat her horse like a martial little statue and looked on. That was sufficient for her, you see. She would not miss or forget a detail of the lesson, she would take it all in with her eye and her mind, and apply it afterward with as much certainty and confidence as if she had already practised it.

We now made three night marches of twelve or thirteen leagues each, riding in peace and undisturbed, being taken for a roving band of Free Companions. Country–folk were glad to have that sort of people go by without stopping. Still, they were very wearying marches, and not comfortable, for the bridges were few and the streams many, and as we had to ford them we found the water dismally cold, and afterward had to bed ourselves, still wet, on the frosty or snowy ground, and get warm as we might and sleep if we could, for it would not have been prudent to build fires. Our energies languished under these hardships and deadly fatigues, but Joan's did not. Her step kept its spring and firmness and her eye its fire. We could only wonder at this, we could not explain it.

But if we had had hard times before, I know not what to call the five nights that now followed, for the marches were as fatiguing, the baths as cold, and we were ambuscaded seven times in addition, and lost two novices and three veterans in the resulting fights. The news had leaked out and gone abroad that the inspired Virgin of Vaucouleurs was making for the King with an escort, and all the roads were being watched now.

These five nights disheartened the command a good deal. This was aggravated by a discovery which Noel made, and which he promptly made known at headquarters. Some of the men had been trying to understand why Joan continued to be alert, vigorous, and confident while the strongest men in the company were fagged with the heavy marches and exposure and were become morose and irritable. There, it shows you how men can have eyes and yet not see. All their lives those men had seen their own women–folks hitched up with a cow and dragging the plow in the fields while the men did the driving. They had also seen other evidences that women have far more endurance and patience and fortitude than menbut what good had their seeing these things been to them? None. It had taught them nothing. They were still surprised to see a girl of seventeen bear the fatigues of war better than trained veterans of the army. Moreover, they did not reflect that a great soul, with a great purpose, can make
a weak body strong and keep it so; and here was the greatest soul in the universe; but how could they know that, those dumb creatures? No, they knew nothing, and their reasonings were of a piece with their ignorance. They argued and discussed among themselves, with Noel listening, and arrived at the decision that Joan was a witch, and had her strange pluck and strength from Satan; so they made a plan to watch for a safe opportunity to take her life.

To have secret plottings of this sort going on in our midst was a very serious business, of course, and the knights asked Joan's permission to hang the plotters, but she refused without hesitancy. She said:

"Neither these men nor any others can take my life before my mission is accomplished, therefore why should I have their blood upon my hands? I will inform them of this, and also admonish them. Call them before me."

When they came she made that statement to them in a plain matter– of–fact way, and just as if the thought never entered her mind that any one could doubt it after she had given her word that it was true.

The men were evidently amazed and impressed to hear her say such a thing in such a sure and confident way, for prophecies boldly uttered never fall barren on superstitious ears. Yes, this speech certainly impressed them, but her closing remark impressed them still more. It was for the ringleader, and Joan said it sorrowfully:

"It is a pity that you should plot another's death when your own is so close at hand."

That man's horse stumbled and fell on him in the first ford which we crossed that night, and he was drowned before we could help him. We had no more conspiracies.

This night was harassed with ambuscades, but we got through without having any men killed. One more night would carry us over the hostile frontier if we had good luck, and we saw the night close down with a good deal of solicitude. Always before, we had been more or less reluctant to start out into the gloom and the silence to be frozen in the fords and persecuted by the enemy, but this time we were impatient to get under way and have it over, although there was promise of more and harder fighting than any of the previous nights had furnished. Moreover, in front of us about three leagues there was a deep stream with a frail wooden bridge over it, and as a cold rain mixed with snow had been falling steadily all day we were anxious
to find out whether we were in a trap or not. If the swollen stream had washed away the bridge, we might properly consider ourselves trapped and cut off from escape.

As soon as it was dark we filed out from the depth of the forest where we had been hidden and began the march. From the time that we had begun to encounter ambushes Joan had ridden at the head of the column, and she took this post now. By the time we had gone a league the rain and snow had turned to sleet, and under the impulse of the storm–wind it lashed my face like whips, and I envied Joan and the knights, who could close their visors and shut up their heads in their helmets as in a box. Now, out of the pitchy darkness and close at hand, came the sharp command:

"Halt!"

We obeyed. I made out a dim mass in front of us which might be a body of horsemen, but one could not be sure. A man rode up and said to Joan in a tone of reproof:

"Well, you have taken your time, truly. And what have you found out? Is she still behind us, or in front?"

Joan answered in a level voice: "She is still

behind."

This news softened the stranger's tone. He said:

"If you know that to be true, you have not lost your time, Captain. But are you sure? How do you know?"

"Because I have seen her."

"Seen her! Seen the Virgin herself?" "Yes, I have

been in her camp."

"Is it possible! Captain Raymond, I ask you to pardon me for speaking in that tone just now. You have performed a daring and admirable service. Where was she camped?"

"In the forest, not more than a league from here."

"Good! I was afraid we might be still behind her, but now that we know she is behind us, everything is safe. She is our game. We will hang her. You shall hang her yourself. No one has so well earned the privilege of abolishing this pestilent limb of Satan."

"I do not know how to thank you sufficiently. If we catch her, I"

"If! I will take care of that; give yourself no uneasiness. All I want is just a look at her, to see what the imp is like that has been able to make all this noise, then you and the halter may have her. How many men has she?"

"I counted but eighteen, but she may have had two or three pickets out."

"Is that all? It won't be a mouthful for my force. Is it true that she is only a girl?"

"Yes; she is not more than seventeen."

"It passes belief! Is she robust, or slender?" "Slender."

The officer pondered a moment or two, then he said: "Was she preparing to break camp?"

"Not when I had my last glimpse of her." "What was she doing?"

"She was talking quietly with an officer." "Quietly? Not giving orders?"

"No, talking as quietly as we are now."

"That is good. She is feeling a false security. She would have been restless and fussy elseit is the way of her sex when danger is about. As she was making no preparation to break camp"

"She certainly was not when I saw her last."

"and was chatting quietly and at her ease, it means that this weather is not to her taste. Night–marching in sleet and wind is not for chits of seventeen. No; she will stay where she is. She has my thanks. We will camp, ourselves; here is as good a place as any. Let us get about it."

"If you command itcertainly. But she has two knights with her. They might force her to march, particularly if the weather should improve."

I was scared, and impatient to be getting out of this peril, and it distressed and worried me to have Joan apparently set herself to work to make delay and increase the danger—still, I thought she probably knew better than I what to do. The officer said:

"Well, in that case we are here to block the way."

"Yes, if they come this way. But if they should send out spies, and find out enough to make them want to try for the bridge through the woods? Is it best to allow the bridge to stand?"

It made me shiver to hear her.

The officer considered awhile, then said:

"It might be well enough to send a force to destroy the bridge. I was intending to occupy it with the whole command, but that is not necessary now."

Joan said, tranquilly:

"With your permission, I will go and destroy it myself."

Ah, now I saw her idea, and was glad she had had the cleverness to invent it and the ability to keep her head cool and think of it in that tight place. The officer replied:

"You have it, Captain, and my thanks. With you to do it, it will be well done; I could send another in your place, but not a better."

They saluted, and we moved forward. I breathed freer. A dozen times I had imagined I heard the hoofbeats of the real Captain Raymond's troop arriving behind us, and had been sitting on pins
and needles all the while that that conversation was dragging along. I breathed freer, but was still not comfortable, for Joan had given only the simple command, "Forward!" Consequently we moved in a walk. Moved in a dead walk past a dim and lengthening column of
enemies at our side. The suspense was exhausting, yet it lasted but a short while, for when the enemy's bugles sang the "Dismount!" Joan gave the word to trot, and that was a great relief to me. She was

always at herself, you see. Before the command to dismount had been given, somebody might have wanted the countersign somewhere along that line if we came flying by at speed, but now we seemed to be on our way to our allotted camping position, so we were allowed to pass unchallenged. The further we went the more formidable was the strength revealed by the hostile force. Perhaps it was only a hundred or two, but to me it seemed a thousand. When we passed the last of these people I was thankful, and the deeper we
plowed into the darkness beyond them the better I felt. I came nearer and nearer to feeling good, for an hour; then we found the bridge
still standing, and I felt entirely good. We crossed it and destroyed it, and then I feltbut I cannot describe what I felt. One has to feel it himself in order to know what it is like.

We had expected to hear the rush of a pursuing force behind us, for we thought that the real Captain Raymond would arrive and suggest that perhaps the troop that had been mistaken for his belonged to the Virgin of Vaucouleurs; but he must have been delayed seriously, for when we resumed our march beyond the river there were no sounds behind us except those which the storm was furnishing.

I said that Joan had harvested a good many compliments intended for Captain Raymond, and that he would find nothing of a crop left but a dry stubble of reprimands when he got back, and a commander just in the humor to superintend the gathering of it in.

Joan said:

"It will be as you say, no doubt; for the commander took a troop for granted, in the night and unchallenged, and would have camped without sending a force to destroy the bridge if he had been left unadvised, and none are so ready to find fault with others as those who do things worthy of blame themselves."

The Sieur Bertrand was amused at Joan's naive way of referring to her advice as if it had been a valuable present to a hostile leader who was saved by it from making a censurable blunder of omission, and then he went on to admire how ingeniously she had deceived that man and yet had not told him anything that was not the truth. This troubled Joan, and she said:

"I thought he was deceiving himself. I forbore to tell him lies, for that would have been wrong; but if my truths deceived him, perhaps that made them lies, and I am to blame. I would God I knew if I have done wrong."

She was assured that she had done right, and that in the perils and necessities of war deceptions that help one's own cause and hurt the enemy's were always permissible; but she was not quite satisfied with that, and thought that even when a great cause was in danger one ought to have the privilege of trying honorable ways first. Jean said:

"Joan, you told us yourself that you were going to Uncle Laxart's to nurse his wife, but you didn't say you were going further, yet you did go on to Vaucouleurs. There!"

"I see now," said Joan, sorrowfully. "I told no lie, yet I deceived. I had tried all other ways first, but I could not get away, and I had to get away. My mission required it. I did wrong, I think, and am to blame."

She was silent a moment, turning the matter over in her mind, then she added, with quiet decision, "But the thing itself was right, and I would do it again."

It seemed an over–nice distinction, but nobody said anything. If we had known her as well as she knew herself, and as her later history revealed her to us, we should have perceived that she had a clear meaning there, and that her position was not identical with ours, as we were supposing, but occupied a higher plane. She would sacrifice herself and her best self; that is, her truthfulness to save her cause; but only that; she would not buy her life at that cost; whereas our war– ethics permitted the purchase of our lives, or any mere military advantage, small or great, by deception. Her saying seemed a commonplace at the time, the essence of its meaning escaping us;
but one sees now that it contained a principle which lifted it above that and made it great and fine.

Presently the wind died down, the sleet stopped falling, and the cold was less severe. The road was become a bog, and the horses labored through it at a walk—they could do no better. As the heavy time wore on, exhaustion overcame us, and we slept in our saddles. Not even the dangers that threatened us could keep us awake.

This tenth night seemed longer than any of the others, and of course it was the hardest, because we had been accumulating fatigue from the beginning, and had more of it on hand now than at any previous time. But we were not molested again. When the dull dawn came at last we saw a river before us and we knew it was the Loire; we entered the town of Gien, and knew we were in a friendly land, with the hostiles all behind us. That was a glad morning for us.

We were a worn and bedraggled and shabby–looking troop; and still, as always, Joan was the freshest of us all, in both body and spirits. We had averaged above thirteen leagues a night, by tortuous and wretched roads. It was a remarkable march, and shows what men can do when they have a leader with a determined purpose and a resolution that never flags.

Chapter 5.

We Pierce the Last Ambuscades

WE RESTED and otherwise refreshed ourselves two or three hours at Gien, but by that time the news was abroad that the young girl commissioned of God to deliver France was come; wherefore, such a press of people flocked to our quarters to get sight of her that it seemed best to seek a quieter place; so we pushed on and halted at a small village called Fierbois.

We were now within six leagues of the King, who was at the Castle of Chinon. Joan dictated a letter to him at once, and I wrote it. In it she said she had come a hundred and fifty leagues to bring him good news, and begged the privilege of delivering it in person. She added that although she had never seen him she would know him in any disguise and would point him out.

The two knights rode away at once with the letter. The troop slept all the afternoon, and after supper we felt pretty fresh and fine, especially our little group of young Domremians. We had the comfortable tap–room of the village inn to ourselves, and for the
first time in ten unspeakably long days were exempt from bodings and terrors and hardships and fatiguing labors. The Paladin was suddenly become his ancient self again, and was swaggering up and down, a very monument of self–complacency. Noel Rainguesson said:

"I think it is wonderful, the way he has brought us through." "Who?"

asked Jean.

"Why, the Paladin."

The Paladin seemed not to hear.

"What had he to do with it?" asked Pierre d'Arc.

"Everything. It was nothing but Joan's confidence in his discretion that enabled her to keep up her heart. She could depend on us and on herself for valor, but discretion is the winning thing in war, after all; discretion is the rarest and loftiest of qualities, and he has got more
of it than any other man in France—more of it, perhaps, than any other sixty men in France."

"Now you are getting ready to make a fool of yourself, Noel Rainguesson," said the Paladin, "and you want to coil some of that long tongue of yours around your neck and stick the end of it in your ear, then you'll be the less likely to get into trouble."

"I didn't know he had more discretion than other people," said Pierre, "for discretion argues brains, and he hasn't any more brains than the rest of us, in my opinion."

"No, you are wrong there. Discretion hasn't anything to do with brains; brains are an obstruction to it, for it does not reason, it feels. Perfect discretion means absence of brains. Discretion is a quality of the heart—solely a quality of the heart; it acts upon us through feeling. We know this because if it were an intellectual quality it would only perceive a danger, for instance, where a danger exists; whereas"

"Hear him twaddle—the damned idiot!" muttered the Paladin. "whereas, it being

purely a quality of the heart, and proceeding by
feeling, not reason, its reach is correspondingly wider and sublimer, enabling it to perceive and avoid dangers that haven't any existence at all; as, for instance, that night in the fog, when the Paladin took his horse's ears for hostile lances and got off and climbed a tree"

"It's a lie! a lie without shadow of foundation, and I call upon you all to beware you give credence to the malicious inventions of this ramshackle slander–mill that has been doing its best to destroy my character for years, and will grind up your own reputations for you next. I got off to tighten my saddle–girth—I wish I may die in my
tracks if it isn't so—and whoever wants to believe it can, and whoever don't can let it alone."

"There, that is the way with him, you see; he never can discuss a theme temperately, but always flies off the handle and becomes disagreeable. And you notice his defect of memory. He remembers getting off his horse, but forgets all the rest, even the tree. But that is natural; he would remember getting off the horse because he was so used to doing it. He always did it when there was an alarm and the clash of arms at the front."

"Why did he choose that time for it?" asked Jean.

"I don't know. To tighten up his girth, he thinks, to climb a tree, I think; I saw him climb nine trees in a single night."

"You saw nothing of the kind! A person that can lie like that deserves no one's respect. I ask you all to answer me. Do you believe what this reptile has said?"

All seemed embarrassed, and only Pierre replied. He said, hesitatingly:

"Iwell, I hardly know what to say. It is a delicate situation. It seems offensive to me to refuse to believe a person when he makes so direct a statement, and yet I am obliged to say, rude as it may appear, that I am not able to believe the whole of itno, I am not able to believe that you climbed nine trees."

"There!" cried the Paladin; "now what do you think of yourself, Noel Rainguesson? How many do you believe I climbed, Pierre?" "Only eight."

The laughter that followed inflamed the Paladin's anger to white heat, and he said:

"I bide my timeI bide my time. I will reckon with you all, I promise you that!"

"Don't get him started," Noel pleaded; "he is a perfect lion when he gets started. I saw enough to teach me that, after the third skirmish. After it was over I saw him come out of the bushes and attack a dead man single–handed."

"It is another lie; and I give you fair warning that you are going too far. You will see me attack a live one if you are not careful."

"Meaning me, of course. This wounds me more than any number of injurious and unkind speeches could do. In gratitude to one's benefactor"

"Benefactor? What do I owe you, I should like to know?"

"You owe me your life. I stood between the trees and the foe, and kept hundreds and thousands of the enemy at bay when they were thirsting for your blood. And I did not do it to display my daring. I did it because I loved you and could not live without you."

"Thereyou have said enough! I will not stay here to listen to these infamies. I can endure your lies, but not your love. Keep that corruption for somebody with a stronger stomach than mine. And I want to say this, before I go. That you people's small performances might appear the better and win you the more glory, I hid my own deeds through all the march. I went always to the front, where the fighting was thickest, to be remote from you in order that you might not see and be discouraged by the things I did to the enemy. It was my purpose to keep this a secret in my own breast, but you force me to reveal it. If you ask for my witnesses, yonder they lie, on the road we have come. I found that road mud, I paved it with corpses. I found that country sterile, I fertilized it with blood. Time and again I was urged to go to the rear because the command could not proceed on account of my dead. And yet you, you miscreant, accuse me of climbing trees! Pah!"

And he strode out, with a lofty air, for the recital of his imaginary deeds had already set him up again and made him feel good.

Next day we mounted and faced toward Chinon. Orleans was at our back now, and close by, lying in the strangling grip of the English; soon, please God, we would face about and go to their relief. From Gien the news had spread to Orleans that the peasant Maid of Vaucouleurs was on her way, divinely commissioned to raise the siege. The news made a great excitement and raised a great hope–the first breath of hope those poor souls had breathed in five months. They sent commissioners at once to the King to beg him to consider this matter, and not throw this help lightly away. These commissioners were already at Chinon by this time.

When we were half–way to Chinon we happened upon yet one more squad of enemies. They burst suddenly out of the woods, and in considerable force, too; but we were not the apprentices we were ten or twelve days before; no, we were seasoned to this kind of adventure now; our hearts did not jump into our throats and our
weapons tremble in our hands. We had learned to be always in battle array, always alert, and always ready to deal with any emergency
that might turn up. We were no more dismayed by the sight of those people than our commander was. Before they could form, Joan had delivered the order, "Forward!" and we were down upon them with a rush. They stood no chance; they turned tail and scattered, we plowing through them as if they had been men of straw. That was
our last ambuscade, and it was probably laid for us by that treacherous
rascal, the King's own minister and favorite, De la Tremouille.

We housed ourselves in an inn, and soon the town came flocking to get a glimpse of the Maid.

Ah, the tedious King and his tedious people! Our two good knights came presently, their patience well wearied, and reported. They and we reverently stood–as becomes persons who are in the presence of kings and the superiors of kings–until Joan, troubled by this mark of homage and respect, and not content with it nor yet used to it, although we had not permitted ourselves to do otherwise since the day she prophesied that wretched traitor's death and he was straightway drowned, thus confirming many previous signs that she was indeed an ambassador commissioned of God, commanded us to sit; then the Sieur de Metz said to Joan:

"The King has got the letter, but they will not let us have speech with him."

"Who is it that forbids?"

"None forbids, but there be three or four that are nearest his person—schemers and traitors every one—that put obstructions in the way, and seek all ways, by lies and pretexts, to make delay. Chiefest of these are Georges de la Tremouille and that plotting fox, the Archbishop of Rheims. While they keep the King idle and in bondage to his sports and follies, they are great and their importance grows; whereas if ever he assert himself and rise and strike for
crown and country like a man, their reign is done. So they but thrive, they care not if the crown go to destruction and the King with it."

"You have spoken with others besides these?"

"Not of the Court, no—the Court are the meek slaves of those reptiles, and watch their mouths and their actions, acting as they act, thinking as they think, saying as they say; wherefore they are cold to us, and turn aside and go another way when we appear. But we have spoken with the commissioners from Orleans. They said with heat: 'It is a marvel that any man in such desperate case as is the King can moon around in this torpid way, and see his all go to ruin without lifting a finger to stay the disaster. What a most strange spectacle it is! Here he is, shut up in this wee corner of the realm like a rat in a trap; his royal shelter this huge gloomy tomb of a castle, with wormy rags for upholstery and crippled furniture for use, a very house of desolation; in his treasure forty francs, and not a farthing more, God be witness! no army, nor any shadow of one; and by contrast with his hungry poverty you behold this crownless pauper and his shoals of fools and favorites tricked out in the gaudiest silks and velvets you shall find
in any Court in Christendom. And look you, he knows that when our city falls—as fall it surely will except succor come swiftly—France falls; he knows that when that day comes he will be an outlaw and a fugitive, and that behind him the English flag will float unchallenged over every acre of his great heritage; he knows these things, he
knows that our faithful city is fighting all solitary and alone against disease, starvation, and the sword to stay this awful calamity, yet he will not strike one blow to save her, he will not hear our prayers, he will not even look upon our faces.' That is what the commissioners said, and they are in despair."

Joan said, gently:

"It is pity, but they must not despair. The Dauphin will hear them presently. Tell them so."

She almost always called the King the Dauphin. To her mind he was not King yet, not being crowned.

"We will tell them so, and it will content them, for they believe you come from God. The Archbishop and his confederate have for backer that veteran soldier Raoul de Gaucourt, Grand Master of the Palace, a worthy man, but simply a soldier, with no head for any greater matter. He cannot make out to see how a country–girl,
ignorant of war, can take a sword in her small hand and win victories where the trained generals of France have looked for defeats only,
for fifty yearsand always found them. And so he lifts his frosty mustache and scoffs."

"When God fights it is but small matter whether the hand that bears His sword is big or little. He will perceive this in time. Is there none in that Castle of Chinon who favors us?"

"Yes, the King's mother–in–law, Yolande, Queen of Sicily, who is wise and good. She spoke with the Sieur Bertrand."

"She favors us, and she hates those others, the King's beguilers," said Bertrand. "She was full of interest, and asked a thousand questions, all of which I answered according to my ability. Then she sat
thinking over these replies until I thought she was lost in a dream and would wake no more. But it was not so. At last she said, slowly, and as if she were talking to herself: 'A child of seventeena girlcountry–breduntaughtignorant of war, the use of arms, and the conduct of battlesmodest, gentle, shrinkingyet throws away her shepherd's crook and clothes herself in steel, and fights her way through a hundred and fifty leagues of fear, and comesshe to whom a king must be a dread and awful presenceand will stand up before
such an one and say, Be not afraid, God has sent me to save you! Ah, whence could come a courage and conviction so sublime as this but from very God Himself!' She was silent again awhile, thinking and making up her mind; then she said, 'And whether she comes of

God or no, there is that in her heart that raises her above men—high above all men that breathe in France to-day—for in her is that mysterious something that puts heart into soldiers, and turns mobs of cowards into armies of fighters that forget what fear is when they are in that presence—fighters who go into battle with joy in their eyes and songs on their lips, and sweep over the field like a storm—that is the spirit that can save France, and that alone, come it whence it may! It is in her, I do truly believe, for what else could have borne up that child on that great march, and made her despise its dangers and fatigues? The King must see her face to face—and shall!' She
dismissed me with those good words, and I know her promise will be kept. They will delay her all they can—those animals—but she will not fail in the end."

"Would she were King!" said the other knight, fervently. "For there is little hope that the King himself can be stirred out of his lethargy. He is wholly without hope, and is only thinking of throwing away everything and flying to some foreign land. The commissioners say there is a spell upon him that makes him hopeless—yes, and that it is shut up in a mystery which they cannot fathom."

"I know the mystery," said Joan, with quiet confidence; "I know it, and he knows it, but no other but God. When I see him I will tell him a secret that will drive away his trouble, then he will hold up his
head again."

I was miserable with curiosity to know what it was that she would
tell him, but she did not say, and I did not expect she would. She was but a child, it is true; but she was not a chatterer to tell great matters and make herself important to little people; no, she was reserved,
and kept things to herself, as the truly great always do.

The next day Queen Yolande got one victory over the King's keepers, for, in spite of their protestations and obstructions, she procured an audience for our two knights, and they made the most they could out of their opportunity. They told the King what a spotless and beautiful character Joan was, and how great and noble a spirit animated her, and they implored him to trust in her, believe in her, and have faith that she was sent to save France. They begged him to consent to see her. He was strongly moved to do this, and promised that he would not drop the matter out of his mind, but would consult with his council about it. This began to look encouraging. Two hours later there was a great stir below, and the innkeeper came flying up to say a commission of illustrious ecclesiastics was come from the Kingfrom the King his very self, understand!think of this vast honor to his humble little hostelry!and he was so overcome with the glory of it that he could hardly find breath enough in his excited body to put the facts into words. They were come from the King to speak with the Maid of Vaucouleurs. Then he flew downstairs, and presently appeared again, backing into the room, and bowing to the ground with every step, in front of four imposing and austere bishops and their train of servants.

Joan rose, and we all stood. The bishops took seats, and for a while no word was said, for it was their prerogative to speak first, and they were so astonished to see what a child it was that was making such a noise in the world and degrading personages of their dignity to the base function of ambassadors to her in her plebeian tavern, that they could not find any words to say at first. Then presently their spokesman told Joan they were aware that she had a message for the King, wherefore she was now commanded to put it into words, briefly and without waste of time or embroideries of speech.

As for me, I could hardly contain my joyour message was to reach
the King at last! And there was the same joy and pride and exultation in the faces of our knights, too, and in those of Joan's brothers. And I knew that they were all prayingas I wasthat the awe which we felt in the presence of these great dignitaries, and which would have tied
our tongues and locked our jaws, would not affect her in the like degree, but that she would be enabled to word her message well, and with little stumbling, and so make a favorable impression here,
where it would be so valuable and so important.

Ah, dear, how little we were expecting what happened then! We were aghast to hear her say what she said. She was standing in a reverent attitude, with her head down and her hands clasped in front of her; for she was always reverent toward the consecrated servants of God. When the spokesman had finished, she raised her head and set her calm eye on those faces, not any more disturbed by their state and grandeur than a princess would have been, and said, with all her ordinary simplicity and modesty of voice and manner:

"Ye will forgive me, reverend sirs, but I have no message save for the King's ear alone."

Those surprised men were dumb for a moment, and their faces flushed darkly; then the spokesman said:

"Hark ye, to you fling the King's command in his face and refuse to deliver this message of yours to his servants appointed to receive it?"

"God has appointed me to receive it, and another's commandment may not take precedence of that. I pray you let me have speech for his grace the Dauphin."

"Forbear this folly, and come at your message! Deliver it, and waste no more time about it."

"You err indeed, most reverend fathers in God, and it is not well. I am not come hither to talk, but to deliver Orleans, and lead the Dauphin to his good city of Rheims, and set the crown upon his head."

"Is that the message you send to the King?"

But Joan only said, in the simple fashion which was her wont:

"Ye will pardon me for reminding you againbut I have no message to send to any one."

The King's messengers rose in deep anger and swept out of the place without further words, we and Joan kneeling as they passed.

Our countenances were vacant, our hearts full of a sense of disaster. Our precious opportunity was thrown away; we could not understand Joan's conduct, she who had been so wise until this fatal hour. At last the Sieur Bertrand found courage to ask her why she had let this
great chance to get her message to the King go by.

"Who sent them here?" she asked. "The King."

"Who moved the King to send them?" She waited for an answer; none came, for we began to see what was in her mindso she answered herself: "The Dauphin's council moved him to it. Are they enemies to me and to the Dauphin's weal, or are they friends?"

"Enemies," answered the Sieur Bertrand.

"If one would have a message go sound and ungarbled, does one choose traitors and tricksters to send it by?"

I saw that we had been fools, and she wise. They saw it too, so none found anything to say. Then she went on:

"They had but small wit that contrived this trap. They thought to get my message and seem to deliver it straight, yet deftly twist it from its purpose. You know that one part of my message is but thisto move the Dauphin by argument and reasonings to give me men–at– arms and send me to the siege. If an enemy carried these in the right words, the exact words, and no word missing, yet left out the persuasions of gesture and supplicating tone and beseeching looks that inform the words and make them live, where were the value of that argumentwhom could it convince? Be patient, the Dauphin will hear me presently; have no fear."

The Sieur de Metz nodded his head several times, and muttered as to himself:

"She was right and wise, and we are but dull fools, when all is said." It was just

my thought; I could have said it myself; and indeed it was
the thought of all there present. A sort of awe crept over us, to think how that untaught girl, taken suddenly and unprepared, was yet able to penetrate the cunning devices of a King's trained advisers and defeat them. Marveling over this, and astonished at it, we fell silent and spoke no more. We had come to know that she was great in courage, fortitude, endurance, patience, conviction, fidelity to all

dutiesin all things, indeed, that make a good and trusty soldier and perfect him for his post; now we were beginning to feel that maybe there were greatnesses in her brain that were even greater than these great qualities of the heart. It set us thinking.

What Joan did that day bore fruit the very day after. The King was obliged to respect the spirit of a young girl who could hold her own and stand her ground like that, and he asserted himself sufficiently to put his respect into an act instead of into polite and empty words. He moved Joan out of that poor inn, and housed her, with us her servants, in the Castle of Courdray, personally confiding her to the care of Madame de Bellier, wife of old Raoul de Gaucourt, Master
of the Palace. Of course, this royal attention had an immediate result: all the great lords and ladies of the Court began to flock there to see and listen to the wonderful girl–soldier that all the world was talking about, and who had answered the King's mandate with a bland
refusal to obey. Joan charmed them every one with her sweetness and simplicity and unconscious eloquence, and all the best and capablest among them recognized that there was an indefinable something about her that testified that she was not made of common clay, that she was built on a grander plan than the mass of mankind, and moved on a loftier plane. These spread her fame. She always made friends and advocates that way; neither the high nor the low could come within the sound of her voice and the sight of her face and go out from her presence indifferent.

Chapter 6.

Joan Convinces the King

WELL, anything to make delay. The King's council advised him against arriving at a decision in our matter too precipitately. He arrive at a decision too precipitately! So they sent a committee of priests—always priests—into Lorraine to inquire into Joan's character and history—a matter which would consume several weeks, of course. You see how fastidious they were. It was as if people should come to put out the fire when a man's house was burning down, and they waited till they could send into another country to find out if he had always kept the Sabbath or not, before letting him try.

So the days poked along; dreary for us young people in some ways, but not in all, for we had one great anticipation in front of us; we had never seen a king, and now some day we should have that prodigious spectacle to see and to treasure in our memories all our lives; so we were on the lookout, and always eager and watching for the chance. The others were doomed to wait longer than I, as it turned out. One day great news came—the Orleans commissioners, with Yolande and our knights, had at last turned the council's position and persuaded the King to see Joan.

Joan received the immense news gratefully but without losing her head, but with us others it was otherwise; we could not eat or sleep or do any rational thing for the excitement and the glory of it. During two days our pair of noble knights were in distress and trepidation on Joan's account, for the audience was to be at night, and they were afraid that Joan would be so paralyzed by the glare of light from the long files of torches, the solemn pomps and ceremonies, the great concourse of renowned personages, the brilliant costumes, and the other splendors of the Court, that she, a simple country-maid, and all unused to such things, would be overcome by these terrors and make a piteous failure.

No doubt I could have comforted them, but I was not free to speak. Would Joan be disturbed by this cheap spectacle, this tinsel show, with its small King and his butterfly dukelets?she who had spoken face to face with the princes of heaven, the familiars of God, and
seen their retinue of angels stretching back into the remoteness of the sky, myriads upon myriads, like a measureless fan of light, a glory like the glory of the sun streaming from each of those innumerable heads, the massed radiance filling the deeps of space with a blinding splendor? I thought not.

Queen Yolande wanted Joan to make the best possible impression upon the King and the Court, so she was strenuous to have her clothed in the richest stuffs, wrought upon the princeliest pattern, and set off with jewels; but in that she had to be disappointed, of course, Joan not being persuadable to it, but begging to be simply and sincerely dressed, as became a servant of God, and one sent upon a mission of a serious sort and grave political import. So then
the gracious Queen imagined and contrived that simple and witching costume which I have described to you so many times, and which I cannot think of even now in my dull age without being moved just as rhythmical and exquisite music moves one; for that was music, that dressthat is what it wasmusic that one saw with the eyes and felt in the heart. Yes, she was a poem, she was a dream, she was a spirit when she was clothed in that.

She kept that raiment always, and wore it several times upon occasions of state, and it is preserved to this day in the Treasury of Orleans, with two of her swords, and her banner, and other things now sacred because they had belonged to her.

At the appointed time the Count of Vendome, a great lord of the court, came richly clothed, with his train of servants and assistants,
to conduct Joan to the King, and the two knights and I went with her, being entitled to this privilege by reason of our official positions
near her person.

When we entered the great audience–hall, there it all was just as I have already painted it. Here were ranks of guards in shining armor and with polished halberds; two sides of the hall were like flower–

gardens for variety of color and the magnificence of the costumes; light streamed upon these masses of color from two hundred and fifty flambeaux. There was a wide free space down the middle of the hall, and at the end of it was a throne royally canopied, and upon it sat a crowned and sceptered figure nobly clothed and blazing with jewels.

It is true that Joan had been hindered and put off a good while, but now that she was admitted to an audience at last, she was received with honors granted to only the greatest personages. At the entrance door stood four heralds in a row, in splendid tabards, with long slender silver trumpets at their mouths, with square silken banners depending from them embroidered with the arms of France. As Joan and the Count passed by, these trumpets gave forth in unison one long rich note, and as we moved down the hall under the pictured and gilded vaulting, this was repeated at every fifty feet of our progress—six times in all. It made our good knights proud and happy, and they held themselves erect, and stiffened their stride, and looked fine and soldierly. They were not expecting this beautiful and honorable tribute to our little country—maid.

Joan walked two yards behind the Count, we three walked two yards behind Joan. Our solemn march ended when we were as yet some eight or ten steps from the throne. The Count made a deep
obeisance, pronounced Joan's name, then bowed again and moved to his place among a group of officials near the throne. I was devouring the crowned personage with all my eyes, and my heart almost stood still with awe.

The eyes of all others were fixed upon Joan in a gaze of wonder which was half worship, and which seemed to say, "How sweet—how lovely—how divine!" All lips were parted and motionless, which was a sure sign that those people, who seldom forget themselves, had forgotten themselves now, and were not conscious of anything but the one object they were gazing upon. They had the look of people who are under the enchantment of a vision.

Then they presently began to come to life again, rousing themselves out of the spell and shaking it off as one drives away little by little a clinging drowsiness or intoxication. Now they fixed their attention upon Joan with a strong new interest of another sort; they were full of curiosity to see what she would do—they having a secret and particular reason for this curiosity. So they watched. This is what they saw:

She made no obeisance, nor even any slight inclination of her head, but stood looking toward the throne in silence. That was all there was to see at present.

I glanced up at De Metz, and was shocked at the paleness of his face. I whispered and said:

"What is it, man, what is it?"

His answering whisper was so weak I could hardly catch it:

"They have taken advantage of the hint in her letter to play a trick upon her! She will err, and they will laugh at her. That is not the King that sits there."

Then I glanced at Joan. She was still gazing steadfastly toward the throne, and I had the curious fancy that even her shoulders and the back of her head expressed bewilderment. Now she turned her head slowly, and her eye wandered along the lines of standing courtiers till it fell upon a young man who was very quietly dressed; then her face lighted joyously, and she ran and threw herself at his feet, and clasped his knees, exclaiming in that soft melodious voice which was her birthright and was now charged with deep and tender feeling:

"God of his grace give you long life, O dear and gentle Dauphin!" In his

astonishment and exultation De Metz cried out:

"By the shadow of God, it is an amazing thing!" Then he mashed all the bones of my hand in his grateful grip, and added, with a proud shake of his mane, "Now, what have these painted infidels to say!"

Meantime the young person in the plain clothes was saying to Joan:

"Ah, you mistake, my child, I am not the King. There he is," and he pointed to the throne.

The knight's face clouded, and he muttered in grief and indignation: "Ah, it is a

shame to use her so. But for this lie she had gone through safe. I will go and proclaim to all the house what"

"Stay where you are!" whispered I and the Sieur Bertrand in a breath, and made him stop in his place.

Joan did not stir from her knees, but still lifted her happy face toward the King, and said:

"No, gracious liege, you are he, and none other." De Metz's

troubles vanished away, and he said:

"Verily, she was not guessing, she knew. Now, how could she know? It is a miracle. I am content, and will meddle no more, for I perceive that she is equal to her occasions, having that in her head that cannot profitably be helped by the vacancy that is in mine."

This interruption of his lost me a remark or two of the other talk; however, I caught the King's next question:

"But tell me who you are, and what would you?"

"I am called Joan the Maid, and am sent to say that the King of Heaven wills that you be crowned and consecrated in your good city of Rheims, and be thereafter Lieutenant of the Lord of Heaven, who is King of France. And He willeth also that you set me at my appointed work and give me men–at–arms." After a slight pause she added, her eye lighting at the sound of her words, "For then will I raise the siege of Orleans and break the English power!"

The young monarch's amused face sobered a little when this martial speech fell upon that sick air like a breath blown from embattled camps and fields of war, and this trifling smile presently faded wholly away and disappeared. He was grave now, and thoughtful.

After a little he waved his hand lightly, and all the people fell away and left those two by themselves in a vacant space. The knights and I moved to the opposite side of the hall and stood there. We saw Joan rise at a sign, then she and the King talked privately together.

All that host had been consumed with curiosity to see what Joan would do. Well, they had seen, and now they were full of astonishment to see that she had really performed that strange miracle according to the promise in her letter; and they were fully as much astonished to find that she was not overcome by the pomps and splendors about her, but was even more tranquil and at her ease in holding speech with a monarch than ever they themselves had been, with all their practice and experience.

As for our two knights, they were inflated beyond measure with pride in Joan, but nearly dumb, as to speech, they not being able to think out any way to account for her managing to carry herself through this imposing ordeal without ever a mistake or an awkwardness of any kind to mar the grace and credit of her great performance.

The talk between Joan and the King was long and earnest, and held in low voices. We could not hear, but we had our eyes and could note effects; and presently we and all the house noted one effect which was memorable and striking, and has been set down in memoirs and histories and in testimony at the Process of Rehabilitation by some who witnessed it; for all knew it was big with meaning, though none knew what that meaning was at that
time, of course. For suddenly we saw the King shake off his indolent attitude and straighten up like a man, and at the same time look immeasurably astonished. It was as if Joan had told him something almost too wonderful for belief, and yet of a most uplifting and welcome nature.

It was long before we found out the secret of this conversation, but we know it now, and all the world knows it. That part of the talk was like this—as one may read in all histories. The perplexed King asked Joan for a sign. He wanted to believe in her and her mission, and that her Voices were supernatural and endowed with knowledge hidden from mortals, but how could he do this unless these Voices could prove their claim in some absolutely unassailable way? It was then that Joan said:

"I will give you a sign, and you shall no more doubt. There is a secret trouble in your heart which you speak of to nonea doubt which wastes away your courage, and makes you dream of throwing all away and fleeing from your realm. Within this little while you have been praying, in your own breast, that God of his grace would resolve that doubt, even if the doing of it must show you that no kingly right is lodged in you."

It was that that amazed the King, for it was as she had said: his prayer was the secret of his own breast, and none but God could know about it. So he said:

"The sign is sufficient. I know now that these Voices are of God. They have said true in this matter; if they have said more, tell it meI will believe."

"They have resolved that doubt, and I bring their very words, which are these: Thou art lawful heir to the King thy father, and true heir of France. God has spoken it. Now lift up thy head, and doubt no more, but give me men–at–arms and let me get about my work."

Telling him he was of lawful birth was what straightened him up and made a man of him for a moment, removing his doubts upon that head and convincing him of his royal right; and if any could have hanged his hindering and pestiferous council and set him free, he would have answered Joan's prayer and set her in the field. But no, those creatures were only checked, not checkmated; they could invent some more delays.

We had been made proud by the honors which had so distinguished Joan's entrance into that placehonors restricted to personages of very high rank and worthbut that pride was as nothing compared with the pride we had in the honor done her upon leaving it. For whereas those first honors were shown only to the great, these last, up to this time, had been shown only to the royal. The King himself led Joan by the hand down the great hall to the door, the glittering multitude standing and making reverence as they passed, and the silver trumpets sounding those rich notes of theirs. Then he dismissed her with gracious words, bending low over her hand and kissing it. Alwaysfrom all companies, high or lowshe went forth richer in honor and esteem than when she came.

And the King did another handsome thing by Joan, for he sent us back to Courdray Castle torch–lighted and in state, under escort of his own troophis guard of honorthe only soldiers he had; and finely equipped and bedizened they were, too, though they hadn't seen the color of their wages since they were children, as a body might say. The wonders which Joan had been performing before the King had been carried all around by this time, so the road was so packed with people who wanted to get a sight of her that we could hardly dig through; and as for talking together, we couldn't, all attempts at talk being drowned in the storm of shoutings and huzzas that broke out all along as we passed, and kept abreast of us like a wave the whole way.

Chapter 7.

Our Paladin in His Glory

WE WERE doomed to suffer tedious waits and delays, and we settled ourselves down to our fate and bore it with a dreary patience, counting the slow hours and the dull days and hoping for a turn
when God should please to send it. The Paladin was the only exception—that is to say, he was the only one who was happy and had no heavy times. This was partly owing to the satisfaction he got out of his clothes. He bought them at second hand—a Spanish cavalier's complete suit, wide-brimmed hat with flowing plumes, lace collar and cuffs, faded velvet doublet and trunks, short cloak hung from the shoulder, funnel-topped buskins, long rapier, and all that—a graceful and picturesque costume, and the Paladin's great frame was the right place to hang it for effect. He wore it when off duty; and when he swaggered by with one hand resting on the hilt of his rapier, and twirling his new mustache with the other, everybody stopped to look and admire; and well they might, for he was a fine and stately contrast to the small French gentlemen of the day squeezed into the trivial French costume of the time.

He was king bee of the little village that snuggled under the shelter of the frowning towers and bastions of Courdray Castle, and acknowledged lord of the tap-room of the inn. When he opened his mouth there, he got a hearing. Those simple artisans and peasants listened with deep and wondering interest; for he was a traveler and had seen the world—all of it that lay between Chinon and Domremy, at any rate—and that was a wide stretch more of it than they might ever hope to see; and he had been in battle, and knew how to paint its shock and struggle, its perils and surprises, with an art that was all
his own. He was cock of that walk, hero of that hostelry; he drew custom as honey draws flies; so he was the pet of the innkeeper, and of his wife and daughter, and they were his obliged and willing servants.

Most people who have the narrative gift—that great and rare endowment—have with it the defect of telling their choice things over the same way every time, and this injures them and causes them to sound stale and wearisome after several repetitions; but it was not so with the Paladin, whose art was of a finer sort; it was more stirring and interesting to hear him tell about a battle the tenth time than it was the first time, because he did not tell it twice the same way, but always made a new battle of it and a better one, with more casualties on the enemy's side each time, and more general wreck and disaster all around, and more widows and orphans and suffering in the neighborhood where it happened. He could not tell his battles apart himself, except by their names; and by the time he had told one of then ten times it had grown so that there wasn't room enough in France for it any more, but was lapping over the edges. But up to
that point the audience would not allow him to substitute a new battle, knowing that the old ones were the best, and sure to improve as long as France could hold them; and so, instead of saying to him
as they would have said to another, "Give us something fresh, we are fatigued with that old thing," they would say, with one voice and
with a strong interest, "Tell about the surprise at Beaulieu again—tell it three or four times!" That is a compliment which few narrative experts have heard in their lifetime.

At first when the Paladin heard us tell about the glories of the Royal Audience he was broken-hearted because he was not taken with us to it; next, his talk was full of what he would have done if he had been there; and within two days he was telling what he did do when he was there. His mill was fairly started, now, and could be trusted to take care of its affair. Within three nights afterward all his battles were taking a rest, for already his worshipers in the tap-room were so infatuated with the great tale of the Royal Audience that they would have nothing else, and so besotted with it were they that they would have cried if they could not have gotten it.

Noel Rainguesson hid himself and heard it, and came and told me, and after that we went together to listen, bribing the inn hostess to let us have her little private parlor, where we could stand at the wickets in the door and see and hear.

The tap-room was large, yet had a snug and cozy look, with its inviting little tables and chairs scattered irregularly over its red brick floor, and its great fire flaming and crackling in the wide chimney. It was a comfortable place to be in on such chilly and blustering March nights as these, and a goodly company had taken shelter there, and were sipping their wine in contentment and gossiping one with another in a neighborly way while they waited for the historian. The host, the hostess, and their pretty daughter were flying here and there and yonder among the tables and doing their best to keep up with the orders. The room was about forty feet square, and a space or aisle down the center of it had been kept vacant and reserved for the Paladin's needs. At the end of it was a platform ten or twelve feet wide, with a big chair and a small table on it, and three steps leading up to it.

Among the wine-sippers were many familiar faces: the cobbler, the farrier, the blacksmith, the wheelwright, the armorer, the maltster, the weaver, the baker, the miller's man with his dusty coat, and so on; and conscious and important, as a matter of course, was the barber-surgeon, for he is that in all villages. As he has to pull everybody's teeth and purge and bleed all the grown people once a month to keep their health sound, he knows everybody, and by constant contact with all sorts of folk becomes a master of etiquette and manners and a conversationalist of large facility. There were plenty of carriers, drovers, and their sort, and journeymen artisans.

When the Paladin presently came sauntering indolently in, he was received with a cheer, and the barber hustled forward and greeted him with several low and most graceful and courtly bows, also taking his hand and touching his lips to it. Then he called in a loud voice for a stoup of wine for the Paladin, and when the host's
daughter brought it up on the platform and dropped her courtesy and departed, the barber called after her, and told her to add the wine to his score. This won him ejaculations of approval, which pleased him very much and made his little rat-eyes shine; and such applause is right and proper, for when we do a liberal and gallant thing it is but natural that we should wish to see notice taken of it.

The barber called upon the people to rise and drink the Paladin's health, and they did it with alacrity and affectionate heartiness, clashing their metal flagons together with a simultaneous crash, and heightening the effect with a resounding cheer. It was a fine thing to see how that young swashbuckler had made himself so popular in a strange land in so little a while, and without other helps to his advancement than just his tongue and the talent to use it given him by Goda talent which was but one talent in the beginning, but was now become ten through husbandry and the increment and usufruct that do naturally follow that and reward it as by a law.

The people sat down and began to hammer on the tables with their flagons and call for "the King's Audience!the King's Audience!the King's Audience!" The Paladin stood there in one of his best attitudes, with his plumed great hat tipped over to the left, the folds of his short cloak drooping from his shoulder, and the one hand resting upon the hilt of his rapier and the other lifting his beaker. As the noise died down he made a stately sort of a bow, which he had picked up somewhere, then fetched his beaker with a sweep to his lips and tilted his head back and drained it to the bottom. The barber jumped for it and set it upon the Paladin's table. Then the Paladin began to walk up and down his platform with a great deal of dignity and quite at his ease; and as he walked he talked, and every little while stopped and stood facing his house and so standing continued his talk.

We went three nights in succession. It was plain that there was a charm about the performance that was apart from the mere interest which attaches to lying. It was presently discoverable that this charm lay in the Paladin's sincerity. He was not lying consciously; he believed what he was saying. To him, his initial statements were facts, and whenever he enlarged a statement, the enlargement became a fact too. He put his heart into his extravagant narrative, just as a poet puts his heart into a heroic fiction, and his earnestness disarmed criticismdisarmed it as far as he himself was concerned. Nobody believed his narrative, but all believed that he believed it.

He made his enlargements without flourish, without emphasis, and so casually that often one failed to notice that a change had been made. He spoke of the governor of Vaucouleurs, the first night,

simply as the governor of Vaucouleurs; he spoke of him the second night as his uncle the governor of Vaucouleurs; the third night he was his father. He did not seem to know that he was making these extraordinary changes; they dropped from his lips in a quite natural and effortless way. By his first night's account the governor merely attached him to the Maid's military escort in a general and unofficial way; the second night his uncle the governor sent him with the Maid as lieutenant of her rear guard; the third night his father the governor put the whole command, Maid and all, in his special charge. The
first night the governor spoke of him as a youth without name or ancestry, but "destined to achieve both"; the second night his uncle the governor spoke of him as the latest and worthiest lineal descendent of the chiefest and noblest of the Twelve Paladins of Charlemagne; the third night he spoke of him as the lineal descendent of the whole dozen. In three nights he promoted the Count of Vendome from a fresh acquaintance to a schoolmate, and then brother–in–law.

At the King's Audience everything grew, in the same way. First the four silver trumpets were twelve, then thirty–five, finally ninety–six; and by that time he had thrown in so many drums and cymbals that he had to lengthen the hall from five hundred feet to nine hundred to accommodate them. Under his hand the people present multiplied in the same large way.

The first two nights he contented himself with merely describing and exaggerating the chief dramatic incident of the Audience, but the third night he added illustration to description. He throned the barber in his own high chair to represent the sham King; then he told how the Court watched the Maid with intense interest and suppressed merriment, expecting to see her fooled by the deception and get herself swept permanently out of credit by the storm of scornful laughter which would follow. He worked this scene up till he got his house in a burning fever of excitement and anticipation, then came his climax. Turning to the barber, he said:

"But mark you what she did. She gazed steadfastly upon that sham's villain face as I now gaze upon yours—this being her noble and simple attitude, just as I stand now—then turned she—thus—to me, and stretching her arm outso and pointing with her finger, she said, in that firm, calm tone which she was used to use in directing the conduct of a battle, 'Pluck me this false knave from the throne!' I, striding forward as I do now, took him by the collar and lifted him out and held him aloft thus as if he had been but a child." (The house rose, shouting, stamping, and banging with their flagons, and went fairly mad over this magnificent exhibition of strength and there was not the shadow of a laugh anywhere, though the spectacle of the limp but proud barber hanging there in the air like a puppy held by the scruff of its neck was a thing that had nothing of solemnity about it.) "Then I set him down upon his feet thus being minded to get him by a better hold and heave him out of the window, but she bid me forbear, so by that error he escaped with his life.

"Then she turned her about and viewed the throng with those eyes of hers, which are the clear-shining windows whence her immortal wisdom looketh out upon the world, resolving its falsities and coming at the kernel of truth that is hid within them, and presently they fell upon a young man modestly clothed, and him she proclaimed for what he truly was, saying, 'I am thy servant thou art the King!' Then all were astonished, and a great shout went up, the whole six thousand joining in it, so that the walls rocked with the volume and the tumult of it."

He made a fine and picturesque thing of the march-out from the Audience, augmenting the glories of it to the last limit of the impossibilities; then he took from his finger and held up a brass nut from a bolt-head which the head ostler at the castle had given him that morning, and made his conclusion thus:

"Then the King dismissed the Maid most graciously as indeed was her desert and, turning to me, said, 'Take this signet-ring, son of the Paladins, and command me with it in your day of need; and look you,' said he, touching my temple, 'preserve this brain, France has use for it; and look well to its casket also, for I foresee that it will be hooped with a ducal coronet one day.' I took the ring, and knelt and kissed his hand, saying, 'Sire, where glory calls, there will I be found; where danger and death are thickest, that is my native air; when France and the throne need help well, I say nothing, for I am not of the talking sort—let my deeds speak for me, it is all I ask.'

"So ended the most fortunate and memorable episode, so big with future weal for the crown and the nation, and unto God be the thanks! Rise! Fill your flagons! Now—to France and the King—drink!"

They emptied them to the bottom, then burst into cheers and huzzas, and kept it up as much as two minutes, the Paladin standing at
stately ease the while and smiling benignantly from his platform.

Chapter 8.

Joan Persuades Her Inquisitors

WHEN JOAN told the King what that deep secret was that was torturing his heart, his doubts were cleared away; he believed she was sent of God, and if he had been let alone he would have set her upon her great mission at once. But he was not let alone. Tremouille and the holy fox of Rheims knew their man. All they needed to say was this—and they said it:

"Your Highness says her Voices have revealed to you, by her mouth, a secret known only to yourself and God. How can you know that
her Voices are not of Satan, and she his mouthpiece?—for does not Satan know the secrets of men and use his knowledge for the destruction of their souls? It is a dangerous business, and your Highness will do well not to proceed in it without probing the matter to the bottom."

That was enough. It shriveled up the King's little soul like a raisin, with terrors and apprehensions, and straightway he privately appointed a commission of bishops to visit and question Joan daily until they should find out whether her supernatural helps hailed from heaven or from hell.

The King's relative, the Duke of Alencon, three years prisoner of war to the English, was in these days released from captivity through promise of a great ransom; and the name and fame of the Maid having reached him—for the same filled all mouths now, and
penetrated to all parts—he came to Chinon to see with his own eyes what manner of creature she might be. The King sent for Joan and introduced her to the Duke. She said, in her simple fashion:

"You are welcome; the more of the blood of France that is joined to this cause, the better for the cause and it."

Then the two talked together, and there was just the usual result: when they departed, the Duke was her friend and advocate.

Joan attended the King's mass the next day, and afterward dined with the King and the Duke. The King was learning to prize her company and value her conversation; and that might well be, for, like other kings, he was used to getting nothing out of people's talk but guarded phrases, colorless and non-committal, or carefully tinted to tally
with the color of what he said himself; and so this kind of conversation only vexes and bores, and is wearisome; but Joan's talk was fresh and free, sincere and honest, and unmarred by timorous self-watching and constraint. She said the very thing that was in her mind, and said it in a plain, straightforward way. One can believe that to the King this must have been like fresh cold water from the mountains to parched lips used to the water of the sun-baked
puddles of the plain.

After dinner Joan so charmed the Duke with her horsemanship and lance practice in the meadows by the Castle of Chinon whither the King also had come to look on, that he made her a present of a great black war-steed.

Every day the commission of bishops came and questioned Joan about her Voices and her mission, and then went to the King with their report. These pryings accomplished but little. She told as much as she considered advisable, and kept the rest to herself. Both threats and trickeries were wasted upon her. She did not care for the threats, and the traps caught nothing. She was perfectly frank and childlike about these things. She knew the bishops were sent by the King, that their questions were the King's questions, and that by all law and custom a King's questions must be answered; yet she told the King
in her naive way at his own table one day that she answered only such of those questions as suited her.

The bishops finally concluded that they couldn't tell whether Joan was sent by God or not. They were cautious, you see. There were two powerful parties at Court; therefore to make a decision either way would infallibly embroil them with one of those parties; so it seemed to them wisest to roost on the fence and shift the burden to other shoulders. And that is what they did. They made final report that Joan's case was beyond their powers, and recommended that it be put into the hands of the learned and illustrious doctors of the University of Poitiers. Then they retired from the field, leaving behind them this little item of testimony, wrung from them by Joan's wise reticence: they said she was a "gentle and simple little shepherdess, very candid, but not given to talking."

It was quite true in their case. But if they could have looked back and seen her with us in the happy pastures of Domremy, they would have perceived that she had a tongue that could go fast enough when no harm could come of her words.

So we traveled to Poitiers, to endure there three weeks of tedious delay while this poor child was being daily questioned and badgered before a great bench of what? Military experts?since what she had come to apply for was an army and the privilege of leading it to battle against the enemies of France. Oh no; it was a great bench of priests and monksprofoundly leaned and astute casuistsrenowned professors of theology! Instead of setting a military commission to find out if this valorous little soldier could win victories, they set a company of holy hair–splitters and phrase–mongers to work to find out if the soldier was sound in her piety and had no doctrinal leaks.
The rats were devouring the house, but instead of examining the cat's teeth and claws, they only concerned themselves to find out if it was
a holy cat. If it was a pious cat, a moral cat, all right, never mind about the other capacities, they were of no consequence.

Joan was as sweetly self–possessed and tranquil before this grim tribunal, with its robed celebrities, its solemn state and imposing ceremonials, as if she were but a spectator and not herself on trial. She sat there, solitary on her bench, untroubled, and disconcerted the science of the sages with her sublime ignorancean ignorance which was a fortress; arts, wiles, the learning drawn from books, and all like missiles rebounded from its unconscious masonry and fell to the ground harmless; they could not dislodge the garrison which was withinJoan's serene great heart and spirit, the guards and keepers of her mission.

She answered all questions frankly, and she told all the story of her visions and of her experiences with the angels and what they said to her; and the manner of the telling was so unaffected, and so earnest and sincere, and made it all seem so lifelike and real, that even that hard practical court forgot itself and sat motionless and mute, listening with a charmed and wondering interest to the end. And if you would have other testimony than mine, look in the histories and you will find where an eyewitness, giving sworn testimony in the Rehabilitation process, says that she told that tale "with a noble dignity and simplicity," and as to its effect, says in substance what I have said. Seventeen, she was seventeen, and all alone on her bench by herself; yet was not afraid, but faced that great company of erudite doctors of law and theology, and by the help of no art learned in the schools, but using only the enchantments which were hers by nature, of youth, sincerity, a voice soft and musical, and an eloquence whose source was the heart, not the head, she laid that spell upon them. Now was not that a beautiful thing to see? If I could, I would put it before you just as I saw it; then I know what you would say.

As I have told you, she could not read. "One day they harried and pestered her with arguments, reasonings, objections, and other windy and wordy trivialities, gathered out of the works of this and that and the other great theological authority, until at last her patience vanished, and she turned upon them sharply and said:

"I don't know A from B; but I know this: that I am come by command of the Lord of Heaven to deliver Orleans from the English power and crown the King of Rheims, and the matters ye are puttering over are of no consequence!"

Necessarily those were trying days for her, and wearing for everybody that took part; but her share was the hardest, for she had no holidays, but must be always on hand and stay the long hours through, whereas this, that, and the other inquisitor could absent himself and rest up from his fatigues when he got worn out. And yet she showed no wear, no weariness, and but seldom let fly her temper. As a rule she put her day through calm, alert, patient, fencing with those veteran masters of scholarly sword–play and coming out always without a scratch.

One day a Dominican sprung upon her a question which made everybody cock up his ears with interest; as for me, I trembled, and said to myself she is done this time, poor Joan, for there is no way of answering this. The sly Dominican began in this way in a sort of indolent fashion, as if the thing he was about was a matter of no moment:

"You assert that God has willed to deliver France from this English bondage?"

"Yes, He has willed it."

"You wish for men–at–arms, so that you may go to the relief of Orleans, I believe?"

"Yes and the sooner the better."

"God is all–powerful, and able to do whatsoever thing He wills to do, is it not so?"

"Most surely. None doubts it."

The Dominican lifted his head suddenly, and sprung that question I have spoken of, with exultation:

"Then answer me this. If He has willed to deliver France, and is able to do whatsoever He wills, where is the need for men–at–arms?"

There was a fine stir and commotion when he said that, and a sudden thrusting forward of heads and putting up of hands to ears to catch the answer; and the Dominican wagged his head with satisfaction, and looked about him collecting his applause, for it shone in every face. But Joan was not disturbed. There was no note of disquiet in her voice when she answered:

"He helps who help themselves. The sons of France will fight the battles, but He will give the victory!"

You could see a light of admiration sweep the house from face to face like a ray from the sun. Even the Dominican himself looked pleased, to see his master–stroke so neatly parried, and I heard a venerable bishop mutter, in the phrasing common to priest and people in that robust time, "By God, the child has said true. He
willed that Goliath should be slain, and He sent a child like this to do it!"

Another day, when the inquisition had dragged along until everybody looked drowsy and tired but Joan, Brother Seguin, professor of theology at the University of Poitiers, who was a sour and sarcastic man, fell to plying Joan with all sorts of nagging questions in his bastard Limousin Frenchfor he was from Limoges. Finally he said:

"How is it that you understand those angels? What language did they speak?"

"French."

"In–deed! How pleasant to know that our language is so honored! Good French?"

"Yesperfect."

"Perfect, eh? Well, certainly you ought to know. It was even better than your own, eh?"

"As to that, II believe I cannot say," said she, and was going on, but stopped. Then she added, almost as if she were saying it to herself, "Still, it was an improvement on yours!"

I knew there was a chuckle back of her eyes, for all their innocence. Everybody shouted. Brother Seguin was nettled, and asked brusquely:

"Do you believe in God?"

Joan answered with an irritating nonchalance:

"Oh, well, yes—better than you, it is likely."

Brother Seguin lost his patience, and heaped sarcasm after sarcasm upon her, and finally burst out in angry earnest, exclaiming:

"Very well, I can tell you this, you whose belief in God is so great: God has not willed that any shall believe in you without a sign. Where is your sign?—show it!"

This roused Joan, and she was on her feet in a moment, and flung out her retort with spirit:

"I have not come to Poitiers to show signs and do miracles. Send me to Orleans and you shall have signs enough. Give me men–at– arms—few or many—and let me go!"

The fire was leaping from her eyes—ah, the heroic little figure! can't you see her? There was a great burst of acclamations, and she sat down blushing, for it was not in her delicate nature to like being conspicuous.

This speech and that episode about the French language scored two points against Brother Seguin, while he scored nothing against Joan; yet, sour man as he was, he was a manly man, and honest, as you can see by the histories; for at the Rehabilitation he could have hidden those unlucky incidents if he had chosen, but he didn't do it, but
spoke them right out in his evidence.

On one of the latter days of that three–weeks session the gowned scholars and professors made one grand assault all along the line, fairly overwhelming Joan with objections and arguments culled from the writings of every ancient and illustrious authority of the Roman Church. She was well–nigh smothered; but at last she shook herself free and struck back, crying out:

"Listen! The Book of God is worth more than all these ye cite, and I stand upon it. And I tell ye there are things in that Book that not one among ye can read, with all your learning!"

From the first she was the guest, by invitation, of the dame De

Rabateau, wife of a councilor of the Parliament of Poitiers; and to that house the great ladies of the city came nightly to see Joan and talk with her; and not these only, but the old lawyers, councilors and scholars of the Parliament and the University. And these grave men, accustomed to weigh every strange and questionable thing, and cautiously consider it, and turn it about this way and that and still doubt it, came night after night, and night after night, falling ever deeper and deeper under the influence of that mysterious something, that spell, that elusive and unwordable fascination, which was the supremest endowment of Joan of Arc, that winning and persuasive and convincing something which high and low alike recognized and felt, but which neither high nor low could explain or describe, and one by one they all surrendered, saying, "This child is sent of God."

All day long Joan, in the great court and subject to its rigid rules of procedure, was at a disadvantage; her judges had things their own way; but at night she held court herself, and matters were reversed, she presiding, with her tongue free and her same judges there before her. There could not be but one result: all the objections and hindrances they could build around her with their hard labors of the day she would charm away at night. In the end, she carried her judges with her in a mass, and got her great verdict without a dissenting voice.

The court was a sight to see when the president of it read it from his throne, for all the great people of the town were there who could get admission and find room. First there were some solemn ceremonies, proper and usual at such times; then, when there was silence again, the reading followed, penetrating the deep hush so that every word was heard in even the remotest parts of the house:

"It is found, and is hereby declared, that Joan of Arc, called the Maid, is a good Christian and a good Catholic; that there is nothing in her person or her words contrary to the faith; and that the King may and ought to accept the succor she offers; for to repel it would be to offend the Holy Spirit, and render him unworthy of the air of God."

The court rose, and then the storm of plaudits burst forth unrebuked, dying down and bursting forth again and again, and I lost sight of Joan, for she was swallowed up in a great tide of people who rushed to congratulate her and pour out benedictions upon her and upon the cause of France, now solemnly and irrevocably delivered into her little hands.

Chapter 9.

She is Made General-in-chief

IT WAS indeed a great day, and a stirring thing to see.

She had won! It was a mistake of Tremouille and her other ill-wishers to let her hold court those nights.

The commission of priests sent to Lorraine ostensibly to inquire into Joan's characterin fact to weary her with delays and wear out her purpose and make her give it uparrived back and reported her character perfect. Our affairs were in full career now, you see.

The verdict made a prodigious stir. Dead France woke suddenly to life, wherever the great news traveled. Whereas before, the spiritless and cowed people hung their heads and slunk away if one mentioned war to them, now they came clamoring to be enlisted under the banner of the Maid of Vaucouleurs, and the roaring of war-songs
and the thundering of the drums filled all the air. I remembered now what she had said, that time there in our village when I proved by facts and statistics that France's case was hopeless, and nothing could ever rouse the people from their lethargy:

"They will hear the drumsand they will answer, they will march!" It has been

said that misfortunes never come one at a time, but in a
body. In our case it was the same with good luck. Having got a start, it came flooding in, tide after tide. Our next wave of it was of this sort. There had been grave doubts among the priests as to whether the Church ought to permit a female soldier to dress like a man. But now came a verdict on that head. Two of the greatest scholars and theologians of the timeone of whom had been Chancellor of the University of Parisrendered it. They decided that since Joan "must
do the work of a man and a soldier, it is just and legitimate that her apparel should conform to the situation."

It was a great point gained, the Church's authority to dress as a man. Oh, yes, wave on wave the good luck came sweeping in. Never mind about the smaller waves, let us come to the largest one of all, the wave that swept us small fry quite off our feet and almost drowned
us with joy. The day of the great verdict, couriers had been despatched to the King with it, and the next morning bright and early the clear notes of a bugle came floating to us on the crisp air, and we pricked up our ears and began to count them. Onetwothree; pause; onetwo; pause; onetwothree, againand out we skipped and went flying; for that formula was used only when the King's herald–at– arms would deliver a proclamation to the people. As we hurried along, people came racing out of every street and house and alley, men, women, and children, all flushed, excited, and throwing
lacking articles of clothing on as they ran; still those clear notes pealed out, and still the rush of people increased till the whole town was abroad and streaming along the principal street. At last we reached the square, which was now packed with citizens, and there, high on the pedestal of the great cross, we saw the herald in his brilliant costume, with his servitors about him. The next moment he began his delivery in the powerful voice proper to his office:

"Know all men, and take heed therefore, that the most high, the most illustrious Charles, by the grace of God King of France, hath been pleased to confer upon his well–beloved servant Joan of Arc, called the Maid, the title, emoluments, authorities, and dignity of General– in–Chief of the Armies of France"

Here a thousand caps flew in the air, and the multitude burst into a hurricane of cheers that raged and raged till it seemed as if it would never come to an end; but at last it did; then the herald went on and finished:"and hath appointed to be her lieutenant and chief of staff a prince of his royal house, his grace the Duke of Alencon!"

That was the end, and the hurricane began again, and was split up into innumerable strips by the blowers of it and wafted through all the lanes and streets of the town.

General of the Armies of France, with a prince of the blood for subordinate! Yesterday she was nothingto–day she was this.

Yesterday she was not even a sergeant, not even a corporal, not even a private—to-day, with one step, she was at the top. Yesterday she was less than nobody to the newest recruit—to-day her command was law to La Hire, Saintrailles, the Bastard of Orleans, and all those others, veterans of old renown, illustrious masters of the trade of war. These were the thoughts I was thinking; I was trying to realize this strange and wonderful thing that had happened, you see.

My mind went travelling back, and presently lighted upon a picture—a picture which was still so new and fresh in my memory that it seemed a matter of only yesterday—and indeed its date was no further back than the first days of January. This is what it was. A peasant- girl in a far-off village, her seventeenth year not yet quite
completed, and herself and her village as unknown as if they had been on the other side of the globe. She had picked up a friendless wanderer somewhere and brought it home—a small gray kitten in a forlorn and starving condition—and had fed it and comforted it and got its confidence and made it believe in her, and now it was curled up
in her lap asleep, and she was knitting a coarse stocking and thinking—dreaming—about what, one may never know. And now—the kitten had hardly had time to become a cat, and yet already the girl is General of the Armies of France, with a prince of the blood to give orders to, and out of her village obscurity her name has climbed up like the sun and is visible from all corners of the land! It made me dizzy to think of these things, they were so out of the common order, and seemed so impossible.

Chapter 10.

The Maid's Sword and Banner

JOAN'S first official act was to dictate a letter to the English commanders at Orleans, summoning them to deliver up all strongholds in their possession and depart out of France. She must have been thinking it all out before and arranging it in her mind, it flowed from her lips so smoothly, and framed itself into such vivacious and forcible language. Still, it might not have been so; she always had a quick mind and a capable tongue, and her faculties were constantly developing in these latter weeks. This letter was to be forwarded presently from Blois. Men, provisions, and money were offering in plenty now, and Joan appointed Blois as a recruiting–station and depot of supplies, and ordered up La Hire from the front to take charge.

The Great Bastardhim of the ducal house, and governor of Orleanshad been clamoring for weeks for Joan to be sent to him, and now came another messenger, old D'Aulon, a veteran officer, a
trusty man and fine and honest. The King kept him, and gave him to Joan to be chief of her household, and commanded her to appoint the rest of her people herself, making their number and dignity accord with the greatness of her office; and at the same time he gave order that they should be properly equipped with arms, clothing, and horses.

Meantime the King was having a complete suit of armor made for her at Tours. It was of the finest steel, heavily plated with silver, richly ornamented with engraved designs, and polished like a mirror.

Joan's Voices had told her that there was an ancient sword hidden somewhere behind the altar of St. Catherine's at Fierbois, and she sent De Metz to get it. The priests knew of no such sword, but a search was made, and sure enough it was found in that place, buried a little way under the ground. It had no sheath and was very rusty,

but the priests polished it up and sent it to Tours, whither we were now to come. They also had a sheath of crimson velvet made for it, and the people of Tours equipped it with another, made of cloth–of– gold. But Joan meant to carry this sword always in battle; so she laid the showy sheaths away and got one made of leather. It was
generally believed that this sword had belonged to Charlemagne, but that was only a matter of opinion. I wanted to sharpen that old blade, but she said it was not necessary, as she should never kill anybody, and should carry it only as a symbol of authority.

At Tours she designed her Standard, and a Scotch painter named James Power made it. It was of the most delicate white boucassin, with fringes of silk. For device it bore the image of God the Father throned in the clouds and holding the world in His hand; two angels knelt at His feet, presenting lilies; inscription, JESUS, MARIA; on the reverse the crown of France supported by two angels.

She also caused a smaller standard or pennon to be made, whereon was represented an angel offering a lily to the Holy Virgin.

Everything was humming there at Tours. Every now and then one heard the bray and crash of military music, every little while one heard the measured tramp of marching mensquads of recruits leaving for Blois; songs and shoutings and huzzas filled the air night and
day, the town was full of strangers, the streets and inns were thronged, the bustle of preparation was everywhere, and everybody carried a glad and cheerful face. Around Joan's headquarters a crowd of people was always massed, hoping for a glimpse of the new General, and when they got it, they went wild; but they seldom got
it, for she was busy planning her campaign, receiving reports, giving orders, despatching couriers, and giving what odd moments she could spare to the companies of great folk waiting in the drawing– rooms. As for us boys, we hardly saw her at all, she was so
occupied.

We were in a mixed state of mindsometimes hopeful, sometimes not; mostly not. She had not appointed her household yetthat was our trouble. We knew she was being overrun with applications for places in it, and that these applications were backed by great names and

weighty influence, whereas we had nothing of the sort to recommend us. She could fill her humblest places with titled folkfolk whose relationships would be a bulwark for her and a valuable support at
all times. In these circumstances would policy allow her to consider us? We were not as cheerful as the rest of the town, but were inclined to be depressed and worried. Sometimes we discussed our
slim chances and gave them as good an appearance as we could. But the very mention of the subject was anguish to the Paladin; for whereas we had some little hope, he had none at all. As a rule Noel Rainguesson was quite willing to let the dismal matter alone; but not when the Paladin was present. Once we were talking the thing over, when Noel said:

"Cheer up, Paladin, I had a dream last night, and you were the only one among us that got an appointment. It wasn't a high one, but it was an appointment, anwaysome kind of a lackey or body-servant, or something of that kind."

The Paladin roused up and looked almost cheerful; for he was a believer in dreams, and in anything and everything of a superstitious sort, in fact. He said, with a rising hopefulness:

"I wish it might come true. Do you think it will come true?" "Certainly; I might

almost say I know it will, for my dreams hardly
ever fail."

"Noel, I could hug you if that dream could come true, I could, indeed! To be servant of the first General of France and have all the world hear of it, and the news go back to the village and make those gawks stare that always said I wouldn't ever amount to anythingwouldn't it be great! Do you think it will come true, Noel? Don't you believe it will?"

"I do. There's my hand on it."

"Noel, if it comes true I'll never forget youshake again! I should be dressed in a noble livery, and the news would go to the village, and those animals would say, 'Him, lackey to the General–in–Chief, with the eyes of the whole world on him, admiringwell, he has shot up into the sky now, hasn't he!"

He began to walk the floor and pile castles in the air so fast and so high that we could hardly keep up with him. Then all of a sudden all the joy went out of his face and misery took its place, and he said:

"Oh, dear, it is all a mistake, it will never come true. I forgot that foolish business at Toul. I have kept out of her sight as much as I could, all these weeks, hoping she would forget that and forgive itbut I know she never will. She can't, of course. And, after all, I wasn't to blame. I did say she promised to marry me, but they put me up to it and persuaded me. I swear they did!" The vast creature was almost crying. Then he pulled himself together and said, remorsefully, "It was the only lie I've ever told, and"

He was drowned out with a chorus of groans and outraged exclamations; and before he could begin again, one of D'Aulon's liveried servants appeared and said we were required at headquarters. We rose, and Noel said:

"Therewhat did I tell you? I have a presentimentthe spirit of prophecy is upon me. She is going to appoint him, and we are to go there and do him homage. Come along!"

But the Paladin was afraid to go, so we left him.

When we presently stood in the presence, in front of a crowd of glittering officers of the army, Joan greeted us with a winning smile, and said she appointed all of us to places in her household, for she wanted her old friends by her. It was a beautiful surprise to have ourselves honored like this when she could have had people of birth and consequence instead, but we couldn't find our tongues to say so, she was become so great and so high above us now. One at a time we stepped forward and each received his warrant from the hand of our chief, D'Aulon. All of us had honorable places; the two knights stood highest; then Joan's two brothers; I was first page and secretary, a young gentleman named Raimond was second page; Noel was her messenger; she had two heralds, and also a chaplain and almoner, whose name was Jean Pasquerel. She had previously appointed a maitre d'hotel and a number of domestics. Now she looked around and said: "But where is the Paladin?" The Sieur Bertrand said:

"He thought he was not sent for, your Excellency." "Now that is not well. Let him be called."

The Paladin entered humbly enough. He ventured no farther than just within the door. He stopped there, looking embarrassed and afraid. Then Joan spoke pleasantly, and said:

"I watched you on the road. You began badly, but improved. Of old you were a fantastic talker, but there is a man in you, and I will bring it out." It was fine to see the Paladin's face light up when she said that. "Will you follow where I lead?"

"Into the fire!" he said; and I said to myself, "By the ring of that, I think she has turned this braggart into a hero. It is another of her miracles, I make no doubt of it."

"I believe you," said Joan. "Heretake my banner. You will ride with me in every field, and when France is saved, you will give it me back."

He took the banner, which is now the most precious of the memorials that remain of Joan of Arc, and his voice was unsteady with emotion when he said:

"If I ever disgrace this trust, my comrades here will know how to do a friend's office upon my body, and this charge I lay upon them, as knowing they will not fail me."

Chapter 11.

The War March is Begun

NOEL and I went back together—silent at first, and impressed. Finally Noel came up out of his thinkings and said:

"The first shall be last and the last first—there's authority for this surprise. But at the same time wasn't it a lofty hoist for our big bull!"

"It truly was; I am not over being stunned yet. It was the greatest place in her gift."

"Yes, it was. There are many generals, and she can create more; but there is only one Standard–Bearer."

"True. It is the most conspicuous place in the army, after her own." "And the most coveted and honorable. Sons of two dukes tried to get it, as we know. And of all people in the world, this majestic windmill carries it off. Well, isn't it a gigantic promotion, when you come to look at it!"

"There's no doubt about it. It's a kind of copy of Joan's own in miniature."

"I don't know how to account for it—do you?" "Yes—without any trouble at all—that is, I think I do."

Noel was surprised at that, and glanced up quickly, as if to see if I was in earnest. He said:

"I thought you couldn't be in earnest, but I see you are. If you can make me understand this puzzle, do it. Tell me what the explanation is."

"I believe I can. You have noticed that our chief knight says a good many wise things and has a thoughtful head on his shoulders. One day, riding along, we were talking about Joan's great talents, and he said, 'But, greatest of all her gifts, she has the seeing eye.' I said, like an unthinking fool, 'The seeing eye?I shouldn't count on that for muchI suppose we all have it.' 'No,' he said; 'very few have it.' Then he explained, and made his meaning clear. He said the common eye sees only the outside of things, and judges by that, but the seeing eye pierces through and reads the heart and the soul, finding there capacities which the outside didn't indicate or promise, and which
the other kind of eye couldn't detect. He said the mightiest military genius must fail and come to nothing if it have not the seeing eyethat is to say, if it cannot read men and select its subordinates with an infallible judgment. It sees as by intuition that this man is good for strategy, that one for dash and daredevil assault, the other for patient bulldog persistence, and it appoints each to his right place and wins, while the commander without the seeing eye would give to each the other's place and lose. He was right about Joan, and I saw it. When she was a child and the tramp came one night, her father and all of
us took him for a rascal, but she saw the honest man through the rags. When I dined with the governor of Vaucouleurs so long ago, I saw nothing in our two knights, though I sat with them and talked with them two hours; Joan was there five minutes, and neither spoke with them nor heard them speak, yet she marked them for men of worth and fidelity, and they have confirmed her judgment. Whom has she sent for to take charge of this thundering rabble of new recruits at Blois, made up of old disbanded Armagnac raiders, unspeakable hellions, every one? Why, she has sent for Satan himselfthat is to say, La Hirethat military hurricane, that godless swashbuckler, that lurid conflagration of blasphemy, that Vesuvius of profanity, forever in eruption. Does he know how to deal with that mob of roaring devils? Better than any man that lives; for he is the head devil of this world his own self, he is the match of the whole of them combined, and probably the father of most of them. She places him in temporary command until she can get to Blois herselfand
then! Why, then she will certainly take them in hand personally, or I don't know her as well as I ought to, after all these years of intimacy. That will be a sight to seethat fair spirit in her white armor,
delivering her will to that muck–heap, that rag–pile, that abandoned

refuse of perdition."

"La Hire!" cried Noel, "our hero of all these years I do want to see that man!"

"I too. His name stirs me just as it did when I was a little boy." "I want to

hear him swear."

"Of course, I would rather hear him swear than another man pray. He is the frankest man there is, and the naivest. Once when he was rebuked for pillaging on his raids, he said it was nothing. Said he, 'If God the Father were a soldier, He would rob.' I judge he is the right man to take temporary charge there at Blois. Joan has cast the seeing eye upon him, you see."

"Which brings us back to where we started. I have an honest affection for the Paladin, and not merely because he is a good fellow, but because he is my child I made him what he is, the windiest blusterer and most catholic liar in the kingdom. I'm glad of his luck, but I hadn't the seeing eye. I shouldn't have chosen him for the most dangerous post in the army. I should have placed him in the rear to kill the wounded and violate the dead."

"Well, we shall see. Joan probably knows what is in him better than we do. And I'll give you another idea. When a person in Joan of Arc's position tells a man he is brave, he believes it; and believing it is enough; in fact, to believe yourself brave is to be brave; it is the one only essential thing."

"Now you've hit it!" cried Noel. "She's got the creating mouth as well as the seeing eye! Ah, yes, that is the thing. France was cowed and a coward; Joan of Arc has spoken, and France is marching, with her head up!"

I was summoned now to write a letter from Joan's dictation. During the next day and night our several uniforms were made by the
tailors, and our new armor provided. We were beautiful to look upon now, whether clothed for peace or war. Clothed for peace, in costly stuffs and rich colors, the Paladin was a tower dyed with the glories

of the sunset; plumed and sashed and iron–clad for war, he was a still statelier thing to look at.

Orders had been issued for the march toward Blois. It was a clear, sharp, beautiful morning. As our showy great company trotted out in column, riding two and two, Joan and the Duke of Alencon in the lead, D'Aulon and the big standard–bearer next, and so on, we made a handsome spectacle, as you may well imagine; and as we plowed through the cheering crowds, with Joan bowing her plumed head to left and right and the sun glinting from her silver mail, the spectators realized that the curtain was rolling up before their eyes upon the
first act of a prodigious drama, and their rising hopes were expressed in an enthusiasm that increased with each moment, until at last one seemed to even physically feel the concussion of the huzzas as well as hear them. Far down the street we heard the softened strains of wind–blown music, and saw a cloud of lancers moving, the sun glowing with a subdued light upon the massed armor, but striking bright upon the soaring lance–headsa vaguely luminous nebula, so to speak, with a constellation twinkling above itand that was our guard of honor. It joined us, the procession was complete, the first war– march of Joan of Arc was begun, the curtain was up.

Chapter 12.

Joan Puts Heart in Her Army

WE WERE at Blois three days. Oh, that camp, it is one of the treasures of my memory! Order? There was no more order among those brigands than there is among the wolves and the hyenas. They went roaring and drinking about, whooping, shouting, swearing, and entertaining themselves with all manner of rude and riotous horse– play; and the place was full of loud and lewd women, and they were no whit behind the men for romps and noise and fantastics.

It was in the midst of this wild mob that Noel and I had our first glimpse of La Hire. He answered to our dearest dreams. He was of great size and of martial bearing, he was cased in mail from head to heel, with a bushel of swishing plumes on his helmet, and at his side the vast sword of the time.

He was on his way to pay his respects in state to Joan, and as he passed through the camp he was restoring order, and proclaiming
that the Maid had come, and he would have no such spectacle as this exposed to the head of the army. His way of creating order was his own, not borrowed. He did it with his great fists. As he moved along swearing and admonishing, he let drive this way, that way, and the other, and wherever his blow landed, a man went down.

"Damn you!" he said, "staggering and cursing around like this, and the Commander–in–Chief in the camp! Straighten up!" and he laid the man flat. What his idea of straightening up was, was his own secret.

We followed the veteran to headquarters, listening, observing, admiringyes, devouring, you may say, the pet hero of the boys of France from our cradles up to that happy day, and their idol and ours. I called to mind how Joan had once rebuked the Paladin, there
in the pastures of Domremy, for uttering lightly those mighty names,

La Hire and the Bastard of Orleans, and how she said that if she could but be permitted to stand afar off and let her eyes rest once upon those great men, she would hold it a privilege. They were to her and the other girls just what they were to the boys. Well, here was one of them at last—and what was his errand? It was hard to realize it, and yet it was true; he was coming to uncover his head before her and take her orders.

While he was quieting a considerable group of his brigands in his soothing way, near headquarters, we stepped on ahead and got a glimpse of Joan's military family, the great chiefs of the army, for they had all arrived now. There they were, six officers of wide renown, handsome men in beautiful armor, but the Lord High Admiral of France was the handsomest of them all and had the most gallant bearing.

When La Hire entered, one could see the surprise in his face at Joan's beauty and extreme youth, and one could see, too, by Joan's glad smile, that it made her happy to get sight of this hero of her childhood at last. La Hire bowed low, with his helmet in his gauntleted hand, and made a bluff but handsome little speech with hardly an oath in it, and one could see that those two took to each other on the spot.

The visit of ceremony was soon over, and the others went away; but La Hire stayed, and he and Joan sat there, and he sipped her wine, and they talked and laughed together like old friends. And presently she gave him some instructions, in his quality as master of the camp, which made his breath stand still. For, to begin with, she said that all those loose women must pack out of the place at once, she wouldn't allow one of them to remain. Next, the rough carousing must stop, drinking must be brought within proper and strictly defined limits, and discipline must take the place of disorder. And finally she climaxed the list of surprises with this—which nearly lifted him out of his armor:

"Every man who joins my standard must confess before the priest and absolve himself from sin; and all accepted recruits must be present at divine service twice a day."

La Hire could not say a word for a good part of a minute, then he said, in deep dejection:

"Oh, sweet child, they were littered in hell, these poor darlings of mine! Attend mass? Why, dear heart, they'll see us both damned first!"

And he went on, pouring out a most pathetic stream of arguments and blasphemy, which broke Joan all up, and made her laugh as she had not laughed since she played in the Domremy pastures. It was good to hear.

But she stuck to her point; so the soldier yielded, and said all right, if such were the orders he must obey, and would do the best that was in him; then he refreshed himself with a lurid explosion of oaths, and said that if any man in the camp refused to renounce sin and lead a pious life, he would knock his head off. That started Joan off again; she was really having a good time, you see. But she would not consent to that form of conversions. She said they must be voluntary.

La Hire said that that was all right, he wasn't going to kill the voluntary ones, but only the others.

No matter, none of them must be killedJoan couldn't have it. She said that to give a man a chance to volunteer, on pain of death if he didn't, left him more or less trammeled, and she wanted him to be entirely free.

So the soldier sighed and said he would advertise the mass, but said he doubted if there was a man in camp that was any more likely to go to it than he was himself. Then there was another surprise for him, for Joan said:

"But, dear man, you are going!"

"I? Impossible! Oh, this is lunacy!"

"Oh, no, it isn't. You are going to the servicetwice a day."

"Oh, am I dreaming? Am I drunkor is my hearing playing me false?

Why, I would rather go to"

"Never mind where. In the morning you are going to begin, and after that it will come easy. Now don't look downhearted like that. Soon you won't mind it."

La Hire tried to cheer up, but he was not able to do it. He sighed like a zephyr, and presently said:

"Well, I'll do it for you, but before I would do it for another, I swear I"

"But don't swear. Break it off."

"Break it off? It is impossible! I beg you totoWhyoh, my General, it is my native speech!"

He begged so hard for grace for his impediment, that Joan left him one fragment of it; she said he might swear by his baton, the symbol of his generalship.

He promised that he would swear only by his baton when in her presence, and would try to modify himself elsewhere, but doubted he could manage it, now that it was so old and stubborn a habit, and
such a solace and support to his declining years.

That tough old lion went away from there a good deal tamed and civilizednot to say softened and sweetened, for perhaps those expressions would hardly fit him. Noel and I believed that when he was away from Joan's influence his old aversions would come up so strong in him that he could not master them, and so wouldn't go to mass. But we got up early in the morning to see.

Satan was converted, you see. Well, the rest followed. Joan rode up and down that camp, and wherever that fair young form appeared in its shining armor, with that sweet face to grace the vision and perfect it, the rude host seemed to think they saw the god of war in person, descended out of the clouds; and first they wondered, then they worshiped. After that, she could do with them what she would.

In three days it was a clean camp and orderly, and those barbarians were herding to divine service twice a day like good children. The women were gone. La Hire was stunned by these marvels; he could not understand them. He went outside the camp when he wanted to swear. He was that sort of a mansinful by nature and habit, but full of superstitious respect for holy places.

The enthusiasm of the reformed army for Joan, its devotion to her, and the hot desire she had aroused in it to be led against the enemy, exceeded any manifestations of this sort which La Hire had ever seen before in his long career. His admiration of it all, and his
wonder over the mystery and miracle of it, were beyond his power to put into words. He had held this army cheap before, but his pride and confidence in it knew no limits now. He said:

"Two or three days ago it was afraid of a hen–roost; one could storm the gates of hell with it now."

Joan and he were inseparable, and a quaint and pleasant contrast they made. He was so big, she so little; he was so gray and so far along in his pilgrimage of life, she so youthful; his face was so bronzed and scarred, hers so fair and pink, so fresh and smooth; she was so gracious, and he so stern; she was so pure, so innocent, he such a cyclopedia of sin. In her eye was stored all charity and compassion, in his lightnings; when her glance fell upon you it seemed to bring benediction and the peace of God, but with his it was different, generally.

They rode through the camp a dozen times a day, visiting every corner of it, observing, inspecting, perfecting; and wherever they appeared the enthusiasm broke forth. They rode side by side, he a great figure of brawn and muscle, she a little masterwork of roundness and grace; he a fortress of rusty iron, she a shining statuette of silver; and when the reformed raiders and bandits caught sight of them they spoke out, with affection and welcome in their voices, and said:

"There they comeSatan and the Page of Christ!"

All the three days that we were in Blois, Joan worked earnestly and tirelessly to bring La Hire to God to rescue him from the bondage of sin to breathe into his stormy heart the serenity and peace of religion. She urged, she begged, she implored him to pray. He stood out, three days of our stay, begging about piteously to be let off to be let off from just that one thing, that impossible thing; he would do anything else anything command, and he would obey he would go through the fire for her if she said the word but spare him this, only this, for he couldn't pray, had never prayed, he was ignorant of how to frame a prayer, he had no words to put it in.

And yet can any believe it?—she carried even that point, she won that incredible victory. She made La Hire pray. It shows, I think, that nothing was impossible to Joan of Arc. Yes, he stood there before her and put up his mailed hands and made a prayer. And it was not borrowed, but was his very own; he had none to help him frame it, he made it out of his own head saying:

"Fair Sir God, I pray you to do by La Hire as he would do by you if you were La Hire and he were God." 1

Then he put on his helmet and marched out of Joan's tent as satisfied with himself as any one might be who had arranged a perplexed and difficult business to the content and admiration of all the parties concerned in the matter.

If I had know that he had been praying, I could have understood why he was feeling so superior, but of course I could not know that.

I was coming to the tent at that moment, and saw him come out, and saw him march away in that large fashion, and indeed it was fine and beautiful to see. But when I got to the tent door I stopped and
stepped back, grieved and shocked, for I heard Joan crying, as I mistakenly thought crying as if she could not contain nor endure the anguish of her soul, crying as if she would die. But it was not so, she was laughing laughing at La Hire's prayer.

It was not until six–and–thirty years afterward that I found that out, and then oh, then I only cried when that picture of young care–free mirth rose before me out of the blur and mists of that long–vanished time; for there had come a day between, when God's good gift of laughter had gone out from me to come again no more in this life.

(1) This prayer has been stolen many times and by many nations in the past four hundred and sixty years, but it originated with La Hire, and the fact is of official record in the National Archives of France. We have the authority of Michelet for this.TRANSLATOR

Chapter 13.

Checked by the Folly of the Wise

WE MARCHED out in great strength and splendor, and took the road toward Orleans. The initial part of Joan's great dream was realizing itself at last. It was the first time that any of us youngsters had ever seen an army, and it was a most stately and imposing spectacle to us. It was indeed an inspiring sight, that interminable column, stretching away into the fading distances, and curving itself in and out of the crookedness of the road like a mighty serpent. Joan rode at the head of it with her personal staff; then came a body of priests singing the Veni Creator, the banner of the Cross rising out of their midst; after these the glinting forest of spears. The several divisions were commanded by the great Armagnac generals, La
Hire, and Marshal de Boussac, the Sire de Retz, Florent d'Illiers, and
Poton de Saintrailles.

Each in his degree was tough, and there were three degreestough, tougher, toughestand La Hire was the last by a shade, but only a shade. They were just illustrious official brigands, the whole party; and by long habits of lawlessness they had lost all acquaintanceship with obedience, if they had ever had any.

But what was the good of saying that? These independent birds knew no law. They seldom obeyed the King; they never obeyed him when it didn't suit them to do it. Would they obey the Maid? In the first place they wouldn't know how to obey her or anybody else, and in the second place it was of course not possible for them to take her military character seriouslythat country–girl of seventeen who had been trained for the complex and terrible business of warhow? By tending sheep.

They had no idea of obeying her except in cases where their veteran military knowledge and experience showed them that the thing she required was sound and right when gauged by the regular military standards. Were they to blame for this attitude? I should think not. Old war–worn captains are hard–headed, practical men. They do not easily believe in the ability of ignorant children to plan campaigns and command armies. No general that ever lived could have taken Joan seriously (militarily) before she raised the siege of Orleans and followed it with the great campaign of the Loire.

Did they consider Joan valueless? Far from it. They valued her as the fruitful earth values the sunthey fully believed she could produce the crop, but that it was in their line of business, not hers, to take it off. They had a deep and superstitious reverence for her as being
endowed with a mysterious supernatural something that was able to do a mighty thing which they were powerless to doblow the breath of life and valor into the dead corpses of cowed armies and turn them into heroes.

To their minds they were everything with her, but nothing without her. She could inspire the soldiers and fit them for battlebut fight the battle herself? Oh, nonsensethat was their function. They, the generals, would fight the battles, Joan would give the victory. That was their ideaan unconscious paraphrase of Joan's reply to the Dominican.

So they began by playing a deception upon her. She had a clear idea of how she meant to proceed. It was her purpose to march boldly upon Orleans by the north bank of the Loire. She gave that order to her generals. They said to themselves, "The idea is insaneit is blunder No. 1; it is what might have been expected of this child who is ignorant of war." They privately sent the word to the Bastard of Orleans. He also recognized the insanity of itat least he thought he didand privately advised the generals to get around the order in some way.

They did it by deceiving Joan. She trusted those people, she was not expecting this sort of treatment, and was not on the lookout for it. It was a lesson to her; she saw to it that the game was not played a second time.

Why was Joan's idea insane, from the generals' point of view, but not from hers? Because her plan was to raise the siege immediately, by fighting, while theirs was to besiege the besiegers and starve them out by closing their communicationsa plan which would require months in the consummation.

The English had built a fence of strong fortresses called bastilles around Orleansfortresses which closed all the gates of the city but one. To the French generals the idea of trying to fight their way past those fortresses and lead the army into Orleans was preposterous; they believed that the result would be the army's destruction. One may not doubt that their opinion was militarily soundno, would have been, but for one circumstance which they overlooked. That was this: the English soldiers were in a demoralized condition of superstitious terror; they had become satisfied that the Maid was in league with Satan. By reason of this a good deal of their courage had oozed out and vanished. On the other hand, the Maid's soldiers were full of courage, enthusiasm, and zeal.

Joan could have marched by the English forts. However, it was not to be. She had been cheated out of her first chance to strike a heavy blow for her country.

In camp that night she slept in her armor on the ground. It was a cold night, and she was nearly as stiff as her armor itself when we resumed the march in the morning, for iron is not good material for a blanket. However, her joy in being now so far on her way to the theater of her mission was fire enough to warm her, and it soon did it.

Her enthusiasm and impatience rose higher and higher with every mile of progress; but at last we reached Olivet, and down it went, and indignation took its place. For she saw the trick that had been played upon herthe river lay between us and Orleans.

She was for attacking one of the three bastilles that were on our side of the river and forcing access to the bridge which it guarded (a project which, if successful, would raise the siege instantly), but the long–ingrained fear of the English came upon her generals and they implored her not to make the attempt. The soldiers wanted to attack, but had to suffer disappointment. So we moved on and came to a halt at a point opposite Checy, six miles above Orleans.

Dunois, Bastard of Orleans, with a body of knights and citizens, came up from the city to welcome Joan. Joan was still burning with resentment over the trick that had been put upon her, and was not in the mood for soft speeches, even to revered military idols of her childhood. She said:

"Are you the bastard?"

"Yes, I am he, and am right glad of your coming."

"And did you advise that I be brought by this side of the river instead of straight to Talbot and the English?"

Her high manner abashed him, and he was not able to answer with anything like a confident promptness, but with many hesitations and partial excuses he managed to get out the confession that for what he and the council had regarded as imperative military reasons they so advised.

"In God's name," said Joan, "my Lord's counsel is safer and wiser than yours. You thought to deceive me, but you have deceived yourselves, for I bring you the best help that ever knight or city had; for it is God's help, not sent for love of me, but by God's pleasure. At the prayer of St. Louis and St. Charlemagne He has had pity on Orleans, and will not suffer the enemy to have both the Duke of Orleans and his city. The provisions to save the starving people are here, the boats are below the city, the wind is contrary, they cannot come up hither. Now then, tell me, in God's name, you who are so wise, what that council of yours was thinking about, to invent this foolish difficulty."

Dunois and the rest fumbled around the matter a moment, then gave in and conceded that a blunder had been made.

"Yes, a blunder has been made," said Joan, "and except God take your proper work upon Himself and change the wind and correct your blunder for you, there is none else that can devise a remedy."

Some of these people began to perceive that with all her technical ignorance she had practical good sense, and that with all her native sweetness and charm she was not the right kind of a person to play with.

Presently God did take the blunder in hand, and by His grace the wind did change. So the fleet of boats came up and went away loaded with provisions and cattle, and conveyed that welcome succor to the hungry city, managing the matter successfully under protection of a sortie from the walls against the bastille of St. Loup. Then Joan began on the Bastard again:

"You see here the army?" "Yes."

"It is here on this side by advice of your council?" "Yes."

"Now, in God's name, can that wise council explain why it is better to have it here than it would be to have it in the bottom of the sea?"

Dunois made some wandering attempts to explain the inexplicable and excuse the inexcusable, but Joan cut him short and said:

"Answer me this, good sirhas the army any value on this side of the river?"

The Bastard confessed that it hadn'tthat is, in view of the plan of campaign which she had devised and decreed.

"And yet, knowing this, you had the hardihood to disobey my orders. Since the army's place is on the other side, will you explain to me how it is to get there?"

The whole size of the needless muddle was apparent. Evasions were of no use; therefore Dunois admitted that there was no way to
correct the blunder but to send the army all the way back to Blois, and let it begin over again and come up on the other side this time,

according to Joan's original plan.

Any other girl, after winning such a triumph as this over a veteran soldier of old renown, might have exulted a little and been excusable for it, but Joan showed no disposition of this sort. She dropped a word or two of grief over the precious time that must be lost, then began at once to issue commands for the march back. She sorrowed to see her army go; for she said its heart was great and its enthusiasm high, and that with it at her back she did not fear to face all the might of England.

All arrangements having been completed for the return of the main body of the army, she took the Bastard and La Hire and a thousand men and went down to Orleans, where all the town was in a fever of impatience to have sight of her face. It was eight in the evening when she and the troops rode in at the Burgundy gate, with the Paladin preceding her with her standard. She was riding a white horse, and she carried in her hand the sacred sword of Fierbois. You should have seen Orleans then. What a picture it was! Such black seas of people, such a starry firmament of torches, such roaring whirlwinds of welcome, such booming of bells and thundering of cannon! It was as if the world was come to an end. Everywhere in the glare of the torches one saw rank upon rank of upturned white faces, the mouths wide open, shouting, and the unchecked tears running down; Joan forged her slow way through the solid masses,
her mailed form projecting above the pavement of heads like a silver statue. The people about her struggled along, gazing up at her through their tears with the rapt look of men and women who
believe they are seeing one who is divine; and always her feet were being kissed by grateful folk, and such as failed of that privilege touched her horse and then kissed their fingers.

Nothing that Joan did escaped notice; everything she did was commented upon and applauded. You could hear the remarks going all the time.

"Thereshe's smilingsee!"

"Now she's taking her little plumed cap off to somebodyah, it's fine and graceful!"

"She's patting that woman on the head with her gauntlet."

"Oh, she was born on a horse—see her turn in her saddle, and kiss the hilt of her sword to the ladies in the window that threw the flowers down."

"Now there's a poor woman lifting up a child—she's kissed it—oh, she's divine!"

"What a dainty little figure it is, and what a lovely face—and such color and animation!"

Joan's slender long banner streaming backward had an accident—the fringe caught fire from a torch. She leaned forward and crushed the flame in her hand.

"She's not afraid of fire nor anything!" they shouted, and delivered a storm of admiring applause that made everything quake.

She rode to the cathedral and gave thanks to God, and the people crammed the place and added their devotions to hers; then she took up her march again and picked her slow way through the crowds and the wilderness of torches to the house of Jacques Boucher, treasurer of the Duke of Orleans, where she was to be the guest of his wife as long as she stayed in the city, and have his young daughter for comrade and room–mate. The delirium of the people went on the rest of the night, and with it the clamor of the joy–bells and the welcoming cannon.

Joan of Arc had stepped upon her stage at last, and was ready to begin.

CHAPTER 14.

What the English Answered

SHE WAS ready, but must sit down and wait until there was an army to work with.

Next morning, Saturday, April 30, 1429, she set about inquiring after the messenger who carried her proclamation to the English from Bloisthe one which she had dictated at Poitiers. Here is a copy of it.
It is a remarkable document, for several reasons: for its matter–of– fact directness, for its high spirit and forcible diction, and for its naive confidence in her ability to achieve the prodigious task which
she had laid upon herself, or which had been laid upon herwhich you please. All through it you seem to see the pomps of war and hear the rumbling of the drums. In it Joan's warrior soul is revealed, and for the moment the soft little shepherdess has disappeared from your view. This untaught country–damsel, unused to dictating anything at all to anybody, much less documents of state to kings and generals, poured out this procession of vigorous sentences as fluently as if this sort of work had been her trade from childhood:

JESUS MARIA King of England and you Duke of Bedford who call yourself Regent of France; William de la Pole, Earl of Suffolk; and you Thomas Lord Scales, who style yourselves lieutenants of the
said Bedforddo right to the King of Heaven. Render to the Maid who is sent by God the keys of all the good towns you have taken and violated in France. She is sent hither by God, to restore the blood royal. She is very ready to make peace if you will do her right by giving up France and paying for what you have held. And you archers, companions of war, noble and otherwise, who are before the good city of Orleans, begone into your own land in God's name, or expect news from the Maid who will shortly go to see you to your very great hurt. King of England, if you do not so, I am chief of war, and whenever I shall find your people in France, I will drive them out, willing or not willing; and if they do not obey I will slay them

all, but if they obey, I will have them to mercy. I am come hither by God, the King of Heaven, body for body, to put you out of France, in spite of those who would work treason and mischief against the kingdom. Think not you shall ever hold the kingdom from the King of Heaven, the Son of the Blessed Mary; King Charles shall hold it, for God wills it so, and has revealed it to him by the Maid. If you believe not the news sent by God through the Maid, wherever we shall meet you we will strike boldly and make such a noise as has
not been in France these thousand years. Be sure that God can send more strength to the Maid than you can bring to any assault against her and her good men–at–arms; and then we shall see who has the better right, the King of Heaven, or you. Duke of Bedford, the Maid prays you not to bring about your own destruction. If you do her right, you may yet go in her company where the French shall do the finest deed that has been done in Christendom, and if you do not, you shall be reminded shortly of your great wrongs.

In that closing sentence she invites them to go on crusade with her to rescue the Holy Sepulcher. No answer had been returned to this proclamation, and the messenger himself had not come back.

So now she sent her two heralds with a new letter warning the English to raise the siege and requiring them to restore that missing messenger. The heralds came back without him. All they brought was notice from the English to Joan that they would presently catch her and burn her if she did not clear out now while she had a chance, and "go back to her proper trade of minding cows."

She held her peace, only saying it was a pity that the English would persist in inviting present disaster and eventual destruction when she was "doing all she could to get them out of the country with their lives still in their bodies."

Presently she thought of an arrangement that might be acceptable, and said to the heralds, "Go back and say to Lord Talbot this, from me: 'Come out of your bastilles with your host, and I will come with mine; if I beat you, go in peace out of France; if you beat me, burn me, according to your desire.'"

I did not hear this, but Dunois did, and spoke of it. The challenge was refused.

Sunday morning her Voices or some instinct gave her a warning, and she sent Dunois to Blois to take command of the army and hurry it to Orleans. It was a wise move, for he found Regnault de Chartres and some more of the King's pet rascals there trying their best to disperse the army, and crippling all the efforts of Joan's generals to head it for Orleans. They were a fine lot, those miscreants. They turned their attention to Dunois now, but he had balked Joan once, with unpleasant results to himself, and was not minded to meddle in that way again. He soon had the army moving.

Chapter 15.

My Exquisite Poem Goes to Smash

WE OF the personal staff were in fairyland now, during the few days that we waited for the return of the army. We went into society. To our two knights this was not a novelty, but to us young villagers it was a new and wonderful life. Any position of any sort near the person of the Maid of Vaucouleurs conferred high distinction upon the holder and caused his society to be courted; and so the D'Arc brothers, and Noel, and the Paladin, humble peasants at home, were gentlemen here, personages of weight and influence. It was fine to
see how soon their country diffidences and awkwardnesses melted away under this pleasant sun of deference and disappeared, and how lightly and easily they took to their new atmosphere. The Paladin was as happy as it was possible for any one in this earth to be. His tongue went all the time, and daily he got new delight out of hearing himself talk. He began to enlarge his ancestry and spread it out all around, and ennoble it right and left, and it was not long until it consisted almost entirely of dukes. He worked up his old battles and tricked them out with fresh splendors; also with new terrors, for he added artillery now. We had seen cannon for the first time at Bloisa few pieceshere there was plenty of it, and now and then we had the impressive spectacle of a huge English bastille hidden from sight in a mountain of smoke from its own guns, with lances of red flame darting through it; and this grand picture, along with the quaking thunders pounding away in the heart of it, inflamed the Paladin's imagination and enabled him to dress out those ambuscade– skirmishes of ours with a sublimity which made it impossible for any to recognize them at all except people who had not been there.

You may suspect that there was a special inspiration for these great efforts of the Paladin's, and there was. It was the daughter of the house, Catherine Boucher, who was eighteen, and gentle and lovely in her ways, and very beautiful. I think she might have been as beautiful as Joan herself, if she had had Joan's eyes. But that could never be. There was never but that one pair, there will never be another. Joan's eyes were deep and rich and wonderful beyond anything merely earthly. They spoke all the languages—they had no need of words. They produced all effects—and just by a glance, just a single glance; a glance that could convict a liar of his lie and make him confess it; that could bring down a proud man's pride and make him humble; that could put courage into a coward and strike dead the courage of the bravest; that could appease resentments and real hatreds; that could make the doubter believe and the hopeless hope again; that could purify the impure mind; that could persuade—ah, there it is—persuasion! that is the word; what or who is it that it couldn't persuade? The maniac of Domremy—the fairy-banishing priest—the reverend tribunal of Toul—the doubting and superstitious Laxart—the obstinate veteran of Vaucouleurs—the characterless heir of France—the sages and scholars of the Parliament and University of Poitiers—the darling of Satan, La Hire—the masterless Bastard of Orleans, accustomed to acknowledge no way as right and rational but his own—these were the trophies of that great gift that made her the wonder and mystery that she was.

We mingled companionably with the great folk who flocked to the big house to make Joan's acquaintance, and they made much of us and we lived in the clouds, so to speak. But what we preferred even to this happiness was the quieter occasions, when the formal guests were gone and the family and a few dozen of its familiar friends were gathered together for a social good time. It was then that we did our best, we five youngsters, with such fascinations as we had, and the chief object of them was Catherine. None of us had ever
been in love before, and now we had the misfortune to all fall in love with the same person at the same time—which was the first moment
we saw her. She was a merry heart, and full of life, and I still remember tenderly those few evenings that I was permitted to have my share of her dear society and of comradeship with that little company of charming people.

The Paladin made us all jealous the first night, for when he got fairly started on those battles of his he had everything to himself, and there was no use in anybody else's trying to get any attention. Those
people had been living in the midst of real war for seven months;

and to hear this windy giant lay out his imaginary campaigns and fairly swim in blood and spatter it all around, entertained them to the verge of the grave. Catherine was like to die, for pure enjoyment.
She didn't laugh loudwe, of course, wished she wouldbut kept in the shelter of a fan, and shook until there was danger that she would unhitch her ribs from her spine. Then when the Paladin had got done with a battle and we began to feel thankful and hope for a change, she would speak up in a way that was so sweet and persuasive that it rankled in me, and ask him about some detail or other in the early part of his battle which she said had greatly interested her, and
would he be so good as to describe that part again and with a little more particularity?which of course precipitated the whole battle on us, again, with a hundred lies added that had been overlooked before.

I do not know how to make you realize the pain I suffered. I had never been jealous before, and it seemed intolerable that this creature should have this good fortune which he was so ill entitled to, and I have to sit and see myself neglected when I was so longing for the least little attention out of the thousand that this beloved girl was lavishing on him. I was near her, and tried two or three times to get started on some of the things that I had done in those battlesand I felt ashamed of myself, too, for stooping to such a businessbut she cared for nothing but his battles, and could not be got to listen; and presently when one of my attempts caused her to lose some precious rag or other of his mendacities and she asked him to repeat, thus bringing on a new engagement, of course, and increasing the havoc and carnage tenfold, I felt so humiliated by this pitiful miscarriage of mine that I gave up and tried no more.

The others were as outraged by the Paladin's selfish conduct as I wasand by his grand luck, too, of courseperhaps, indeed, that was the main hurt. We talked our trouble over together, which was natural,
for rivals become brothers when a common affliction assails them and a common enemy bears off the victory.

Each of us could do things that would please and get notice if it were not for this person, who occupied all the time and gave others no chance. I had made a poem, taking a whole night to ita poem in

which I most happily and delicately celebrated that sweet girl's charms, without mentioning her name, but any one could see who was meant; for the bare title "The Rose of Orleans" would reveal that, as it seemed to me. It pictured this pure and dainty white rose as growing up out of the rude soil of war and looking abroad out of its tender eyes upon the horrid machinery of death, and then note this conceit it blushes for the sinful nature of man, and turns red in a single night. Becomes a red rose, you see a rose that was white before. The idea was my own, and quite new. Then it sent its sweet perfume out over the embattled city, and when the beleaguering forces smelt it they laid down their arms and wept. This was also my own idea, and new. That closed that part of the poem; then I put her into the similitude of the firmament not the whole of it, but only part. That is to say, she was the moon, and all the constellations were following her about, their hearts in flames for love of her, but she would not halt, she would not listen, for 'twas thought she loved another. 'Twas thought she loved a poor unworthy suppliant who
was upon the earth, facing danger, death, and possible mutilation in the bloody field, waging relentless war against a heartless foe to save her from an all too early grave, and her city from destruction. And when the sad pursuing constellations came to know and realize the bitter sorrow that was come upon them note this idea their hearts
broke and their tears gushed forth, filling the vault of heaven with a fiery splendor, for those tears were falling stars. It was a rash idea, but beautiful; beautiful and pathetic; wonderfully pathetic, the way I had it, with the rhyme and all to help. At the end of each verse there was a two-line refrain pitying the poor earthly lover separated so far, and perhaps forever, from her he loved so well, and growing always paler and weaker and thinner in his agony as he neared the cruel grave the most touching thing even the boys themselves could hardly keep back their tears, the way Noel said those lines. There were
eight four-line stanzas in the first end of the poem the end about the rose, the horticultural end, as you may say, if that is not too large a name for such a little poem and eight in the astronomical end sixteen stanzas altogether, and I could have made it a hundred and fifty if I had wanted to, I was so inspired and so all swelled up with beautiful thoughts and fancies; but that would have been too many to sing or recite before a company that way, whereas sixteen was just right,
and could be done over again if desired. The boys were amazed that

I could make such a poem as that out of my own head, and so was I, of course, it being as much a surprise to me as it could be to anybody, for I did not know that it was in me. If any had asked me a single day before if it was in me, I should have told them frankly no, it was not.

That is the way with us; we may go on half of our life not knowing such a thing is in us, when in reality it was there all the time, and all we needed was something to turn up that would call for it. Indeed, it was always so without family. My grandfather had a cancer, and they never knew what was the matter with him till he died, and he didn't know himself. It is wonderful how gifts and diseases can be concealed in that way. All that was necessary in my case was for this lovely and inspiring girl to cross my path, and out came the poem, and no more trouble to me to word it and rhyme it and perfect it than it is to stone a dog. No, I should have said it was not in me; but it was.

The boys couldn't say enough about it, they were so charmed and astonished. The thing that pleased them the most was the way it would do the Paladin's business for him. They forgot everything in their anxiety to get him shelved and silenced. Noel Rainguesson was clear beside himself with admiration of the poem, and wished he could do such a thing, but it was out of his line, and he couldn't, of course. He had it by heart in half an hour, and there was never anything so pathetic and beautiful as the way he recited it. For that was just his gift–that and mimicry. He could recite anything better than anybody in the world, and he could take of La Hire to the very
life–or anybody else, for that matter. Now I never could recite worth a farthing; and when I tried with this poem the boys wouldn't let me finish; they would have nobody but Noel. So then, as I wanted the poem to make the best possible impression on Catherine and the company, I told Noel he might do the reciting. Never was anybody
so delighted. He could hardly believe that I was in earnest, but I was. I said that to have them know that I was the author of it would be enough for me. The boys were full of exultation, and Noel said if he could just get one chance at those people it would be all he would ask; he would make them realize that there was something higher
and finer than war–lies to be had here.

But how to get the opportunitythat was the difficulty. We invented several schemes that promised fairly, and at last we hit upon one that was sure. That was, to let the Paladin get a good start in a manufactured battle, and then send in a false call for him, and as
soon as he was out of the room, have Noel take his place and finish the battle himself in the Paladin's own style, imitated to a shade. That would get great applause, and win the house's favor and put it in the right mood to hear the poem. The two triumphs together with finish the Standard–Bearermodify him, anyway, to a certainty, and give the rest of us a chance for the future.

So the next night I kept out of the way until the Paladin had got his start and was sweeping down upon the enemy like a whirlwind at the head of his corps, then I stepped within the door in my official uniform and announced that a messenger from General La Hire's quarters desired speech with the Standard–Bearer. He left the room, and Noel took his place and said that the interruption was to be deplored, but that fortunately he was personally acquainted with the details of the battle himself, and if permitted would be glad to state them to the company. Then without waiting for the permission he turned himself to the Paladina dwarfed Paladin, of coursewith manner, tones, gestures, attitudes, everything exact, and went right
on with the battle, and it would be impossible to imagine a more perfectly and minutely ridiculous imitation than he furnished to
those shrieking people. They went into spasms, convulsions, frenzies of laughter, and the tears flowed down their cheeks in rivulets. The more they laughed, the more inspired Noel grew with his theme and the greater marvels he worked, till really the laughter was not properly laughing any more, but screaming. Blessedest feature of all, Catherine Boucher was dying with ecstasies, and presently there was little left of her but gasps and suffocations. Victory? It was a perfect Agincourt.

The Paladin was gone only a couple of minutes; he found out at once that a trick had been played on him, so he came back. When he approached the door he heard Noel ranting in there and recognized the state of the case; so he remained near the door but out of sight, and heard the performance through to the end. The applause Noel
got when he finished was wonderful; and they kept it up and kept it

up, clapping their hands like mad, and shouting to him to do it over again.

But Noel was clever. He knew the very best background for a poem of deep and refined sentiment and pathetic melancholy was one where great and satisfying merriment had prepared the spirit for the powerful contrast.

So he paused until all was quiet, then his face grew grave and assumed an impressive aspect, and at once all faces sobered in sympathy and took on a look of wondering and expectant interest. Now he began in a low but distinct voice the opening verses of The Rose. As he breathed the rhythmic measures forth, and one gracious line after another fell upon those enchanted ears in that deep hush, one could catch, on every hand, half-audible ejaculations of "How lovelyhow beautifulhow exquisite!"

By this time the Paladin, who had gone away for a moment with the opening of the poem, was back again, and had stepped within the door. He stood there now, resting his great frame against the wall and gazing toward the reciter like one entranced. When Noel got to the second part, and that heart-breaking refrain began to melt and move all listeners, the Paladin began to wipe away tears with the back of first one hand and then the other. The next time the refrain was repeated he got to snuffling, and sort of half sobbing, and went to wiping his eyes with the sleeves of his doublet. He was so conspicuous that he embarrassed Noel a little, and also had an ill effect upon the audience. With the next repetition he broke quite down and began to cry like a calf, which ruined all the effect and started many to the audience to laughing. Then he went on from bad to worse, until I never saw such a spectacle; for he fetched out a towel from under his doublet and began to swab his eyes with it and let go the most infernal bellowings mixed up with sobbings and groanings and retchings and barkings and coughings and snortings and screamings and howlingsand he twisted himself about on his heels and squirmed this way and that, still pouring out that brutal clamor and flourishing his towel in the air and swabbing again and wringing it out. Hear? You couldn't hear yourself think. Noel was wholly drowned out and silenced, and those people were laughing

the very lungs out of themselves. It was the most degrading sight that ever was. Now I heard the clankety–clank that plate–armor makes when the man that is in it is running, and then alongside my head there burst out the most inhuman explosion of laughter that ever rent the drum of a person's ear, and I looked, and it was La Hire; and the stood there with his gauntlets on his hips and his head tilted back and his jaws spread to that degree to let out his hurricanes and his thunders that it amounted to indecent exposure, for you
could see everything that was in him. Only one thing more and worse could happen, and it happened: at the other door I saw the flurry and bustle and bowings and scrapings of officials and flunkeys which means that some great personage is comingthen Joan of Arc stepped in, and the house rose! Yes, and tried to shut its indecorous mouth and make itself grave and proper; but when it saw the Maid herself go to laughing, it thanked God for this mercy and the earthquake that followed.

Such things make a life of bitterness, and I do not wish to dwell upon them. The effect of the poem was spoiled.

Chapter 16.

The Finding of the Dwarf

THIS EPISODE disagreed with me and I was not able to leave my bed the next day. The others were in the same condition. But for this, one or another of us might have had the good luck that fell to the Paladin's share that day; but it is observable that God in His compassion sends the good luck to such as are ill equipped with
gifts, as compensation for their defect, but requires such as are more fortunately endowed to get by labor and talent what those others get by chance. It was Noel who said this, and it seemed to me to be well and justly thought.

The Paladin, going about the town all the day in order to be followed and admired and overhear the people say in an awed voice, "'Ssh! look, it is the Standard–Bearer of Joan of Arc!" had speech with all sorts and conditions of folk, and he learned from some boatmen that there was a stir of some kind going on in the bastilles on the other side of the river; and in the evening, seeking further, he found a deserter from the fortress called the "Augustins," who said that the English were going to send me over to strengthen the garrisons on our side during the darkness of the night, and were exulting greatly, for they meant to spring upon Dunois and the army when it was passing the bastilles and destroy it; a thing quite easy to do, since the "Witch" would not be there, and without her presence the army would do like the French armies of these many years past—drop their weapons and run when they saw an English face.

It was ten at night when the Paladin brought this news and asked leave to speak to Joan, and I was up and on duty then. It was a bitter stroke to me to see what a chance I had lost. Joan made searching inquiries, and satisfied herself that the word was true, then she made this annoying remark:

"You have done well, and you have my thanks. It may be that you have prevented a disaster. Your name and service shall receive official mention."

Then he bowed low, and when he rose he was eleven feet high. As he swelled out past me he covertly pulled down the corner of his eye with his finger and muttered part of that defiled refrain, "Oh, tears, ah, tears, oh, sad sweet tears!name in General Orderspersonal mention to the King, you see!"

I wished Joan could have seen his conduct, but she was busy thinking what she would do. Then she had me fetch the knight Jean de Metz, and in a minute he was off for La Hire's quarters with orders for him and the Lord de Villars and Florent d'Illiers to report to her at five o'clock next morning with five hundred picked men well mounted. The histories say half past four, but it is not true, I heard the order given.

We were on our way at five to the minute, and encountered the head of the arriving column between six and seven, a couple of leagues from the city. Dunois was pleased, for the army had begun to get restive and show uneasiness now that it was getting so near to the dreaded bastilles. But that all disappeared now, as the word ran
down the line, with a huzza that swept along the length of it like a wave, that the Maid was come. Dunois asked her to halt and let the column pass in review, so that the men could be sure that the reports of her presence was not a ruse to revive their courage. So she took position at the side of the road with her staff, and the battalions swung by with a martial stride, huzzaing. Joan was armed, except her head. She was wearing the cunning little velvet cap with the mass of curved white ostrich plumes tumbling over its edges which the city of Orleans had given her the night she arrivedthe one that is in the picture that hangs in the Hotel de Ville at Rouen. She was looking about fifteen. The sight of soldiers always set her blood to leaping, and lit the fires in her eyes and brought the warm rich color to her cheeks; it was then that you saw that she was too beautiful to be of the earth, or at any rate that there was a subtle something somewhere about her beauty that differed it from the human types of your experience and exalted it above them.

In the train of wains laden with supplies a man lay on top of the goods. He was stretched out on his back, and his hands were tied together with ropes, and also his ankles. Joan signed to the officer in charge of that division of the train to come to her, and he rode up
and saluted.

"What is he that is bound there?" she asked. "A prisoner,

General."

"What is his offense?" "He is a

deserter."

"What is to be done with him?"

"He will be hanged, but it was not convenient on the march, and there was no hurry."

"Tell me about him."

"He is a good soldier, but he asked leave to go and see his wife who was dying, he said, but it could not be granted; so he went without leave. Meanwhile the march began, and he only overtook us yesterday evening."

"Overtook you? Did he come of his own will?" "Yes, it was

of his own will."

"He a deserter! Name of God! Bring him to me."

The officer rode forward and loosed the man's feet and brought him back with his hands still tied. What a figure he was a good seven feet high, and built for business! He had a strong face; he had an
unkempt shock of black hair which showed up a striking way when the officer removed his morion for him; for weapon he had a big ax in his broad leathern belt. Standing by Joan's horse, he made Joan look littler than ever, for his head was about on a level with her own. His face was profoundly melancholy; all interest in life seemed to be

dead in the man. Joan said: "Hold up

your hands."

The man's head was down. He lifted it when he heard that soft friendly voice, and there was a wistful something in his face which made one think that there had been music in it for him and that he would like to hear it again. When he raised his hands Joan laid her sword to his bonds, but the officer said with apprehension:

"Ah, madammy General!" "What is it?"

she said.

"He is under sentence!"

"Yes, I know. I am responsible for him"; and she cut the bonds. They had lacerated his wrists, and they were bleeding. "Ah, pitiful!" she said; "bloodI do not like it"; and she shrank from the sight. But only for a moment. "Give me something, somebody, to bandage his wrists with."

The officer said:

"Ah, my General! it is not fitting. Let me bring another to do it." "Another? De par le Dieu! You would seek far to find one that can
do it better than I, for I learned it long ago among both men and beasts. And I can tie better than those that did this; if I had tied him the ropes had not cut his flesh."

The man looked on silent, while he was being bandaged, stealing a furtive glance at Joan's face occasionally, such as an animal might that is receiving a kindness form an unexpected quarter and is gropingly trying to reconcile the act with its source. All the staff had forgotten the huzzaing army drifting by in its rolling clouds of dust, to crane their necks and watch the bandaging as if it was the most interesting and absorbing novelty that ever was. I have often seen people do like thatget entirely lost in the simplest trifle, when it is something that is out of their line. Now there in Poitiers, once, I saw

two bishops and a dozen of those grave and famous scholars grouped together watching a man paint a sign on a shop; they didn't breathe, they were as good as dead; and when it began to sprinkle they didn't know it at first; then they noticed it, and each man hove a deep sigh, and glanced up with a surprised look as wondering to see the others there, and how he came to be there himselfbut that is the way with people, as I have said. There is no way of accounting for people.
You have to take them as they are.

"There," said Joan at last, pleased with her success; "another could have done it no betternot as well, I think. Tell mewhat is it you did? Tell me all."

The giant said:

"It was this way, my angel. My mother died, then my three little children, one after the other, all in two years. It was the famine; others fared soit was God's will. I saw them die; I had that grace; and I buried them. Then when my poor wife's fate was come, I begged
for leave to go to hershe who was so dear to meshe who was all I had; I begged on my knees. But they would not let me. Could I let her die, friendless and alone? Could I let her die believing I would not come? Would she let me die and she not comewith her feet free to do it if she would, and no cost upon it but only her life? Ah, she would comeshe would come through the fire! So I went. I saw her. She died in my arms. I buried her. Then the army was gone. I had trouble to overtake it, but my legs are long and there are many hours in a day; I overtook it last night."

Joan said, musingly, as if she were thinking aloud:

"It sounds true. If true, it were no great harm to suspend the law this one timeany would say that. It may not be true, but if it is true" She turned suddenly to the man and said, "I would see your eyeslook
up!" The eyes of the two met, and Joan said to the officer, "This man is pardoned. Give you good day; you may go." Then she said to the man, "Did you know it was death to come back to the army?"

"Yes," he said, "I knew it."

"Then why did you do it?" The man said,

quite simply:

"Because it was death. She was all I had. There was nothing left to love."

"Ah, yes, there wasFrance! The children of France have always their motherthey cannot be left with nothing to love. You shall liveand you shall serve France"

"I will serve you!""you shall fight for France" "I will fight

for you!"

"You shall be France's soldier"

"I will be your soldier!""you shall give all your heart to France"

"I will give all my heart to youand all my soul, if I have oneand all my strength, which is greatfor I was dead and am alive again; I had nothing to live for, but now I have! You are France for me. You are my France, and I will have no other."

Joan smiled, and was touched and pleased at the man's grave enthusiasmsolemn enthusiasm, one may call it, for the manner of it was deeper than mere gravityand she said:

"Well, it shall be as you will. What are you called?" The man

answered with unsmiling simplicity:

"They call me the Dwarf, but I think it is more in jest than otherwise."

It made Joan laugh, and she said:

"It has something of that look truly! What is the office of that vast ax?"

The soldier replied with the same gravitywhich must have been born to him, it sat upon him so naturally:

"It is to persuade persons to respect France." Joan laughed

again, and said:

"Have you given many lessons?" "Ah, indeed,

yes—many."

"The pupils behaved to suit you, afterward?"

"Yes; it made them quiet—quite pleasant and quiet."

"I should think it would happen so. Would you like to be my man–at–arms?—orderly, sentinel, or something like that?" "If I may!"

"Then you shall. You shall have proper armor, and shall go on teaching your art. Take one of those led horses there, and follow the staff when we move."

That is how we came by the Dwarf; and a good fellow he was. Joan picked him out on sight, but it wasn't a mistake; no one could be faithfuler than he was, and he was a devil and the son of a devil when he turned himself loose with his ax. He was so big that he made the Paladin look like an ordinary man. He liked to like people, therefore people liked him. He liked us boys from the start; and he liked the knights, and liked pretty much everybody he came across; but he thought more of a paring of Joan's finger–nail than he did of all the rest of the world put together.

Yes, that is where we got him—stretched on the wain, going to his death, poor chap, and nobody to say a good word for him. He was a good find. Why, the knights treated him almost like an equal—it is the honest truth; that is the sort of a man he was. They called him the Bastille sometimes, and sometimes they called him Hellfire, which was on account of his warm and sumptuous style in battle, and you know they wouldn't have given him pet names if they hadn't had a good deal of affection for him.

To the Dwarf, Joan was France, the spirit of France made flesh—he never got away from that idea that he had started with; and God knows it was the true one. That was a humble eye to see so great a truth where some others failed. To me that seems quite remarkable. And yet, after all, it was, in a way, just what nations do. When they love a great and noble thing, they embody it—they want it so that they can see it with their eyes; like liberty, for instance. They are not content with the cloudy abstract idea, they make a beautiful statue of it, and then their beloved idea is substantial and they can look at it and worship it. And so it is as I say; to the Dwarf, Joan was our country embodied, our country made visible flesh cast in a gracious form. When she stood before others, they saw Joan of Arc, but he saw France.

Sometimes he would speak of her by that name. It shows you how the idea was embedded in his mind, and how real it was to him. The world has called our kings by it, but I know of none of them who has had so good a right as she to that sublime title.

When the march past was finished, Joan returned to the front and rode at the head of the column. When we began to file past those grim bastilles and could glimpse the men within, standing to their guns and ready to empty death into our ranks, such a faintness came over me and such a sickness that all things seemed to turn dim and swim before my eyes; and the other boys looked droopy, too, I thought—including the Paladin, although I do not know this for certain, because he was ahead of me and I had to keep my eyes out toward the bastille side, because I could wince better when I saw what to wince at.

But Joan was at home—in Paradise, I might say. She sat up straight, and I could see that she was feeling different from me. The awfulest thing was the silence; there wasn't a sound but the screaking of the saddles, the measured tramplings, and the sneezing of the horses, afflicted by the smothering dust-clouds which they kicked up. I wanted to sneeze myself, but it seemed to me that I would rather go unsneezed, or suffer even a bitterer torture, if there is one, than attract attention to myself.

I was not of a rank to make suggestions, or I would have suggested that if we went faster we should get by sooner. It seemed to me that it was an ill-judged time to be taking a walk. Just as we were drifting in that suffocating stillness past a great cannon that stood just within a raised portcullis, with nothing between me and it but the moat, a most uncommon jackass in there split the world with his bray, and I fell out of the saddle. Sir Bertrand grabbed me as I went, which was well, for if I had gone to the ground in my armor I could not have gotten up again by myself. The English warders on the battlements laughed a coarse laugh, forgetting that every one must begin, and that there had been a time when they themselves would have fared no better when shot by a jackass.

The English never uttered a challenge nor fired a shot. It was said afterward that when their men saw the Maid riding at the front and saw how lovely she was, their eager courage cooled down in many cases and vanished in the rest, they feeling certain that the creature was not mortal, but the very child of Satan, and so the officers were prudent and did not try to make them fight. It was said also that some of the officers were affected by the same superstitious fears. Well, in any case, they never offered to molest us, and we poked by all the grisly fortresses in peace. During the march I caught up on my devotions, which were in arrears; so it was not all loss and no profit for me after all.

It was on this march that the histories say Dunois told Joan that the English were expecting reinforcements under the command of Sir John Fastolfe, and that she turned upon him and said:

"Bastard, Bastard, in God's name I warn you to let me know of his coming as soon as you hear of it; for if he passes without my knowledge you shall lose your head!"

It may be so; I don't deny it; but I didn't her it. If she really said it I think she only meant she would take off his official headdegrade him from his command. It was not like her to threaten a comrade's life. She did have her doubts of her generals, and was entitled to them, for she was all for storm and assault, and they were for holding still and tiring the English out. Since they did not believe in her way and were experienced old soldiers, it would be natural for them to prefer their own and try to get around carrying hers out.

But I did hear something that the histories didn't mention and don't know about. I heard Joan say that now that the garrisons on the other wide had been weakened to strengthen those on our side, the most effective point of operations had shifted to the south shore; so she meant to go over there and storm the forts which held the bridge end, and that would open up communication with our own dominions and raise the siege. The generals began to balk, privately, right away, but they only baffled and delayed her, and that for only four days.

All Orleans met the army at the gate and huzzaed it through the bannered streets to its various quarters, but nobody had to rock it to sleep; it slumped down dog-tired, for Dunois had rushed it without mercy, and for the next twenty-four hours it would be quiet, all but the snoring.

Chapter 17.

Sweet Fruit of Bitter Truth

WHEN WE got home, breakfast for us minor fry was waiting in our mess–room and the family honored us by coming in to eat it with us. The nice old treasurer, and in fact all three were flatteringly eager to hear about our adventures. Nobody asked the Paladin to begin, but
he did begin, because now that his specially ordained and peculiar military rank set him above everybody on the personal staff but old D'Aulon, who didn't eat with us, he didn't care a farthing for the knights' nobility no mine, but took precedence in the talk whenever it suited him, which was all the time, because he was born that way. He said:

"God be thanked, we found the army in admirable condition I think I
have never seen a finer body of animals." "Animals!"

said Miss Catherine.

"I will explain to you what he means," said Noel. "He"

"I will trouble you not to trouble yourself to explain anything for me," said the Paladin, loftily. "I have reason to think"

"That is his way," said Noel; "always when he thinks he has reason to think, he thinks he does think, but this is an error. He didn't see the army. I noticed him, and he didn't see it. He was troubled by his old complaint."

"What's his old complaint?" Catherine asked. "Prudence," I

said, seeing my chance to help.

But it was not a fortunate remark, for the Paladin said:

"It probably isn't your turn to criticize people's prudenceyou who fall out of the saddle when a donkey brays."

They all laughed, and I was ashamed of myself for my hasty smartness. I said:

"It isn't quite fair for you to say I fell out on account of the donkey's braying. It was emotion, just ordinary emotion."

"Very well, if you want to call it that, I am not objecting. What would you call it, Sir Bertrand?"

"Well, it—well, whatever it was, it was excusable, I think. All of you have learned how to behave in hot hand–to–hand engagements, and you don't need to be ashamed of your record in that matter; but to walk along in front of death, with one's hands idle, and no noise, no music, and nothing going on, is a very trying situation. If I were you, De Conte, I would name the emotion; it's nothing to be ashamed of."

It was as straight and sensible a speech as ever I heard, and I was grateful for the opening it gave me; so I came out and said:

"It was fear—and thank you for the honest idea, too."

"It was the cleanest and best way out," said the old treasurer; "you've done well, my lad."

That made me comfortable, and when Miss Catherine said, "It's what I think, too," I was grateful to myself for getting into that scrape. Sir Jean de

Metz said:

"We were all in a body together when the donkey brayed, and it was dismally still at the time. I don't see how any young campaigner could escape some little touch of that emotion."

He looked about him with a pleasant expression of inquiry on his good face, and as each pair of eyes in turn met his head they were in nodded a confession. Even the Paladin delivered his nod. That surprised everybody, and saved the Standard–Bearer's credit. It was clever of him; nobody believed he could tell the truth that way without practice, or would tell that particular sort of a truth either with or without practice. I suppose he judged it would favorably impress the family. Then the old treasurer said:

"Passing the forts in that trying way required the same sort of nerve that a person must have when ghosts are about him in the dark, I should think. What does the Standard–Bearer think?"

"Well, I don't quite know about that, sir. I've often thought I would like to see a ghost if I"

"Would you?" exclaimed the young lady. "We've got one! Would you try that one? Will you?"

She was so eager and pretty that the Paladin said straight out that he would; and then as none of the rest had bravery enough to expose the fear that was in him, one volunteered after the other with a prompt mouth and a sick heart till all were shipped for the voyage; then the girl clapped her hands in glee, and the parents were gratified, too, saying that the ghosts of their house had been a dread and a misery
to them and their forebears for generations, and nobody had ever been found yet who was willing to confront them and find out what their trouble was, so that the family could heal it and content the poor specters and beguile them to tranquillity and peace.

Chapter 18.

Joan's First Battle-field

ABOUT NOON I was chatting with Madame Boucher; nothing was going on, all was quiet, when Catherine Boucher suddenly entered in great excitement, and said:

"Fly, sir, fly! The Maid was doing in her chair in my room, when she sprang up and cried out, 'French blood is flowing!my arms, give me my arms!' Her giant was on guard at the door, and he brought D'Aulon, who began to arm her, and I and the giant have been warning the staff. Fly!and stay by her; and if there really is a battle, keep her out of itdon't let her risk herselfthere is no needif the men know she is near and looking on, it is all that is necessary. Keep her out of the fightdon't fail of this!"

I started on a run, saying, sarcasticallyfor I was always fond of sarcasm, and it was said that I had a most neat gift that way:

"Oh, yes, nothing easier than thatI'll attend to it!"

At the furthest end of the house I met Joan, fully armed, hurrying toward the door, and she said:

"Ah, French blood is being spilt, and you did not tell me." "Indeed I did not

know it," I said; "there are no sounds of war;
everything is quiet, your Excellency."

"You will hear war–sounds enough in a moment," she said, and was gone.

It was true. Before one could count five there broke upon the stillness the swelling rush and tramp of an approaching multitude of men and horses, with hoarse cries of command; and then out of the distance came the muffled deep boom!boom–boom!boom! of cannon, and straightway that rushing multitude was roaring by the house like a hurricane.

Our knights and all our staff came flying, armed, but with no horses ready, and we burst out after Joan in a body, the Paladin in the lead with the banner. The surging crowd was made up half of citizens and half of soldiers, and had no recognized leader. When Joan was seen
a huzza went up, and she shouted: "A horsea

horse!"

A dozen saddles were at her disposal in a moment. She mounted, a hundred people shouting:

"Way, thereway for the MAID OF ORLEANS!" The first time that that immortal name was ever utteredand I, praise God, was there to hear it! The mass divided itself like the waters of the Red Sea, and down this lane Joan went skimming like a bird, crying, "Forward, French heartsfollow me!" and we came winging in her wake on the rest of the borrowed horses, the holy standard streaming above us, and the lane closing together in our rear.

This was a different thing from the ghastly march past the dismal bastilles. No, we felt fine, now, and all awhirl with enthusiasm. The explanation of this sudden uprising was this. The city and the little garrison, so long hopeless and afraid, had gone wild over Joan's coming, and could no longer restrain their desire to get at the enemy; so, without orders from anybody, a few hundred soldiers and citizens had plunged out at the Burgundy gate on a sudden impulse and made a charge on one of Lord Talbot's most formidable fortressesSt. Loupand were getting the worst of it. The news of this had swept through the city and started this new crowd that we were with.

As we poured out at the gate we met a force bringing in the wounded from the front. The sight moved Joan, and she said:

"Ah, French blood; it makes my hair rise to see it!"

We were soon on the field, soon in the midst of the turmoil. Joan was seeing her first real battle, and so were we.

It was a battle in the open field; for the garrison of St. Loup had sallied confidently out to meet the attack, being used to victories when "witches" were not around. The sally had been reinforced by troops from the "Paris" bastille, and when we approached the French were getting whipped and were falling back. But when Joan came charging through the disorder with her banner displayed, crying "Forward, menfollow me!" there was a change; the French turned about and surged forward like a solid wave of the sea, and swept the English before them, hacking and slashing, and being hacked and slashed, in a way that was terrible to see.

In the field the Dwarf had no assignment; that is to say, he was not under orders to occupy any particular place, therefore he chose his place for himself, and went ahead of Joan and made a road for her. It was horrible to see the iron helmets fly into fragments under his dreadful ax. He called it cracking nuts, and it looked like that. He made a good road, and paved it well with flesh and iron. Joan and the rest of us followed it so briskly that we outspeeded our forces and had the English behind us as well as before. The knights commanded us to face outward around Joan, which we did, and then there was work done that was fine to see. One was obliged to respect the Paladin, now. Being right under Joan's exalting and transforming eye, he forgot his native prudence, he forgot his diffidence in the presence of danger, he forgot what fear was, and he never laid about him in his imaginary battles in a more tremendous way that he did in this real one; and wherever he struck there was an enemy the less.

We were in that close place only a few minutes; then our forces to the rear broke through with a great shout and joined us, and then the English fought a retreating fight, but in a fine and gallant way, and we drove them to their fortress foot by foot, they facing us all the time, and their reserves on the walls raining showers of arrows, cross–bow bolts, and stone cannon–balls upon us.

The bulk of the enemy got safely within the works and left us outside with piles of French and English dead and wounded for companya sickening sight, an awful sight to us youngsters, for our little ambush fights in February had been in the night, and the blood and the mutilations and the dead faces were mercifully dim, whereas we saw these things now for the first time in all their naked ghastliness.

Now arrived Dunois from the city, and plunged through the battle on his foam-flecked horse and galloped up to Joan, saluting, and uttering handsome compliments as he came. He waved his hand toward the distant walls of the city, where a multitude of flags were flaunting gaily in the wind, and said the populace were up there observing her fortunate performance and rejoicing over it, and added that she and the forces would have a great reception now.

"Now? Hardly now, Bastard. Not yet!" "Why not yet?

Is there more to be done?"

"More, Bastard? We have but begun! We will take this fortress."

"Ah, you can't be serious! We can't take this place; let me urge you not to make the attempt; it is too desperate. Let me order the forces back."

Joan's heart was overflowing with the joys and enthusiasms of war, and it made her impatient to hear such talk. She cried out:

"Bastard, Bastard, will ye play always with these English? Now verily I tell you we will not budge until this place is ours. We will carry it by storm. Sound the charge!"

"Ah, my General"

"Waste no more time, manlet the bugles sound the assault!" and we saw that strange deep light in her eye which we named the battle- light, and learned to know so well in later fields.

The martial notes pealed out, the troops answered with a yell, and down they came against that formidable work, whose outlines were lost in its own cannon-smoke, and whose sides were spouting flame and thunder.

We suffered repulse after repulse, but Joan was here and there and everywhere encouraging the men, and she kept them to their work. During three hours the tide ebbed and flowed, flowed and ebbed; but at last La Hire, who was now come, made a final and resistless charge, and the bastille St. Loup was ours. We gutted it, taking all its stores and artillery, and then destroyed it.

When all our host was shouting itself hoarse with rejoicings, and there went up a cry for the General, for they wanted to praise her and glorify her and do her homage for her victory, we had trouble to find her; and when we did find her, she was off by herself, sitting among
a ruck of corpses, with her face in her hands, cryingfor she was a young girl, you know, and her hero heart was a young girl's heart too, with the pity and the tenderness that are natural to it. She was thinking of the mothers of those dead friends and enemies.

Among the prisoners were a number of priests, and Joan took these under her protection and saved their lives. It was urged that they were most probably combatants in disguise, but she said:

"As to that, how can any tell? They wear the livery of God, and if even one of these wears it rightfully, surely it were better that all the guilty should escape than that we have upon our hands the blood of that innocent man. I will lodge them where I lodge, and feed them, and sent them away in safety."

We marched back to the city with our crop of cannon and prisoners on view and our banners displayed. Here was the first substantial bit of war–work the imprisoned people had seen in the seven months that the siege had endured, the first chance they had had to rejoice over a French exploit. You may guess that they made good use of it. They and the bells went mad. Joan was their darling now, and the press of people struggling and shouldering each other to get a glimpse of her was so great that we could hardly push our way through the streets at all. Her new name had gone all about, and was on everybody's lips. The Holy Maid of Vaucouleurs was a forgotten title; the city had claimed her for its own, and she was the MAID OF ORLEANS now. It is a happiness to me to remember that I heard
that name the first time it was ever uttered. Between that first utterance and the last time it will be uttered on this earthah, think

how many moldering ages will lie in that gap!

The Boucher family welcomed her back as if she had been a child of the house, and saved from death against all hope or probability. They chided her for going into the battle and exposing herself to danger during all those hours. They could not realize that she had meant to carry her warriorship so far, and asked her if it had really been her purpose to go right into the turmoil of the fight, or hadn't she got swept into it by accident and the rush of the troops? They begged her to be more careful another time. It was good advice, maybe, but it
fell upon pretty unfruitful soil.

Chapter 19.

We Burst in Upon Ghosts

BEING WORN out with the long fight, we all slept the rest of the afternoon away and two or three hours into the night. Then we got up refreshed, and had supper. As for me, I could have been willing to let the matter of the ghost drop; and the others were of a like mind, no doubt, for they talked diligently of the battle and said nothing of that other thing. And indeed it was fine and stirring to hear the Paladin rehearse his deeds and see him pile his dead, fifteen here, eighteen there, and thirty–five yonder; but this only postponed the trouble; it could not do more. He could not go on forever; when he had carried the bastille by assault and eaten up the garrison there was nothing for it but to stop, unless Catherine Boucher would give him a new start and have it all done over againas we hoped she would, this timebut she was otherwise minded. As soon as there was a good opening and a fair chance, she brought up her unwelcome subject, and we faced it the best we could.

We followed her and her parents to the haunted room at eleven o'clock, with candles, and also with torches to place in the sockets on the walls. It was a big house, with very thick walls, and this room
was in a remote part of it which had been left unoccupied for nobody knew how many years, because of its evil repute.

This was a large room, like a salon, and had a big table in it of enduring oak and well preserved; but the chair were worm–eaten and the tapestry on the walls was rotten and discolored by age. The dusty cobwebs under the ceiling had the look of not having had any business for a century.

Catherine said:

"Tradition says that these ghosts have never been seenthey have merely been heard. It is plain that this room was once larger than it is

now, and that the wall at this end was built in some bygone time to make and fence off a narrow room there. There is no communication anywhere with that narrow room, and if it existsand of that there is
no reasonable doubtit has no light and no air, but is an absolute dungeon. Wait where you are, and take note of what happens."

That was all. Then she and her parents left us. When their footfalls had died out in the distance down the empty stone corridors an uncanny silence and solemnity ensued which was dismaler to me than the mute march past the bastilles. We sat looking vacantly at each other, and it was easy to see that no one there was comfortable. The longer we sat so, the more deadly still that stillness got to be; and when the wind began to moan around the house presently, it made me sick and miserable, and I wished I had been brave enough
to be a coward this time, for indeed it is no proper shame to be afraid of ghosts, seeing how helpless the living are in their hands. And then these ghosts were invisible, which made the matter the worse, as it seemed to me. They might be in the room with us at that momentwe could not know. I felt airy touches on my shoulders and my hair, and I shrank from them and cringed, and was not ashamed to show this fear, for I saw the others doing the like, and knew that they were feeling those faint contacts too. As this went onoh, eternities it seemed, the time dragged so drearilyall those faces became as wax, and I seemed sitting with a congress of the dead.

At last, faint and far and weird and slow, came a "boom!boom! boom!"a distant bell tolling midnight. When the last stroke died, that depressing stillness followed again, and as before I was staring at those waxen faces and feeling those airy touches on my hair and my shoulders once more.

One minutetwo minutesthree minutes of this, then we heard a long deep groan, and everybody sprang up and stood, with his legs quaking. It came from that little dungeon. There was a pause, then we herd muffled sobbings, mixed with pitiful ejaculations. Then there was a second voice, low and not distinct, and the one seemed trying to comfort the other; and so the two voices went on, with moanings, and soft sobbings, and, ah, the tones were so full of compassion and sorry and despair! Indeed, it made one's heart sore to hear it.

But those sounds were so real and so human and so moving that the idea of ghosts passed straight out of our minds, and Sir Jean de Metz spoke out and said:

"Come! we will smash that wall and set those poor captives free. Here, with your ax!"

The Dwarf jumped forward, swinging his great ax with both hands, and others sprang for torches and brought them.

Bang!whang!slam!smash went the ancient bricks, and there was a hole an ox could pass through. We plunged within and held up the torches.

Nothing there but vacancy! On the floor lay a rusty sword and a rotten fan.

Now you know all that I know. Take the pathetic relics, and weave about them the romance of the dungeon's long-vanished inmates as best you can.

Chapter 20.

Joan Makes Cowards Brave Victors

THE NEXT day Joan wanted to go against the enemy again, but it was the feast of the Ascension, and the holy council of bandit generals were too pious to be willing to profane it with bloodshed. But privately they profaned it with plottings, a sort of industry just in their line. They decided to do the only thing proper to do now in the new circumstances of the casefeign an attack on the most important bastille on the Orleans side, and then, if the English weakened the
far more important fortresses on the other side of the river to come to its help, cross in force and capture those works. This would give
them the bridge and free communication with the Sologne, which was French territory. They decided to keep this latter part of the program secret from Joan.

Joan intruded and took them by surprise. She asked them what they were about and what they had resolved upon. They said they had resolved to attack the most important of the English bastilles on the Orleans side next morningand there the spokesman stopped. Joan said:

"Well, go on."

"There is nothing more. That is all."

"Am I to believe this? That is to say, am I to believe that you have lost your wits?" She turned to Dunois, and said, "Bastard, you have sense, answer me this: if this attack is made and the bastille taken, how much better off would we be than we are now?"

The Bastard hesitated, and then began some rambling talk not quite germane to the question. Joan interrupted him and said:

"That will not do, good Bastard, you have answered. Since the

Bastard is not able to mention any advantage to be gained by taking that bastille and stopping there, it is not likely that any of you could better the matter. You waste much time here in inventing plans that lead to nothing, and making delays that are a damage. Are you concealing something from me? Bastard, this council has a general plan, I take it; without going into details, what is it?"

"It is the same it was in the beginning, seven months ago to get provisions for a long siege, then sit down and tire the English out."

"In the name of God! As if seven months was not enough, you want to provide for a year of it. Now ye shall drop these pusillanimous dreams the English shall go in three days!"

Several exclaimed:

"Ah, General, General, be prudent!"

"Be prudent and starve? Do ye call that war? I tell you this, if you do not already know it: The new circumstances have changed the face
of matters. The true point of attack has shifted; it is on the other side of the river now. One must take the fortifications that command the bridge. The English know that if we are not fools and cowards we will try to do that. They are grateful for your piety in wasting this day. They will reinforce the bridge forts from this side to–night, knowing what ought to happen to–morrow. You have but lost a day and made our task harder, for we will cross and take the bridge forts. Bastard, tell me the truth does not this council know that there is no other course for us than the one I am speaking of?"

Dunois conceded that the council did know it to be the most desirable, but considered it impracticable; and he excused the council as well as he could by saying that inasmuch as nothing was really and rationally to be hoped for but a long continuance of the siege and wearying out of the English, they were naturally a little afraid of Joan's impetuous notions. He said:

"You see, we are sure that the waiting game is the best, whereas you would carry everything by storm."

"That I would!and moreover that I will! You have my ordershere and now. We will move upon the forts of the south bank to—morrow at dawn."

"And carry them by storm?" "Yes, carry

them by storm!"

La Hire came clanking in, and heard the last remark. He cried out:

"By my baton, that is the music I love to hear! Yes, that is the right time and the beautiful words, my Generalwe will carry them by storm!"

He saluted in his large way and came up and shook Joan by the hand.

Some member of the council was heard to say:

"It follows, then, that we must begin with the bastille St. John, and that will give the English time to"

Joan turned and said:

"Give yourselves no uneasiness about the bastille St. John. The English will know enough to retire from it and fall back on the bridge bastilles when they see us coming." She added, with a touch of sarcasm, "Even a war–council would know enough to do that itself."

Then she took her leave. La Hire made this general remark to the council:

"She is a child, and that is all ye seem to see. Keep to that superstition if you must, but you perceive that this child understands this complex game of war as well as any of you; and if you want my opinion without the trouble of asking for it, here you have it without ruffles or embroideryby God, I think she can teach the best of you how to play it!"

Joan had spoken truly; the sagacious English saw that the policy of the French had undergone a revolution; that the policy of paltering and dawdling was ended; that in place of taking blows, blows were ready to be struck now; therefore they made ready for the new state of things by transferring heavy reinforcements to the bastilles of the south bank from those of the north.

The city learned the great news that once more in French history, after all these humiliating years, France was going to take the offensive; that France, so used to retreating, was going to advance; that France, so long accustomed to skulking, was going to face about and strike. The joy of the people passed all bounds. The city walls were black with them to see the army march out in the morning in that strange new positionits front, not its tail, toward an English camp. You shall imagine for yourselves what the excitement was
like and how it expressed itself, when Joan rode out at the head of the host with her banner floating above her.

We crossed the five in strong force, and a tedious long job it was, for the boats were small and not numerous. Our landing on the island of St. Aignan was not disputed. We threw a bridge of a few boats
across the narrow channel thence to the south shore and took up our march in good order and unmolested; for although there was a fortress thereSt. Johnthe English vacated and destroyed it and fell back on the bridge forts below as soon as our first boats were seen to leave the Orleans shore; which was what Joan had said would happen, when she was disputing with the council.

We moved down the shore and Joan planted her standard before the bastille of the Augustins, the first of the formidable works that protected the end of the bridge. The trumpets sounded the assault, and two charges followed in handsome style; but we were too weak, as yet, for our main body was still lagging behind. Before we could gather for a third assault the garrison of St. Prive were seen coming up to reinforce the big bastille. They came on a run, and the Augustins sallied out, and both forces came against us with a rush, and sent our small army flying in a panic, and followed us, slashing and slaying, and shouting jeers and insults at us.

Joan was doing her best to rally the men, but their wits were gone, their hearts were dominated for the moment by the old-time dread of the English. Joan's temper flamed up, and she halted and
commanded the trumpets to sound the advance. Then she wheeled about and cried out:

"If there is but a dozen of you that are not cowards, it is enoughfollow me!"

Away she went, and after her a few dozen who had heard her words and been inspired by them. The pursuing force was astonished to see her sweeping down upon them with this handful of men, and it was their turn now to experience a grisly frightsurely this is a witch, this is a child of Satan! That was their thoughtand without stopping to analyze the matter they turned and fled in a panic.

Our flying squadrons heard the bugle and turned to look; and when they saw the Maid's banner speeding in the other direction and the enemy scrambling ahead of it in disorder, their courage returned and they came scouring after us.

La Hire heard it and hurried his force forward and caught up with us just as we were planting our banner again before the ramparts of the Augustins. We were strong enough now. We had a long and tough piece of work before us, but we carried it through before night, Joan keeping us hard at it, and she and La Hire saying we were able to take that big bastille, and must. The English fought likewell, they fought like the English; when that is said, there is no more to say. We made assault after assault, through the smoke and flame and the deafening cannon-blasts, and at last as the sun was sinking we carried the place with a rush, and planted our standard on its walls.

The Augustins was ours. The Tourelles must be ours, too, if we would free the bridge and raise the siege. We had achieved one great undertaking, Joan was determined to accomplish the other. We must lie on our arms where we were, hold fast to what we had got, and be ready for business in the morning. So Joan was not minded to let the men be demoralized by pillage and riot and carousings; she had the Augustins burned, with all its stores in it, excepting the artillery and ammunition.

Everybody was tired out with this long day's hard work, and of course this was the case with Joan; still, she wanted to stay with the army before the Tourelles, to be ready for the assault in the morning. The chiefs argued with her, and at last persuaded her to go home and prepare for the great work by taking proper rest, and also by having
a leech look to a wound which she had received in her foot. So we crossed with them and went home.

Just as usual, we found the town in a fury of joy, all the bells clanging, everybody shouting, and several people drunk. We never went out or came in without furnishing good and sufficient reasons for one of these pleasant tempests, and so the tempest was always on hand. There had been a blank absence of reasons for this sort of upheavals for the past seven months, therefore the people too to the upheavals with all the more relish on that account.

Chapter 21.

She Gently Reproves Her Dear Friend

TO GET away from the usual crowd of visitors and have a rest, Joan went with Catherine straight to the apartment which the two occupied together, and there they took their supper and there the wound was dressed. But then, instead of going to bed, Joan, weary as she was, sent the Dwarf for me, in spite of Catherine's protests and persuasions. She said she had something on her mind, and must send a courier to Domremy with a letter for our old Pere Fronte to read to her mother. I came, and she began to dictate. After some loving words and greetings to her mother and family, came this:

"But the thing which moves me to write now, is to say that when you presently hear that I am wounded, you shall give yourself no concern about it, and refuse faith to any that shall try to make you believe it is serious."

She was going on, when Catherine spoke up and said:

"Ah, but it will fright her so to read these words. Strike them out, Joan, strike them out, and wait only one day—two days at most—then write and say your foot was wounded but is well again—for it surely be well then, or very near it. Don't distress her, Joan; do as I say."

A laugh like the laugh of the old days, the impulsive free laugh of an untroubled spirit, a laugh like a chime of bells, was Joan's answer; then she said:

"My foot? Why should I write about such a scratch as that? I was not thinking of it, dear heart."

"Child, have you another wound and a worse, and have not spoken of it? What have you been dreaming about, that you—"

She had jumped up, full of vague fears, to have the leech called back at once, but Joan laid her hand upon her arm and made her sit down again, saying:

"There, now, be tranquil, there is no other wound, as yet; I am writing about one which I shall get when we storm that bastille tomorrow."

Catherine had the look of one who is trying to understand a puzzling proposition but cannot quite do it. She said, in a distraught fashion:

"A wound which you are going to get? But--but why grieve your mother when it--when it may not happen?"

"May not? Why, it will."

The puzzle was a puzzle still. Catherine said in that same abstracted way as before:

"Will. It is a strong word. I cannot seem to--my mind is not able to take hold of this. Oh, Joan, such a presentiment is a dreadful thing--it takes one's peace and courage all away. Cast it from you!--drive it out! It will make your whole night miserable, and to no good; for we will hope--"

"But it isn't a presentiment--it is a fact. And it will not make me miserable. It is uncertainties that do that, but this is not an uncertainty."

"Joan, do you know it is going to happen?" "Yes, I know

it. My Voices told me."

"Ah," said Catherine, resignedly, "if they told you--But are you sure it was they?--quite sure?"

"Yes, quite. It will happen--there is no doubt."

"It is dreadful! Since when have you know it?"

"Since I think it is several weeks." Joan turned to me. "Louis, you will remember. How long is it?"

"Your Excellency spoke of it first to the King, in Chinon," I answered; "that was as much as seven weeks ago. You spoke of it again the 20th of April, and also the 22d, two weeks ago, as I see by my record here."

These marvels disturbed Catherine profoundly, but I had long ceased to be surprised at them. One can get used to anything in this world. Catherine said:

"And it is to happen to—morrow?always to—morrow? Is it the same date always? There has been no mistake, and no confusion?"

"No," Joan said, "the 7th of May is the datethere is no other."

"Then you shall not go a step out of this house till that awful day is gone by! You will not dream of it, Joan, will you?promise that you will stay with us."

But Joan was not persuaded. She said:

"It would not help the matter, dear good friend. The wound is to come, and come to—morrow. If I do not seek it, it will seek me. My duty calls me to that place to—morrow; I should have to go if my death were waiting for me there; shall I stay away for only a wound? Oh, no, we must try to do better than that."

"Then you are determined to go?"

"Of a certainty, yes. There is only one thing that I can do for Francehearten her soldiers for battle and victory." She thought a moment, then added, "However, one should not be unreasonable, and I would do much to please you, who are so good to me. Do you love France?"

I wondered what she might be contriving now, but I saw no clue. Catherine said, reproachfully:

"Ah, what have I done to deserve this question?"

"Then you do love France. I had not doubted it, dear. Do not be hurt, but answer me—have you ever told a lie?"

"In my life I have not wilfully told a lie—fibs, but no lies."

"That is sufficient. You love France and do not tell lies; therefore I will trust you. I will go or I will stay, as you shall decide."

"Oh, I thank you from my heart, Joan! How good and dear it is of you to do this for me! Oh, you shall stay, and not go!"

In her delight she flung her arms about Joan's neck and squandered endearments upon her the least of which would have made me rich, but, as it was, they only made me realize how poor I was—how miserably poor in what I would most have prized in this world. Joan said:

"Then you will send word to my headquarters that I am not going?" "Oh, gladly.

Leave that to me."

"It is good of you. And how will you word it?—for it must have proper official form. Shall I word it for you?"

"Oh, do—for you know about these solemn procedures and stately proprieties, and I have had no experience."

"Then word it like this: 'The chief of staff is commanded to make known to the King's forces in garrison and in the field, that the General–in–Chief of the Armies of France will not face the English on the morrow, she being afraid she may get hurt. Signed, JOAN OF ARC, by the hand of CATHERINE BOUCHER, who loves France.'"

There was a pause—a silence of the sort that tortures one into stealing a glance to see how the situation looks, and I did that. There was a loving smile on Joan's face, but the color was mounting in crimson waves into Catherine's, and her lips were quivering and the tears gathering; then she said:

"Oh, I am so ashamed of myself!and you are so noble and brave and wise, and I am so paltryso paltry and such a fool!" and she broke down and began to cry, and I did so want to take her in my arms and comfort her, but Joan did it, and of course I said nothing. Joan did it well, and most sweetly and tenderly, but I could have done it as well, though I knew it would be foolish and out of place to suggest such a thing, and might make an awkwardness, too, and be embarrassing to us all, so I did not offer, and I hope I did right and for the best,
though I could not know, and was many times tortured with doubts afterward as having perhaps let a chance pass which might have changed all my life and made it happier and more beautiful than, alas, it turned out to be. For this reason I grieve yet, when I think of that scene, and do not like to call it up out of the deeps of my memory because of the pangs it brings.

Well, well, a good and wholesome thing is a little harmless fun in this world; it tones a body up and keeps him human and prevents him from souring. To set that little trap for Catherine was as good and effective a way as any to show her what a grotesque thing she was asking of Joan. It was a funny idea now, wasn't it, when you look at it all around? Even Catherine dried up her tears and laughed when she thought of the English getting hold of the French Commander–in–Chief's reason for staying out of a battle. She granted that they could have a good time over a thing like that.

We got to work on the letter again, and of course did not have to strike out the passage about the wound. Joan was in fine spirits; but when she got to sending messages to this, that, and the other playmate and friend, it brought our village and the Fairy Tree and
the flowery plain and the browsing sheep and all the peaceful beauty of our old humble home–place back, and the familiar names began
to tremble on her lips; and when she got to Haumette and Little Mengette it was no use, her voice broke and she couldn't go on. She waited a moment, then said:

"Give them my lovemy warm lovemy deep loveoh, out of my heart of hearts! I shall never see our home any more."

Now came Pasquerel, Joan's confessor, and introduced a gallant knight, the Sire de Rais, who had been sent with a message. He said he was instructed to say that the council had decided that enough had been done for the present; that it would be safest and best to be content with what God had already done; that the city was now well victualed and able to stand a long siege; that the wise course must necessarily be to withdraw the troops from the other side of the river and resume the defensivetherefore they had decided accordingly.

"The incurable cowards!" exclaimed Joan. "So it was to get me away from my men that they pretended so much solicitude about my fatigue. Take this message back, not to the councilI have no
speeches for those disguised ladies' maidsbut to the Bastard and La Hire, who are men. Tell them the army is to remain where it is, and I hold them responsible if this command miscarries. And say the offensive will be resumed in the morning. You may go, good sir."

Then she said to her priest:

"Rise early, and be by me all the day. There will be much work on my hands, and I shall be hurt between my neck and my shoulder."

Chapter 22.

The Fate of France Decided

WE WERE up at dawn, and after mass we started. In the hall we met the master of the house, who was grieved, good man, to see Joan going breakfastless to such a day's work, and begged her to wait and eat, but she couldn't afford the time—that is to say, she couldn't afford the patience, she being in such a blaze of anxiety to get at that last remaining bastille which stood between her and the completion of the first great step in the rescue and redemption of France. Boucher put in another plea:

"But think—we poor beleaguered citizens who have hardly known the flavor of fish for these many months, have spoil of that sort again, and we owe it to you. There's a noble shad for breakfast; wait—be persuaded."

Joan said:

"Oh, there's going to be fish in plenty; when this day's work is done the whole river-front will be yours to do as you please with."

"Ah, your Excellency will do well, that I know; but we don't require quite that much, even of you; you shall have a month for it in place of a day. Now be beguiled—wait and eat. There's a saying that he that would cross a river twice in the same day in a boat, will do well to eat fish for luck, lest he have an accident."

"That doesn't fit my case, for to-day I cross but once in a boat." "Oh, don't

say that. Aren't you coming back to us?"

"Yes, but not in a boat." "How,

then?"

"By the bridge."

"Listen to thatby the bridge! Now stop this jesting, dear General, and do as I would have done you. It's a noble fish."

"Be good then, and save me some for supper; and I will bring one of those Englishmen with me and he shall have his share."

"Ah, well, have your way if you must. But he that fasts must attempt but little and stop early. When shall you be back?"

"When we've raised the siege of Orleans. FORWARD!"

We were off. The streets were full of citizens and of groups and squads of soldiers, but the spectacle was melancholy. There was not a smile anywhere, but only universal gloom. It was as if some vast calamity had smitten all hope and cheer dead. We were not used to
this, and were astonished. But when they saw the Maid, there was an immediate stir, and the eager question flew from mouth to mouth.

"Where is she going? Whither is she bound?" Joan heard it,

and called out:

"Whither would ye suppose? I am going to take the Tourelles."

It would not be possible for any to describe how those few words turned that mourning into joyinto exaltationinto frenzy; and how a storm of huzzas burst out and swept down the streets in every direction and woke those corpse–like multitudes to vivid life and action and turmoil in a moment. The soldiers broke from the crowd and came flocking to our standard, and many of the citizens ran and got pikes and halberds and joined us. As we moved on, our numbers increased steadily, and the hurrahing continuedyes, we moved through a solid cloud of noise, as you may say, and all the windows on both sides contributed to it, for they were filled with excited people.

You see, the council had closed the Burgundy gate and placed a strong force there, under that stout soldier Raoul de Gaucourt, Bailly of Orleans, with orders to prevent Joan from getting out and resuming the attack on the Tourelles, and this shameful thing had plunged the city into sorrow and despair. But that feeling was gone now. They believed the Maid was a match for the council, and they were right.

When we reached the gate, Joan told Gaucourt to open it and let her pass.

He said it would be impossible to do this, for his orders were from the council and were strict. Joan said:

"There is no authority above mine but the King's. If you have an order from the King, produce it."

"I cannot claim to have an order from him, General." "Then make

way, or take the consequences!"

He began to argue the case, for he was like the rest of the tribe, always ready to fight with words, not acts; but in the midst of his gabble Joan interrupted with the terse order:

"Charge!"

We came with a rush, and brief work we made of that small job. It was good to see the Bailly's surprise. He was not used to this unsentimental promptness. He said afterward that he was cut off in the midst of what he was saying in the midst of an argument by which he could have proved that he could not let Joan pass an argument which Joan could not have answered.

"Still, it appears she did answer it," said the person he was talking to. We swung

through the gate in great style, with a vast accession of
noise, the most of which was laughter, and soon our van was over the river and moving down against the Tourelles.

First we must take a supporting work called a boulevard, and which was otherwise nameless, before we could assault the great bastille.

Its rear communicated with the bastille by a drawbridge, under which ran a swift and deep strip of the Loire. The boulevard was strong, and Dunois doubted our ability to take it, but Joan had no such doubt. She pounded it with artillery all the forenoon, then about noon she ordered an assault and led it herself. We poured into the fosse through the smoke and a tempest of missiles, and Joan, shouting encouragements to her men, started to climb a scaling– ladder, when that misfortune happened which we knew was to happenthe iron bolt from an arbaquest struck between her neck and her shoulder, and tore its way down through her armor. When she
felt the sharp pain and saw her blood gushing over her breast, she was frightened, poor girl, and as she sank to the ground she began to cry bitterly.

The English sent up a glad shout and came surging down in strong force to take her, and then for a few minutes the might of both adversaries was concentrated upon that spot. Over her and above her, English and French fought with desperationfor she stood for France, indeed she was France to both sideswhichever won her won France, and could keep it forever. Right there in that small spot, and
in ten minutes by the clock, the fate of France, for all time, was to be decided, and was decided.

If the English had captured Joan then, Charles VII. would have flown the country, the Treaty of Troyes would have held good, and France, already English property, would have become, without further dispute, an English province, to so remain until Judgment Day. A nationality and a kingdom were at stake there, and no more time to decide it in than it takes to hard–boil an egg. It was the most momentous ten minutes that the clock has ever ticked in France, or ever will. Whenever you read in histories about hours or days or weeks in which the fate of one or another nation hung in the balance, do not you fail to remember, nor your French hearts to beat the quicker for the remembrance, the ten minutes that France, called otherwise Joan of Arc, lay bleeding in the fosse that day, with two nations struggling over her for her possession.

And you will not forget the Dwarf. For he stood over her, and did the work of any six of the others. He swung his ax with both hands;

whenever it came down, he said those two words, "For France!" and a splintered helmet flew like eggshells, and the skull that carried it had learned its manners and would offend the French no more. He piled a bulwark of iron-clad dead in front of him and fought from behind it; and at last when the victory was ours we closed about him, shielding him, and he ran up a ladder with Joan as easily as another man would carry a child, and bore her out of the battle, a great crowd following and anxious, for she was drenched with blood to her feet, half of it her own and the other half English, for bodies had fallen across her as she lay and had poured their red life-streams over her. One couldn't see the white armor now, with that awful dressing over it.

The iron bolt was still in the woundsome say it projected out behind the shoulder. It may beI did not wish to see, and did not try to. It was pulled out, and the pain made Joan cry again, poor thing. Some say she pulled it out herself because others refused, saying they could
not bear to hurt her. As to this I do not know; I only know it was pulled out, and that the wound was treated with oil and properly dressed.

Joan lay on the grass, weak and suffering, hour after hour, but still insisting that the fight go on. Which it did, but not to much purpose, for it was only under her eye that men were heroes and not afraid. They were like the Paladin; I think he was afraid of his shadowI mean in the afternoon, when it was very big and long; but when he was under Joan's eye and the inspiration of her great spirit, what was he afraid of? Nothing in this worldand that is just the truth.

Toward night Dunois gave it up. Joan heard the bugles. "What!" she

cried. "Sounding the retreat!"

Her wound was forgotten in a moment. She countermanded the order, and sent another, to the officer in command of a battery, to stand ready to fire five shots in quick succession. This was a signal to the force on the Orleans side of the river under La Hire, who was not, as some of the histories say, with us. It was to be given whenever Joan should feel sure the boulevard was about to fall into her hands—then that force must make a counter–attack on the Tourelles by way of the bridge.

Joan mounted her horse now, with her staff about her, and when our people saw us coming they raised a great shout, and were at once eager for another assault on the boulevard. Joan rode straight to the fosse where she had received her wound, and standing there in the rain of bolts and arrows, she ordered the Paladin to let her long standard blow free, and to note when its fringes should touch the fortress. Presently he said:

"It touches."

"Now, then," said Joan to the waiting battalions, "the place is yours—enter in! Bugles, sound the assault! Now, then—all together—go!"

And go it was. You never saw anything like it. We swarmed up the ladders and over the battlements like a wave—and the place was our property. Why, one might live a thousand years and never see so gorgeous a thing as that again. There, hand to hand, we fought like wild beasts, for there was no give–up to those English—there was no way to convince one of those people but to kill him, and even then
he doubted. At least so it was thought, in those days, and maintained by many.

We were busy and never heard the five cannon–shots fired, but they were fired a moment after Joan had ordered the assault; and so, while we were hammering and being hammered in the smaller
fortress, the reserve on the Orleans side poured across the bridge and attacked the Tourelles from that side. A fire–boat was brought down and moored under the drawbridge which connected the Tourelles with our boulevard; wherefore, when at last we drove our English ahead of us and they tried to cross that drawbridge and join their friends in the Tourelles, the burning timbers gave way under them and emptied them in a mass into the river in their heavy armor—and a pitiful sight it was to see brave men die such a death as that.

"Ah, God pity them!" said Joan, and wept to see that sorrowful spectacle. She said those gentle words and wept those compassionate tears although one of those perishing men had grossly insulted her with a coarse name three days before, when she had sent him a message asking him to surrender. That was their leader, Sir Williams Glasdale, a most valorous knight. He was clothed all in steel; so he plunged under water like a lance, and of course came up no more.

We soon patched a sort of bridge together and threw ourselves against the last stronghold of the English power that barred Orleans from friends and supplies. Before the sun was quite down, Joan's forever memorable day's work was finished, her banner floated from the fortress of the Tourelles, her promise was fulfilled, she had
raised the siege of Orleans!

The seven months' beleaguerment was ended, the thing which the first generals of France had called impossible was accomplished; in spite of all that the King's ministers and war–councils could do to prevent it, this little country–maid at seventeen had carried her immortal task through, and had done it in four days!

Good news travels fast, sometimes, as well as bad. By the time we were ready to start homeward by the bridge the whole city of
Orleans was one red flame of bonfires, and the heavens blushed with satisfaction to see it; and the booming and bellowing of cannon and the banging of bells surpassed by great odds anything that even Orleans had attempted before in the way of noise.

When we arrivedwell, there is no describing that. Why, those acres of people that we plowed through shed tears enough to raise the river; there was not a face in the glare of those fires that hadn't tears streaming down it; and if Joan's feet had not been protected by iron they would have kissed them off of her. "Welcome! welcome to the Maid of Orleans!" That was the cry; I heard it a hundred thousand times. "Welcome to our Maid!" some of them worded it.

No other girl in all history has ever reached such a summit of glory
as Joan of Arc reached that day. And do you think it turned her head, and that she sat up to enjoy that delicious music of homage and applause? No; another girl would have done that, but not this one. That was the greatest heart and the simplest that ever beat. She went straight to bed and to sleep, like any tired child; and when the people

found she was wounded and would rest, they shut off all passage and traffic in that region and stood guard themselves the whole night through, to see that he slumbers were not disturbed. They said, "She has given us peace, she shall have peace herself."

All knew that that region would be empty of English next day, and all said that neither the present citizens nor their posterity would ever cease to hold that day sacred to the memory of Joan of Arc. That word has been true for more than sixty years; it will continue so always. Orleans will never forget the 8th of May, nor ever fail to celebrate it. It is Joan of Arc's dayand holy. (1)

(1)It is still celebrated every year with civic and military pomps and solemnities.TRANSLATOR.

CHAPTER 23.

Joan Inspires the Tawdry King

IN THE earliest dawn of morning, Talbot and his English forces evacuated their bastilles and marched away, not stopping to burn, destroy, or carry off anything, but leaving their fortresses just as they were, provisioned, armed, and equipped for a long siege. It was difficult for the people to believe that this great thing had really happened; that they were actually free once more, and might go and come through any gate they pleased, with none to molest or forbid; that the terrible Talbot, that scourge of the French, that man whose mere name had been able to annul the effectiveness of French
armies, was gone, vanished, retreatingdriven away by a girl.

The city emptied itself. Out of every gate the crowds poured. They swarmed about the English bastilles like an invasion of ants, but noisier than those creatures, and carried off the artillery and stores, then turned all those dozen fortresses into monster bonfires, imitation volcanoes whose lofty columns of thick smoke seemed supporting the arch of the sky.

The delight of the children took another form. To some of the younger ones seven months was a sort of lifetime. They had forgotten what grass was like, and the velvety green meadows seemed paradise to their surprised and happy eyes after the long
habit of seeing nothing but dirty lanes and streets. It was a wonder to themthose spacious reaches of open country to run and dance and tumble and frolic in, after their dull and joyless captivity; so they scampered far and wide over the fair regions on both sides of the river, and came back at eventide weary, but laden with flowers and flushed with new health drawn from the fresh country air and the vigorous exercise.

After the burnings, the grown folk followed Joan from church to church and put in the day in thanksgivings for the city's deliverance, and at night they feted her and her generals and illuminated the town, and high and low gave themselves up to festivities and rejoicings. By the time the populace were fairly in bed, toward dawn, we were in the saddle and away toward Tours to report to the King.

That was a march which would have turned any one's head but Joan's. We moved between emotional ranks of grateful country– people all the way. They crowded about Joan to touch her feet, her horse, her armor, and they even knelt in the road and kissed her horse's hoof–prints.

The land was full of her praises. The most illustrious chiefs of the church wrote to the King extolling the Maid, comparing her to the saints and heroes of the Bible, and warning him not to let "unbelief, ingratitude, or other injustice" hinder or impair the divine help sent through her. One might think there was a touch of prophecy in that, and we will let it go at that; but to my mind it had its inspiration in those great men's accurate knowledge of the King's trivial and treacherous character.

The King had come to Tours to meet Joan. At the present day this poor thing is called Charles the Victorious, on account of victories which other people won for him, but in our time we had a private name for him which described him better, and was sanctified to him by personal deservingCharles the Base. When we entered the presence he sat throned, with his tinseled snobs and dandies around him. He looked like a forked carrot, so tightly did his clothing fit
him from his waist down; he wore shoes with a rope–like pliant toe a foot long that had to be hitched up to the knee to keep it out of the way; he had on a crimson velvet cape that came no lower than his elbows; on his head he had a tall felt thing like a thimble, with a feather it its jeweled band that stuck up like a pen from an inkhorn, and from under that thimble his bush of stiff hair stuck down to his shoulders, curving outward at the bottom, so that the cap and the hair together made the head like a shuttlecock. All the materials of his dress were rich, and all the colors brilliant. In his lap he cuddled a miniature greyhound that snarled, lifting its lip and showing its white teeth whenever any slight movement disturbed it. The King's dandies

were dressed in about the same fashion as himself, and when I remembered that Joan had called the war-council of Orleans "disguised ladies' maids," it reminded me of people who squander all their money on a trifle and then haven't anything to invest when they come across a better chance; that name ought to have been saved for these creatures.

Joan fell on her knees before the majesty of France, and the other frivolous animal in his lapa sight which it pained me to see. What had that man done for his country or for anybody in it, that she or any other person should kneel to him? But sheshe had just done the only great deed that had been done for France in fifty years, and had consecrated it with the libation of her blood. The positions should have been reversed.

However, to be fair, one must grant that Charles acquitted himself very well for the most part, on that occasionvery much better than he was in the habit of doing. He passed his pup to a courtier, and took off his cap to Joan as if she had been a queen. Then he stepped from his throne and raised her, and showed quite a spirited and manly joy and gratitude in welcoming her and thanking her for her extraordinary achievement in his service. My prejudices are of a
later date than that. If he had continued as he was at that moment, I
should not have acquired them. He acted

handsomely. He said:

"You shall not kneel to me, my matchless General; you have wrought royally, and royal courtesies are your due." Noticing that she was pale, he said, "But you must not stand; you have lost blood for France, and your wound is yet greencome." He led her to a seat and sat down by her. "Now, then, speak out frankly, as to one who owes you much and freely confesses it before all this courtly assemblage. What shall be your reward? Name it."

I was ashamed of him. And yet that was not fair, for how could he be expected to know this marvelous child in these few weeks, when we who thought we had known her all her life were daily seeing the clouds uncover some new altitudes of her character whose existence

was not suspected by us before? But we are all that way: when we know a thing we have only scorn for other people who don't happen to know it. And I was ashamed of these courtiers, too, for the way they licked their chops, so to speak, as envying Joan her great chance, they not knowing her any better than the King did. A blush
began to rise in Joan's cheeks at the thought that she was working for her country for pay, and she dropped her head and tried to hide her face, as girls always do when they find themselves blushing; no one knows why they do, but they do, and the more they blush the more they fail to get reconciled to it, and the more they can't bear to have people look at them when they are doing it. The King made it a great deal worse by calling attention to it, which is the unkindest thing a person can do when a girl is blushing; sometimes, when there is a
big crowd of strangers, it is even likely to make her cry if she is as young as Joan was. God knows the reason for this, it is hidden from men. As for me, I would as soon blush as sneeze; in fact, I would rather. However, these meditations are not of consequence: I will go on with what I was saying. The King rallied her for blushing, and
this brought up the rest of the blood and turned her face to fire. Then he was sorry, seeing what he had done, and tried to make her comfortable by saying the blush was exceeding becoming to her and not to mind itwhich caused even the dog to notice it now, so of course the red in Joan's face turned to purple, and the tears overflowed and ran downI could have told anybody that that would happen. The King was distressed, and saw that the best thing to do would be to get away from this subject, so he began to say the finest kind of things about Joan's capture of the Tourelles, and presently when she was more composed he mentioned the reward again and pressed her to name it. Everybody listened with anxious interest to hear what her claim was going to be, but when her answer came
their faces showed that the thing she asked for was not what they had been expecting.

"Oh, dear and gracious Dauphin, I have but one desireonly one. If" "Do not be

afraid, my childname it."

"That you will not delay a day. My army is strong and valiant, and eager to finish its workmarch with me to Rheims and receive your crown." You could see the indolent King shrink, in his butterfly clothes.

"To Rheimsoh, impossible, my General! We march through the heart of England's power?"

Could those be French faces there? Not one of them lighted in response to the girl's brave proposition, but all promptly showed satisfaction in the King's objection. Leave this silken idleness for the rude contact of war? None of these butterflies desired that. They passed their jeweled comfit–boxes one to another and whispered their content in the head butterfly's practical prudence. Joan pleaded with the King, saying:

"Ah, I pray you do not throw away this perfect opportunity. Everything is favorableeverything. It is as if the circumstances were specially made for it. The spirits of our army are exalted with victory, those of the English forces depressed by defeat. Delay will change this. Seeing us hesitate to follow up our advantage, our men will wonder, doubt, lose confidence, and the English will wonder, gather courage, and be bold again. Now is the timepritheee let us march!"

The King shook his head, and La Tremouille, being asked for an opinion, eagerly furnished it:

"Sire, all prudence is against it. Think of the English strongholds along the Loire; think of those that lie between us and Rheims!"

He was going on, but Joan cut him short, and said, turning to him: "If we wait,

they will all be strengthened, reinforced. Will that advantage us?" "Whyno."

"Then what is your suggestion?what is it that you would propose to do?"

"My judgment is to wait."

"Wait for what?"

The minister was obliged to hesitate, for he knew of no explanation that would sound well. Moreover, he was not used to being catechized in this fashion, with the eyes of a crowd of people on him, so he was irritated, and said:

"Matters of state are not proper matters for public discussion." Joan said

placidly:

"I have to beg your pardon. My trespass came of ignorance. I did not know that matters connected with your department of the government were matters of state."

The minister lifted his brows in amused surprise, and said, with a touch of sarcasm:

"I am the King's chief minister, and yet you had the impression that matters connected with my department are not matters of state? Pray, how is that?"

Joan replied, indifferently: "Because

there is no state." "No state!"

"No, sir, there is no state, and no use for a minister. France is shrunk to a couple of acres of ground; a sheriff's constable could take care of it; its affairs are not matters of state. The term is too large."

The King did not blush, but burst into a hearty, careless laugh, and the court laughed too, but prudently turned its head and did it silently. La Tremouille was angry, and opened his mouth to speak, but the King put up his hand, and said:

"ThereI take her under the royal protection. She has spoken the truth, the ungilded truthhow seldom I hear it! With all this tinsel on me and all this tinsel about me, I am but a sheriff after alla poor shabby two–

acre sheriff—and you are but a constable," and he laughed his cordial laugh again. "Joan, my frank, honest General, will you name your reward? I would ennoble you. You shall quarter the crown and the lilies of France for blazon, and with them your victorious sword to defend them—speak the word."

It made an eager buzz of surprise and envy in the assemblage, but Joan shook her head and said:

"Ah, I cannot, dear and noble Dauphin. To be allowed to work for France, to spend one's self for France, is itself so supreme a reward that nothing can add to it—nothing. Give me the one reward I ask, the dearest of all rewards, the highest in your gift—march with me to Rheims and receive your crown. I will beg it on my knees."

But the King put his hand on her arm, and there was a really brave awakening in his voice and a manly fire in his eye when he said:

"No, sit. You have conquered me—it shall be as you"

But a warning sign from his minister halted him, and he added, to the relief of the court:

"Well, well, we will think of it, we will think it over and see. Does that content you, impulsive little soldier?"

The first part of the speech sent a glow of delight to Joan's face, but the end of it quenched it and she looked sad, and the tears gathered in her eyes. After a moment she spoke out with what seemed a sort of terrified impulse, and said:

"Oh, use me; I beseech you, use me—there is but little time!" "But little time?"

"Only a year—I shall last only a year."

"Why, child, there are fifty good years in that compact little body yet."

"Oh, you err, indeed you do. In one little year the end will come. Ah, the time is so short, so short; the moments are flying, and so much to be done. Oh, use me, and quickly—it is life or death for France."

Even those insects were sobered by her impassioned words. The King looked very grave—grave, and strongly impressed. His eyes lit suddenly with an eloquent fire, and he rose and drew his sword and raised it aloft; then he brought it slowly down upon Joan's shoulder and said:

"Ah, thou art so simple, so true, so great, so noble—and by this accolade I join thee to the nobility of France, thy fitting place! And for thy sake I do hereby ennoble all thy family and all thy kin; and all their descendants born in wedlock, not only in the male but also in the female line. And more!more! To distinguish thy house and honor it above all others, we add a privilege never accorded to any before in the history of these dominions: the females of thy line shall have and hold the right to ennoble their husbands when these shall be of inferior degree." [Astonishment and envy flared up in every countenance when the words were uttered which conferred this extraordinary grace. The King paused and looked around upon these signs with quite evident satisfaction.] "Rise, Joan of Arc, now and henceforth surnamed Du Lis, in grateful acknowledgment of the good blow which you have struck for the lilies of France; and they, and the royal crown, and your own victorious sword, fit and fair company for each other, shall be grouped in you escutcheon and be and remain the symbol of your high nobility forever."

As my Lady Du Lis rose, the gilded children of privilege pressed forward to welcome her to their sacred ranks and call her by her new name; but she was troubled, and said these honors were not meet for one of her lowly birth and station, and by their kind grace she would remain simple Joan of Arc, nothing more—and so be called.

Nothing more! As if there could be anything more, anything higher, anything greater. My Lady Du Lis—why, it was tinsel, petty, perishable. But, JOAN OF ARC! The mere sound of it sets one's pulses leaping.

Chapter 24.

Tinsel Trappings of Nobility

IT WAS vexatious to see what a to–do the whole town, and next the whole country, made over the news. Joan of Arc ennobled by the King! People went dizzy with wonder and delight over it. You cannot imagine how she was gaped at, stared at, envied. Why, one would have supposed that some great and fortunate thing had happened to her. But we did not think any great things of it. To our minds no mere human hand could add a glory to Joan of Arc. To us she was the sun soaring in the heavens, and her new nobility a
candle atop of it; to us it was swallowed up and lost in her own light. And she was as indifferent to it and as unconscious of it as the other sun would have been.

But it was different with her brothers. They were proud and happy in their new dignity, which was quite natural. And Joan was glad it had been conferred, when she saw how pleased they were. It was a
clever thought in the King to outflank her scruples by marching on them under shelter of her love for her family and her kin.

Jean and Pierre sported their coats–of–arms right away; and their society was courted by everybody, the nobles and commons alike. The Standard–Bearer said, with some touch of bitterness, that he could see that they just felt good to be alive, they were so soaked
with the comfort of their glory; and didn't like to sleep at all, because when they were asleep they didn't know they were noble, and so
sleep was a clean loss of time. And then he said:

"They can't take precedence of me in military functions and state ceremonies, but when it comes to civil ones and society affairs I judge they'll cuddle coolly in behind you and the knights, and Noel and I will have to walk behind them—hey?"

"Yes," I said, "I think you are right."

"I was just afraid of it—just afraid of it," said the Standard–Bearer, with a sigh. "Afraid of it? I'm talking like a fool; of course I knew it. Yes, I was talking like a fool."

Noel Rainguesson said, musingly:

"Yes, I noticed something natural about the tone of it." We others

laughed.

"Oh, you did, did you? You think you are very clever, don't you? I'll take and wring your neck for you one of these days, Noel Rainguesson."

The Sieur de Metz said:

"Paladin, your fears haven't reached the top notch. They are away below the grand possibilities. Didn't it occur to you that in civil and society functions they will take precedence of all the rest of the personal staff—every one of us?"

"Oh, come!"

"You'll find it's so. Look at their escutcheon. Its chiefest feature is the lilies of France. It's royal, man, royal—do you understand the size of that? The lilies are there by authority of the Kingdo you
understand the size of that? Though not in detail and in entirety, they do nevertheless substantially quarter the arms of France in their coat. Imagine it! consider it! measure the magnitude of it! We walk in
front of those boys? Bless you, we've done that for the last time. In my opinion there isn't a lay lord in this whole region that can walk in front of them, except the Duke d'Alencon, prince of the blood."

You could have knocked the Paladin down with a feather. He seemed to actually turn pale. He worked his lips a moment without getting anything out; then it came:

"I didn't know that, nor the half of it; how could I? I've been an idiot. I see it now—I've been an idiot. I met them this morning, and sung out hello to them just as I would to anybody. I didn't mean to be ill–

mannered, but I didn't know the half of this that you've been telling. I've been an ass. Yes, that is all there is to itI've been an ass."

Noel Rainguesson said, in a kind of weary way:

"Yes, that is likely enough; but I don't see why you should seem surprised at it."

"You don't, don't you? Well, why don't you?"

"Because I don't see any novelty about it. With some people it is a condition which is present all the time. Now you take a condition which is present all the time, and the results of that condition will be uniform; this uniformity of result will in time become monotonous; monotonousness, by the law of its being, is fatiguing. If you had manifested fatigue upon noticing that you had been an ass, that would have been logical, that would have been rational; whereas it seems to me that to manifest surprise was to be again an ass, because the condition of intellect that can enable a person to be surprised and stirred by inert monotonousness is a"

"Now that is enough, Noel Rainguesson; stop where you are, before you get yourself into trouble. And don't bother me any more for some days or a week an it please you, for I cannot abide your clack."

"Come, I like that! I didn't want to talk. I tried to get out of talking. If you didn't want to hear my clack, what did you keep intruding your conversation on me for?"

"I? I never dreamed of such a thing."

"Well, you did it, anyway. And I have a right to feel hurt, and I do feel hurt, to have you treat me so. It seems to me that when a person goads, and crowds, and in a manner forces another person to talk, it is neither very fair nor very good–mannered to call what he says clack."

"Oh, snuffledo! and break your heart, you poor thing. Somebody fetch this sick doll a sugar–rag. Look you, Sir Jean de Metz, do you feel absolutely certain about that thing?"

"What thing?"

"Why, that Jean and Pierre are going to take precedence of all the lay noblesse hereabouts except the Duke d'Alencon?"

"I think there is not a doubt of it."

The Standard–Bearer was deep in thoughts and dreams a few moments, then the silk–and–velvet expanse of his vast breast rose and fell with a sigh, and he said:

"Dear, dear, what a lift it is! It just shows what luck can do. Well, I don't care. I shouldn't care to be a painted accidentI shouldn't value it. I am prouder to have climbed up to where I am just by sheer natural merit than I would be to ride the very sun in the zenith and have to reflect that I was nothing but a poor little accident, and got shot up there out of somebody else's catapult. To me, merit is everythingin fact, the only thing. All else is dross."

Just then the bugles blew the assembly, and that cut our talk short.

Chapter 25.

At Lastforward!

THE DAYS began to waste awayand nothing decided, nothing done. The army was full of zeal, but it was also hungry. It got no pay, the treasury was getting empty, it was becoming impossible to feed it; under pressure of privation it began to fall apart and dispersewhich pleased the trifling court exceedingly. Joan's distress was pitiful to see. She was obliged to stand helpless while her victorious army dissolved away until hardly the skeleton of it was left.

At last one day she went to the Castle of Loches, where the King was idling. She found him consulting with three of his councilors, Robert le Maton, a former Chancellor of France, Christophe d'Harcourt, and Gerard Machet. The Bastard of Orleans was present also, and it is through him that we know what happened. Joan threw herself at the King's feet and embraced his knees, saying:

"Noble Dauphin, prithee hold no more of these long and numerous councils, but come, and come quickly, to Rheims and receive your crown."

Christophe d'Harcourt asked:

"Is it your Voices that command you to say that to the King?" "Yes, and

urgently."

"Then will you not tell us in the King's presence in what way the Voices communicate with you?"

It was another sly attempt to trap Joan into indiscreet admissions and dangerous pretensions. But nothing came of it. Joan's answer was simple and straightforward, and the smooth Bishop was not able to find any fault with it. She said that when she met with people who doubted the truth of her mission she went aside and prayed, complaining of the distrust of these, and then the comforting Voices were heard at her ear saying, soft and low, "Go forward, Daughter of God, and I will help thee." Then she added, "When I hear that, the joy in my heart, oh, it is insupportable!"

The Bastard said that when she said these words her face lit up as with a flame, and she was like one in an ecstasy.

Joan pleaded, persuaded, reasoned; gaining ground little by little, but opposed step by step by the council. She begged, she implored, leave to march. When they could answer nothing further, they granted that perhaps it had been a mistake to let the army waste away, but how could we help it now? how could we march without an army?

"Raise one!" said Joan.

"But it will take six weeks." "No

matterbegin! let us begin!"

"It is too late. Without doubt the Duke of Bedford has been gathering troops to push to the succor of his strongholds on the Loire."

"Yes, while we have been disbanding oursand pity 'tis. But we must throw away no more time; we must bestir ourselves."

The King objected that he could not venture toward Rheims with those strong places on the Loire in his path. But Joan said:

"We will break them up. Then you can march."

With that plan the King was willing to venture assent. He could sit around out of danger while the road was being cleared.

Joan came back in great spirits. Straightway everything was stirring. Proclamations were issued calling for men, a recruiting–camp was established at Selles in Berry, and the commons and the nobles began to flock to it with enthusiasm.

A deal of the month of May had been wasted; and yet by the 6th of June Joan had swept together a new army and was ready to march. She had eight thousand men. Think of that. Think of gathering together such a body as that in that little region. And these were veteran soldiers, too. In fact, most of the men in France were soldiers, when you came to that; for the wars had lasted generations now. Yes, most Frenchmen were soldiers; and admirable runners, too, both by practice and inheritance; they had done next to nothing but run for near a century. But that was not their fault. They had had no fair and proper leadershipat least leaders with a fair and proper chance. Away back, King and Court got the habit of being treacherous to the leaders; then the leaders easily got the habit of disobeying the King and going their own way, each for himself and nobody for the lot. Nobody could win victories that way. Hence, running became the habit of the French troops, and no wonder. Yet all that those troops needed in order to be good fighters was a leader
who would attend strictly to businessa leader with all authority in his hands in place of a tenth of it along with nine other generals
equipped with an equal tenth apiece. They had a leader rightly clothed with authority now, and with a head and heart bent on war of the most intensely businesslike and earnest sortand there would be results. No doubt of that. They had Joan of Arc; and under that leadership their legs would lose the art and mystery of running.

Yes, Joan was in great spirits. She was here and there and everywhere, all over the camp, by day and by night, pushing things. And wherever she came charging down the lines, reviewing the troops, it was good to hear them break out and cheer. And nobody could help cheering, she was such a vision of young bloom and beauty and grace, and such an incarnation of pluck and life and go! she was growing more and more ideally beautiful every day, as was plain to be seenand these were days of development; for she was
well past seventeen nowin fact, she was getting close upon seventeen and a halfindeed, just a little woman, as you may say.

The two young Counts de Laval arrived one dayfine young fellows allied to the greatest and most illustrious houses of France; and they could not rest till they had seen Joan of Arc. So the King sent for them and presented them to her, and you may believe she filled the bill of their expectations. When they heard that rich voice of hers they must have thought it was a flute; and when they saw her deep eyes and her face, and the soul that looked out of that face, you could see that the sight of her stirred them like a poem, like lofty eloquence, like martial music. One of them wrote home to his people, and in his letter he said, "It seemed something divine to see her and hear her." Ah, yes, and it was a true word. Truer word was never spoken.

He saw her when she was ready to begin her march and open the campaign, and this is what he said about it:

"She was clothed all in white armor save her head, and in her hand she carried a little battle–ax; and when she was ready to mount her great black horse he reared and plunged and would not let her. Then she said, 'Lead him to the cross.' This cross was in front of the church close by. So they led him there. Then she mounted, and he never budged, any more than if he had been tied. Then she turned toward the door of the church and said, in her soft womanly voice, 'You, priests and people of the Church, make processions and pray to God for us!' Then she spurred away, under her standard, with her little ax in her hand, crying 'Forwardmarch!' One of her brothers, who came eight days ago, departed with her; and he also was clad all in white armor."

I was there, and I saw it, too; saw it all, just as he pictures it. And I see it yetthe little battle–ax, the dainty plumed cap, the white armorall in the soft June afternoon; I see it just as if it were yesterday. And I rode with the staffthe personal staffthe staff of Joan of Arc.

That young count was dying to go, too, but the King held him back for the present. But Joan had made him a promise. In his letter he said:

"She told me that when the King starts for Rheims I shall go with him. But God grant I may not have to wait till then, but may have a part in the battles!"

She made him that promise when she was taking leave of my lady the Duchess d'Alencon. The duchess was exacting a promise, so it seemed a proper time for others to do the like. The duchess was troubled for her husband, for she foresaw desperate fighting; and she held Joan to her breast, and stroked her hair lovingly, and said:

"You must watch over him, dear, and take care of him, and send him back to me safe. I require it of you; I will not let you go till you promise."

Joan said:

"I give you the promise with all my heart; and it is not just words, it is a promise; you shall have him back without a hurt. Do you believe? And are you satisfied with me now?"

The duchess could not speak, but she kissed Joan on the forehead; and so they parted.

We left on the 6th and stopped over at Romorantin; then on the 9th Joan entered Orleans in state, under triumphal arches, with the welcoming cannon thundering and seas of welcoming flags fluttering in the breeze. The Grand Staff rode with her, clothed in shining splendors of costume and decorations: the Duke d'Alencon; the Bastard of Orleans; the Sire de Boussac, Marshal of France; the Lord de Granville, Master of the Crossbowmen; the Sire de Culan, Admiral of France; Ambroise de Lor; Etienne de Vignoles, called La Hire; Gautier de Brusac, and other illustrious captains.

It was grand times; the usual shoutings and packed multitudes, the usual crush to get sight of Joan; but at last we crowded through to our old lodgings, and I saw old Boucher and the wife and that dear Catherine gather Joan to their hearts and smother her with kissesand my heart ached for her so! for I could have kissed Catherine better than anybody, and more and longer; yet was not thought of for that office, and I so famished for it. Ah, she was so beautiful, and oh, so sweet! I had loved her the first day I ever saw her, and from that day forth she was sacred to me. I have carried her image in my heart for sixty–three yearsall lonely thee, yes, solitary, for it never has had companyand I am grown so old, so old; but it, oh, it is as fresh and young and merry and mischievous and lovely and sweet and pure and witching and divine as it was when it crept in there, bringing benediction and peace to its habitation so long ago, so long ago—for it has not aged a day!

Chapter 26.

The Last Doubts Scattered

THIS TIME, as before, the King's last command to the generals was this: "See to it that you do nothing without the sanction of the Maid." And this time the command was obeyed; and would continue to be obeyed all through the coming great days of the Loire campaign.

That was a change! That was new! It broke the traditions. It shows you what sort of a reputation as a commander–in–chief the child had made for herself in ten days in the field. It was a conquering of men's doubts and suspicions and a capturing and solidifying of men's belief and confidence such as the grayest veteran on the Grand Staff had
not been able to achieve in thirty years. Don't you remember that when at sixteen Joan conducted her own case in a grim court of law and won it, the old judge spoke of her as "this marvelous child"? It was the right name, you see.

These veterans were not going to branch out and do things without the sanction of the Maid that is true; and it was a great gain. But at
the same time there were some among them who still trembled at her new and dashing war tactics and earnestly desired to modify them. And so, during the 10th, while Joan was slaving away at her plans and issuing order after order with tireless industry, the old–time consultations and arguings and speechifyings were going on among certain of the generals.

In the afternoon of that day they came in a body to hold one of these councils of war; and while they waited for Joan to join them they discussed the situation. Now this discussion is not set down in the histories; but I was there, and I will speak of it, as knowing you will trust me, I not being given to beguiling you with lies.

Gautier de Brusac was spokesman for the timid ones; Joan's side was resolutely upheld by d'Alencon, the Bastard, La Hire, the Admiral of

France, the Marshal de Boussac, and all the other really important chiefs.

De Brusac argued that the situation was very grave; that Jargeau, the first point of attack, was formidably strong; its imposing walls bristling with artillery; with seven thousand picked English veterans behind them, and at their head the great Earl of Suffolk and his two redoubtable brothers, the De la Poles. It seemed to him that the proposal of Joan of Arc to try to take such a place by storm was a most rash and over-daring idea, and she ought to be persuaded to relinquish it in favor of the soberer and safer procedure of
investment by regular siege. It seemed to him that this fiery and furious new fashion of hurling masses of men against impregnable walls of stone, in defiance of the established laws and usages of war, was

But he got no further. La Hire gave his plumed helm an impatient toss and burst out with:

"By God, she knows her trade, and none can teach it her!"

And before he could get out anything more, D'Alencon was on his feet, and the Bastard of Orleans, and a half a dozen others, all thundering at once, and pouring out their indignant displeasure upon any and all that might hold, secretly or publicly, distrust of the wisdom of the Commander-in-Chief. And when they had said their say, La Hire took a chance again, and said:

"There are some that never know how to change. Circumstances may change, but those people are never able to see that they have got to change too, to meet those circumstances. All that they know is the one beaten track that their fathers and grandfathers have followed
and that they themselves have followed in their turn. If an
earthquake come and rip the land to chaos, and that beaten track now lead over precipices and into morasses, those people can't learn that they must strike out a new road no; they will march stupidly along
and follow the old one, to death and perdition. Men, there's a new state of things; and a surpassing military genius has perceived it with her clear eye. And a new road is required, and that same clear eye

has noted where it must go, and has marked it out for us. The man does not live, never has lived, never will live, that can improve upon it! The old state of things was defeat, defeat, defeat—and by consequence we had troops with no dash, no heart, no hope. Would you assault stone walls with such? No—here was but one way with that kind: sit down before a place and wait, wait—starve it out, if you could. The new case is the very opposite; it is this: men all on fire with pluck and dash and vim and fury and energy—a restrained conflagration! What would you do with it? Hold it down and let it smolder and perish and go out? What would Joan of Arc do with it? Turn it loose, by the Lord God of heaven and earth, and let it swallow up the foe in the whirlwind of its fires! Nothing shows the splendor and wisdom of her military genius like her instant comprehension of the size of the change which has come about, and her instant perception of the right and only right way to take advantage of it. With her is no sitting down and starving out; no dilly–dallying and fooling around; no lazying, loafing, and going to sleep; no, it is storm! storm! storm! and still storm! storm! storm! and forever storm! storm! storm! hunt the enemy to his hole, then
turn her French hurricanes loose and carry him by storm! And that is my sort! Jargeau? What of Jargeau, with its battlements and towers, its devastating artillery, its seven thousand picked veterans? Joan of Arc is to the fore, and by the splendor of God its fate is sealed!"

Oh, he carried them. There was not another word said about persuading Joan to change her tactics. They sat talking comfortably enough after that.

By and by Joan entered, and they rose and saluted with their swords, and she asked what their pleasure might be. La Hire said:

"It is settled, my General. The matter concerned Jargeau. There were some who thought we could not take the place."

Joan laughed her pleasant laugh, her merry, carefree laugh; the laugh that rippled so buoyantly from her lips and made old people feel young again to hear it; and she said to the company:

"Have no fears—indeed, there is no need nor any occasion for them.

We will strike the English boldly by assault, and you will see." Then a faraway look came into her eyes, and I think that a picture of her home drifted across the vision of her mind; for she said very gently, and as one who muses, "But that I know God guides us and will give us success, I had liefer keep sheep than endure these perils."

We had a homelike farewell supper that evening just the personal staff and the family. Joan had to miss it; for the city had given a banquet in her honor, and she had gone there in state with the Grand Staff, through a riot of joy–bells and a sparkling Milky Way of illuminations.

After supper some lively young folk whom we knew came in, and we presently forgot that we were soldiers, and only remembered that we were boys and girls and full of animal spirits and long–pent fun; and so there was dancing, and games, and romps, and screams of laughter just as extravagant and innocent and noisy a good time as ever I had in my life. Dear, dear, how long ago it was! and I was young then. And outside, all the while, was the measured tramp of marching battalions, belated odds and ends of the French power gathering for the morrow's tragedy on the grim stage of war. Yes, in those days we had those contrasts side by side. And as I passed
along to bed there was another one: the big Dwarf, in brave new armor, sat sentry at Joan's door the stern Spirit of War made flesh, as it were and on his ample shoulder was curled a kitten asleep.

Chapter 27.

How Joan Took Jargeau

WE MADE a gallant show next day when we filed out through the frowning gates of Orleans, with banners flying and Joan and the Grand Staff in the van of the long column. Those two young De Lavals were come now, and were joined to the Grand Staff. Which was well; war being their proper trade, for they were grandsons of that illustrious fighter Bertrand du Guesclin, Constable of France in earlier days. Louis de Bourbon, the Marshal de Rais, and the Vidame de Chartres were added also. We had a right to feel a little uneasy,
for we knew that a force of five thousand men was on its way under Sir John Fastolfe to reinforce Jargeau, but I think we were not uneasy, nevertheless. In truth, that force was not yet in our neighborhood. Sir John was loitering; for some reason or other he was not hurrying. He was losing precious time—four days at Etampes, and four more at Janville.

We reached Jargeau and began business at once. Joan sent forward a heavy force which hurled itself against the outworks in handsome style, and gained a footing and fought hard to keep it; but it presently began to fall back before a sortie from the city. Seeing this, Joan raised her battle–cry and led a new assault herself under a furious artillery fire. The Paladin was struck down at her side wounded, but she snatched her standard from his failing hand and plunged on through the ruck of flying missiles, cheering her men with encouraging cries; and then for a good time one had turmoil, and clash of steel, and collision and confusion of struggling multitudes, and the hoarse bellowing of the guns; and then the hiding of it all under a rolling firmament of smoke—a firmament through which
veiled vacancies appeared for a moment now and then, giving fitful dim glimpses of the wild tragedy enacting beyond; and always at these times one caught sight of that slight figure in white mail which was the center and soul of our hope and trust, and whenever we saw that, with its back to us and its face to the fight, we knew that all was

well. At last a great shout went up—a joyous roar of shoutings, in fact—and that was sign sufficient that the faubourgs were ours.

Yes, they were ours; the enemy had been driven back within the walls. On the ground which Joan had won we camped; for night was coming on.

Joan sent a summons to the English, promising that if they surrendered she would allow them to go in peace and take their horses with them. Nobody knew that she could take that strong place, but she knew it—knew it well; yet she offered that grace—offered
it in a time when such a thing was unknown in war; in a time when it was custom and usage to massacre the garrison and the inhabitants
of captured cities without pity or compunction—yes, even to the harmless women and children sometimes. There are neighbors all about you who well remember the unspeakable atrocities which Charles the Bold inflicted upon the men and women and children of Dinant when he took that place some years ago. It was a unique and kindly grace which Joan offered that garrison; but that was her way, that was her loving and merciful nature—she always did her best to save her enemy's life and his soldierly pride when she had the mastery of him.

The English asked fifteen days' armistice to consider the proposal in. And Fastolfe coming with five thousand men! Joan said no. But she offered another grace: they might take both their horses and their side–arms—but they must go within the hour.

Well, those bronzed English veterans were pretty hard–headed folk. They declined again. Then Joan gave command that her army be made ready to move to the assault at nine in the morning. Considering the deal of marching and fighting which the men had done that day, D'Alencon thought the hour rather early; but Joan said
it was best so, and so must be obeyed. Then she burst out with one of those enthusiasms which were always burning in her when battle
was imminent, and said:

"Work! work! and God will work with us!"

Yes, one might say that her motto was "Work! stick to it; keep on working!" for in war she never knew what indolence was. And whoever will take that motto and live by it will likely to succeed. There's many a way to win in this world, but none of them is worth much without good hard work back out of it.

I think we should have lost our big Standard–Bearer that day, if our bigger Dwarf had not been at hand to bring him out of the melee when he was wounded. He was unconscious, and would have been trampled to death by our own horse, if the Dwarf had not promptly rescued him and haled him to the rear and safety. He recovered, and was himself again after two or three hours; and then he was happy and proud, and made the most of his wound, and went swaggering around in his bandages showing off like an innocent big–childwhich was just what he was. He was prouder of being wounded than a really modest person would be of being killed. But there was no harm in his vanity, and nobody minded it. He said he was hit by a stone from a catapulta stone the size of a man's head. But the stone grew, of course. Before he got through with it he was claiming that the enemy had flung a building at him.

"Let him alone," said Noel Rainguesson. "Don't interrupt his processes. To–morrow it will be a cathedral."

He said that privately. And, sure enough, to–morrow it was a cathedral. I never saw anybody with such an abandoned imagination.

Joan was abroad at the crack of dawn, galloping here and there and yonder, examining the situation minutely, and choosing what she considered the most effective positions for her artillery; and with such accurate judgment did she place her guns that her Lieutenant– General's admiration of it still survived in his memory when his testimony was taken at the Rehabilitation, a quarter of a century later.

In this testimony the Duke d'Alencon said that at Jargeau that morning of the 12th of June she made her dispositions not like a novice, but "with the sure and clear judgment of a trained general of twenty or thirty years' experience."

The veteran captains of the armies of France said she was great in war in all ways, but greatest of all in her genius for posting and handling artillery.

Who taught the shepherd–girl to do these marvels—she who could not read, and had had no opportunity to study the complex arts of war? I do not know any way to solve such a baffling riddle as that, there being no precedent for it, nothing in history to compare it with and examine it by. For in history there is no great general, however gifted, who arrived at success otherwise than through able teaching and hard study and some experience. It is a riddle which will never be guessed. I think these vast powers and capacities were born in her, and that she applied them by an intuition which could not err.

At eight o'clock all movement ceased, and with it all sounds, all noise. A mute expectancy reigned. The stillness was something awful—because it meant so much. There was no air stirring. The flags on the towers and ramparts hung straight down like tassels. Wherever one saw a person, that person had stopped what he was
doing, and was in a waiting attitude, a listening attitude. We were on a commanding spot, clustered around Joan. Not far from us, on
every hand, were the lanes and humble dwellings of these outlying suburbs. Many people were visible—all were listening, not one was moving. A man had placed a nail; he was about to fasten something with it to the door–post of his shop—but he had stopped. There was his hand reaching up holding the nail; and there was his other hand in
the act of striking with the hammer; but he had forgotten everything—his head was turned aside listening. Even children unconsciously stopped in their play; I saw a little boy with his hoop– stick pointed slanting toward the ground in the act of steering the hoop around the corner; and so he had stopped and was listening—the hoop was rolling away, doing its own steering. I saw a young girl prettily framed in an open window, a watering–pot in her hand and window–boxes of red flowers under its spout—but the water had
ceased to flow; the girl was listening. Everywhere were these impressive petrified forms; and everywhere was suspended movement and that awful stillness.

Joan of Arc raised her sword in the air. At the signal, the silence was torn to rags; cannon after cannon vomited flames and smoke and delivered its quaking thunders; and we saw answering tongues of fire dart from the towers and walls of the city, accompanied by answering deep thunders, and in a minute the walls and the towers disappeared, and in their place stood vast banks and pyramids of snowy smoke, motionless in the dead air. The startled girl dropped her watering–pot and clasped her hands together, and at that moment a stone cannon–ball crashed through her fair body.

The great artillery duel went on, each side hammering away with all its might; and it was splendid for smoke and noise, and most exalting to one's spirits. The poor little town around about us suffered cruelly. The cannon–balls tore through its slight buildings, wrecking them as if they had been built of cards; and every moment or two one would see a huge rock come curving through the upper air above the smoke–clouds and go plunging down through the roofs. Fire broke out, and columns of flame and smoke rose toward the sky.

Presently the artillery concussions changed the weather. The sky became overcast, and a strong wind rose and blew away the smoke that hid the English fortresses.

Then the spectacle was fine; turreted gray walls and towers, and streaming bright flags, and jets of red fire and gushes of white smoke in long rows, all standing out with sharp vividness against the deep leaden background of the sky; and then the whizzing missiles began to knock up the dirt all around us, and I felt no more interest in the scenery. There was one English gun that was getting our position down finer and finer all the time. Presently Joan pointed to it and said:

"Fair duke, step out of your tracks, or that machine will kill you."

The Duke d'Alencon did as he was bid; but Monsieur du Lude rashly took his place, and that cannon tore his head off in a moment.

Joan was watching all along for the right time to order the assault. At last, about nine o'clock, she cried out:

"Nowto the assault!" and the buglers blew the charge.

Instantly we saw the body of men that had been appointed to this service move forward toward a point where the concentrated fire of our guns had crumbled the upper half of a broad stretch of wall to ruins; we saw this force descend into the ditch and begin to plant the scaling-ladders. We were soon with them. The Lieutenant-General thought the assault premature. But Joan said:

"Ah, gentle duke, are you afraid? Do you not know that I have promised to send you home safe?"

It was warm work in the ditches. The walls were crowded with men, and they poured avalanches of stones down upon us. There was one gigantic Englishman who did us more hurt than any dozen of his brethren. He always dominated the places easiest of assault, and flung down exceedingly troublesome big stones which smashed men and ladders boththen he would near burst himself with laughing over what he had done. But the duke settled accounts with him. He went and found the famous cannoneer, Jean le Lorrain, and said:

"Train your gunkill me this demon."

He did it with the first shot. He hit the Englishman fair in the breast and knocked him backward into the city.

The enemy's resistance was so effective and so stubborn that our people began to show signs of doubt and dismay. Seeing this, Joan raised her inspiring battle-cry and descended into the fosse herself, the Dwarf helping her and the Paladin sticking bravely at her side with the standard. She started up a scaling-ladder, but a great stone flung from above came crashing down upon her helmet and stretched her, wounded and stunned, upon the ground. But only for a moment. The Dwarf stood her upon her feet, and straightway she started up the ladder again, crying:

"To the assault, friends, to the assaultthe English are ours! It is the appointed hour!"

There was a grand rush, and a fierce roar of war-cries, and we swarmed over the ramparts like ants. The garrison fled, we pursued; Jargeau was ours!

The Earl of Suffolk was hemmed in and surrounded, and the Duke d'Alencon and the Bastard of Orleans demanded that he surrender himself. But he was a proud nobleman and came of a proud race. He refused to yield his sword to subordinates, saying:

"I will die rather. I will surrender to the Maid of Orleans alone, and to no other."

And so he did; and was courteously and honorably used by her.

His two brothers retreated, fighting step by step, toward the bridge, we pressing their despairing forces and cutting them down by scores. Arrived on the bridge, the slaughter still continued. Alexander de la Pole was pushed overboard or fell over, and was drowned. Eleven hundred men had fallen; John de la Pole decided to give up the struggle. But he was nearly as proud and particular as his brother of Suffolk as to whom he would surrender to. The French officer nearest at hand was Guillaume Renault, who was pressing him closely. Sir John said to him:

"Are you a gentleman?" "Yes."

"And a knight?" "No."

Then Sir John knighted him himself there on the bridge, giving him the accolade with English coolness and tranquillity in the midst of that storm of slaughter and mutilation; and then bowing with high courtesy took the sword by the blade and laid the hilt of it in the man's hand in token of surrender. Ah, yes, a proud tribe, those De la Poles.

It was a grand day, a memorable day, a most splendid victory. We had a crowd of prisoners, but Joan would not allow them to be hurt. We took them with us and marched into Orleans next day through the usual tempest of welcome and joy.

And this time there was a new tribute to our leader. From everywhere in the packed streets the new recruits squeezed their way to her side to touch the sword of Joan of Arc, and draw from it somewhat of that mysterious quality which made it invincible.

Made in the USA
Coppell, TX
26 February 2022